NEW GEPT

新制全民英檢

中級 寫作測驗必考題型

陳頎/著

國際語言中心委員會/監修

完全掌握 40種英檢「常考情境主題」
9大類「必考文法句型」

Step 1

● 9大類必考文法句型

本書精心整理「寫作能力培養」單元，囊括9大類英檢常考文法句型，幫助考生活用英文句型，輕鬆寫出正確又漂亮的英文句子。

Step 2

二大題型

● 英檢寫作2大題型分析

本書逼真模擬「全民英檢中級寫作測驗」的兩大題型：「中譯英」和「英文作文」，幫助考生熟悉兩大題型的作答策略及高分技巧。

Step 3

● 40種常考情境主題

融入最常出現在測驗當中的40種情境主題，精心編寫「中譯英」和「英文作文」的擬真練習題，訓練考生靈活運用前面學到的各種應考重點。

Step 4

● 一回完整模擬試題

收錄一回完整擬真模擬試題，讓考生能實際運用各種作答技巧、及時檢驗所學成果，並逐句詳細分析範文擬答，實際應戰更有把握。

Step 5

● 寫作能力測驗

PASS!!

完全掌握英檢出題趨勢，厚植考生應試寫作能力！

▼ 速見P.18

◆ **題型透視，提高英文應考力！**

中級寫作測驗中只會出現兩種題型：「中譯英」和「英文作文」。其中，「英文作文」有三種類型，包括「看圖寫作」、「故事接龍」、「書信寫作」，本書為考生點出各題型特色及作答技巧，保證大幅提高考生在考場上的應考力。

看圖寫作

題型解說

「看圖寫作」的考題中，會提供一張圖片與一個問題做為作答提示，生必須根據圖片內容與題目要求，建構出一篇完整的文章。考生在撰寫著重於「原因」、「理由」與「結果」，並補充說明以支持自身論點。

▼ 速見P.45

◆ **句型活用，培養英文構句力！**

本書為考生整理並詳細剖析 9 大類「必考文法句型」，讓考生能循序漸進培養構句能力，只要把握最重要的句型與文法概念，再難的句子也難不倒你，讓你能快速寫出讓人眼睛一亮的漂亮英文句子及文章！

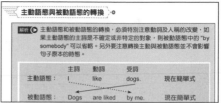

主動語態與被動語態的轉換

解析 ▶ 主動語態和被動語態的轉換，必須特別注意動詞及人稱的改變，如果主動語態的主詞是不確定或非特定的對象，則被動語態中的"by somebody"可以省略。另外要注意轉換主動與被動語態並不會影響句子原本的時態。

	主詞	動詞	受詞	
主動語態：	I	like	dogs.	現在簡單式
被動語態：	Dogs	are liked	by me.	現在簡單式

▼ 速見P.144

◆ **翻譯訓練，增強英文翻譯力！**

本書根據英檢出題方式，編寫了 20 篇連貫式中譯英練習試題，讓考生可以從單句練習開始鍛字鍊句，並提供完整擬答與詳解分析，讓考生能參考並修正自己的翻譯弱點，有效增強翻譯功力。

1-1 模擬試題篇

TEST 1 感冒篇 中譯英

請將下列中文敘述翻譯為正確的英文，將答案寫在答案欄中。

我是一個經常感冒的人。昨天早上我離開家的時候，天氣十分暖和，所以我沒有穿夾克，只穿了一件襯衫與短褲。但是到了傍晚，氣溫卻急速下降。難然晚上我很早就回家，但我還是覺得有點不舒服。今天我不但打噴嚏還頭暈，我想我最好馬上去診所看醫生。

▼ 速見P.213

◆ **主題作文，建構英文表達力！**

本書收錄 20 篇按照近年來英檢出題方向的英文作文主題式練習題，引導考生就該主題靈活思考，有效建構寫作表達能力，訓練考生用英文暢所欲言，而不是枯燥且一再重複的範本作文。

TEST 2 恐怖的旅遊篇 故事接龍

請用 120 字（8 至 12 句）完成以下的故事。主題是 "A Terrible Trip"，故事的開頭如下。答案請寫在答案欄內，開頭的部分不需重謄（評分重點包括內容、組織、文法、用字遣詞、標點行號與大小寫）。

My girlfriend and I took a trip to Hawaii last year. My brother and his wife lived in Hawaii and they wanted us to come to visit them. We had tickets for an early flight to Hawaii, so we got up before the sun rose. This is where our problems started. On our way to the airport, we had a

▼ 速見P.320

◆ **全真模擬，傳授英文高分祕笈！**

本書收錄全新一回擬真模擬試題，讓考生能檢驗學習成果，每一題都提供高分範文，且逐句詳細分析，提供考生絕對完整的模擬演練，讓你實際應戰更有把握！

全民英語能力分級檢定測驗

中級寫作能力測驗

本測驗共有兩部分。第一部分為中譯英，第二部分為英文寫作為 40 分鐘。

一、中譯英 (40%)

Contents

Contents

Contents 目錄 >>>

Look Inside

Contents

- 教育與學習
- 工作與職場
- 餐飲與購物
- 日常生活

Part 3 精選模擬試題

1-2 試題解析篇

Contents

UNIT 2 英文作文 212

2-1 模擬試題篇

2-2 試題解析篇

Contents
目錄 >>

Look Inside

Contents

Part 4 寫作測驗模擬試題

Part

寫作題型模擬透視

1

全民英檢的中級寫作測驗分為「中譯英」與「英文作文」二個部分,兩個部分各考一個題目。第一部分「中譯英」的考題是連貫式翻譯,題目會提供一篇長度約四到六句的中文短文,考生需將其翻譯成英文;第二部分「英文作文」又包括「看圖寫作」、「故事接龍」與「書信寫作」三種題型。中級寫作測驗的目的在於評量考生的英文書寫能力,當然也考驗考生的英文字彙及片語量多寡、文法觀念及對句型的了解度。

Look Inside

寫作題型
　　模擬透視

「全民英檢中級寫作能力測驗」的第一部分「中譯英」考題是連貫式翻譯，題目會提供一篇長度約四到六句的中文短文，考生須將其翻譯成英文。

題型解說

「全民英檢中級寫作測驗」的第一部分是「中譯英」，題目會提供一篇長度約四到六句的中文短文，考生必須將其翻譯成英文，考試重點在於測驗考生對詞彙的了解與熟悉度，因此對於常用的「字彙」與「片語」要十分熟悉，而「文法句型」與「句子的通順程度」也是重點。

要注意中譯英的題型是「連貫式」的，因此句與句之間是有關聯的，而非各自獨立、不相關的句子。所以句與句的對應、時態和語氣的一致性、句間轉折語的運用都是十分重要的。

字彙的使用除了要正確之外，還要能夠完整表達含意；文句除了要合乎文法之外，用法更要符合英文的表達習慣。中譯英的考題包括各式各樣的生活情境主題（見本書例題部分），以下的例題為一般中譯英考題中最常出現的「學習英文」的主題。

示範例題

說明 ▶ 請將下列的一段中文翻譯成通順、達意且前後連貫的英文。請將答案寫在答案欄中。

1 許多正在學英文的學生都不太注意讀書的方法，以至於浪費許多寶貴的時間。2 他們讀英文好幾年了，但還是不會寫很簡單的英文句子。3 其實，只要讀書的方法正確，英文的能力應該不難培養。4 當你在閱讀時，不要一遇到單字就查字典。5 當你在寫作時，要注意你的文法是否正確。

[1]Many students who are learning English pay so little attention to their studies that they waste much precious time. [2]They have been learning English for many years, but they still cannot write relatively easy English sentences. [3]Actually, as long as their methods are correct, their English ability should not be difficult to cultivate. [4]When you read, don't look up in the dictionary as soon as you run into new words. [5]When you write, keep an eye on whether your grammar is correct or not.

範文句型解析

許多正在學英文的學生都不太注意讀書的方法，以至於浪費許多寶貴的時間。

➡ Many students **who** are learning English pay so little attention to their studies that they waste much precious time.

解析 ▶ 主要的句型是以 "so ... that ..." 來表示「太……以致於……」的意思，並且用形容詞子句 "who are learning English" 來修飾先行詞 "Many students"。"so ... that ..." 的句型若有否定的意思，可以改用 "too ... to..." 的句型來表達。例如 "May is so hungry that she cannot walk." 可改寫成 "May is too hungry to walk."，兩句的意思都是「梅太餓了，以致於走不動。」

他們讀英文好幾年了，但還是不會寫很簡單的英文句子。

➡ They have been learning English for many years, **but** they still cannot write relatively easy English sentences.

解析 ▶ 已經持續了多年的動作，須使用現在完成進行式來表示。這裡運用對等連接詞 "but" 連接兩個句子，"but" 前面必須要加逗點。

其實，只要讀書的方法正確，英文的能力應該不難培養。

➡ Actually, as long as their methods are correct, their English ability should not be difficult to cultivate.

解析 ▶ 由連接詞 "as long as" 引導表示條件的副詞子句，記得當副詞子句置於主要子句之前的時候，兩個子句之間要加上逗號。

當你在閱讀時，不要一遇到單字就查字典。

➡ When you read, don't look up in the dictionary **as soon as** you run into new words.

解析 ▶ 先用連接詞 "when" 引導的時間副詞子句修飾主要子句，再用連接詞 "as soon as" 引導的時間副詞子句修飾主要子句。

當你在寫作時，要注意你的文法是否正確。

➡ When you write, keep an eye on **whether** your grammar is correct **or not**.

解析 ▶ 用連接詞 "when" 引導的時間副詞子句修飾主要子句。主要子句之中，連接詞 "whether or not" 引導的名詞子句做為動詞片語 "keep an eye on" 的受詞。

必備字彙 與片語整理

cultivate	[ˋkʌltəˏvet]	v.	培養
grammar	[ˋɡræmɚ]	n.	文法
many	[ˋmɛnɪ]	adj.	許多的
notice	[ˋnotɪs]	v.	注意
precious	[ˋprɛʃəs]	adj.	寶貴的
relatively	[ˋrɛlətɪvlɪ]	adv.	相當
sentence	[ˋsɛntəns]	n.	句子
waste	[west]	v.	浪費
actually	[ˋæktʃʊəlɪ]	adv.	其實，實際上
look up in the dictionary		phr.	查閱字典
pay attention to		phr.	注意
run into		phr.	遇到
keep an eye on		phr.	注意

「全民英檢中級寫作測驗」的第二部分是「英文作文」，其中可分為「看圖寫作」、「故事接龍」與「書信寫作」三種出題型式。

2-1 看圖寫作

題型解說

「看圖寫作」的考題中，會提供一張圖片與一個問題做為作答提示，考生必須根據圖片內容與題目要求，建構出一篇完整的文章。考生在撰寫時要著重於「原因」、「理由」與「結果」，並補充說明以支持自身論點。

示範例題

說明 ▶ 請依照下面所提供的圖片以及文字提示，寫一篇英文作文，長度約 120 字（8 至 12 個句子），答案請寫在寫作能力測驗答案紙上。評分重點包括內容、組織、文法、用字遣詞、標點符號與大小寫。

提示 ▶ 在台灣，有許多學生或上班族經常會到英文補習班加強英文，請說明為何英文在台灣如此重要或受歡迎，並進一步說明學英文到底可以獲得哪些好處。

_____

_____

_____

_____

參考範文

[1]English is an extremely important language in Taiwan. [2]Not only do the students need to learn English for their exams, but also employees need to learn English for their careers. [3]No wonder there are so many language centers and cram schools here in Taiwan. [4]Therefore, why English learning in Taiwan is so popular is indeed an interesting question. [5]First, English is a useful language. [6]With English, we can obtain the latest information and gain more knowledge. [7]Meanwhile, we can't communicate with foreigners without English. [8]English is a tool that helps us to keep in touch with our friends and connect to the whole world. [9]Therefore, many students and employees need to learn English, and that is why cram schools and language centers in Taiwan are so popular.

中文翻譯

[1] 英文在台灣真的是一個十分重要的語言。[2] 不僅學生會為了他們的考試而念英文,上班族也會為了工作而去學。[3] 難怪台灣有如此多的語言中心與補習班。[4] 因此,為何英文學習在台灣如此受歡迎,這是個相當有趣的問題。[5] 第一,英文是一個有用的語言。[6] 藉由英文,我們可以獲得最新的資訊並獲得更多知識。[7] 同時,若沒有英文,我們無法與外國人溝通。[8] 英文是一個我們可以用來與朋友保持聯絡,並與整個世界相連接的工具。[9] 因此,很多學生和上班族都需要學英文,這就是為什麼台灣的補習班與語言中心是如此的受歡迎。

範文句型解析 >●

English is an extremely important language in Taiwan.
英文在台灣真的是一個十分重要的語言。

解析 ► 基本架構是 "S＋V＋SC" 的句型，用 "an extremely important language" 來補充說明 "English"。

Not only do the students need to learn English for their exams, **but also** employees need to learn English for their careers.
不僅學生會為了他們的考試而念英文，上班族也會為了工作而去學。

解析 ► "Not only ..., but also ..." 的句型，意為「不僅……，也……」。後面連接的兩個子句，第一個位於 "Not only" 之後的子句須倒裝，位於 "but also" 後的子句則不須倒裝。

No wonder **there are** so many language centers and cram schools here in Taiwan.
難怪台灣有如此多的語言中心與補習班。

解析 ► 這是 "There + beV + S ..." 的句型。真主詞的部分用 "and" 來連接兩個名詞。

Therefore, why English learning in Taiwan is so popular is indeed an interesting question.
因此，為何英文學習在台灣如此受歡迎，這是個相當有趣的問題。

解析 ► 這裡的基本架構是 "S + V + SC" 的句型，由連接詞 "why" 引導名詞子句做為主詞，在 "why" 的前面其實省略了同義主詞 "the reason"。這裡用補語 "an interesting question" 來補充說明整個名詞子句。

5

First, English **is** a useful language.
第一，英文是一個有用的語言。

解析 ▶ 基本架構是 "S + V + SC" 的句型，補語 "a useful language" 說明整個主詞 "English"。"First/Firstly, Secondly, Thirdly, Fourthly, ..." 是用來舉例的表達方式。

6

With English, we can obtain the latest information **and** gain more knowledge.
藉由英文，我們可以獲得最新的資訊並獲得更多知識。

解析 ▶ "With + N + ..." 的句型，意為「藉由……」。這裡的對等連接詞 "and" 連接助動詞 "can" 之後的兩個原形動詞。

7

Meanwhile, we can't communicate with foreigners **without** English.
同時，若沒有英文，我們無法與外國人溝通。

解析 ▶ "can't ... without ..." 的句型，意為「沒有……就不能……」。"meanwhile" 置於句首當副詞用，用來讓前後文句子間的語氣產生相呼應的感覺。

8

English is a tool that helps us to keep in touch with our friends and connect to the whole world.
英文是一個我們可以用來與朋友保持聯絡，並與整個世界相連接的工具。

解析 ▶ 主要子句為 "English is a tool"，接著用由 "that" 引導的形容詞子句修飾名詞 "tool"。形容詞子句當中的對等連接詞是用來連接在 "to" 後面的兩個原形動詞。

21

9

Therefore, many students and employees need to learn English, and that is why cram schools and language centers in Taiwan are so popular.

因此，很多學生和上班族都需要學英文，這就是為什麼台灣的補習班與語言中心是如此的受歡迎。

解析 由副詞 "therefore" 引導表原因的副詞子句，說明主要子句發生的原因。主要子句的基本架構是 "S + V + SC"，這個句子的主詞是 "cram schools and language centers in Taiwan"。

 必備字彙 與片語整理

career	[kə`rɪr]	n.	職業（生涯）
extremely	[ɪk`strimlɪ]	adv.	極度地，非常地
foreigner	[`fɔrɪnɚ]	n.	外國人
gain	[gen]	v.	獲得，得到
latest	[`letɪst]	adj.	最新的
obtain	[əb`ten]	v.	得到，獲得
useful	[`jusfəl]	adj.	有用的；實用的
communicate with		phr.	與……溝通
cram schools		phr.	補習班
keep in touch with		phr.	與……聯繫

2-2 故事接龍

題型解說

在「故事接龍」的題型中,題目會提供一篇尚未完成的情境短文,考生必須根據題目所提供的英文敘述加以延伸,寫成一個完整的故事。考生在撰寫時要仔細閱讀故事的開端,文章前後的時態、語氣、人稱都要一致。

示範例題

說明 ▶ 請用 120 字(8 至 12 句)完成以下提示欄中未完成的的故事,主題是 "An Unexpected Surprise",提示的部分不須重謄,答案請寫在寫作能力測驗答案紙上。評分重點包括內容、組織、文法、用字遣詞、標點符號與大小寫。

提示 ▶ I will never forget this unexpected surprise. One day I was shopping in a department store and joined a lucky draw. What a surprise! I won the biggest prize, a 5-day-holiday in Guam. I was really happy for the unexpected luck at that moment ...

我永遠不會忘記這個出乎意料的驚喜。有一天我在百貨公司裡購物,參加了抽獎。驚喜的是!我中了「關島五日遊」的第一特獎!當時真是令我喜出望外⋯⋯

¹I just could not believe it! ²I had longed for an overseas vacation for a long time. ³To my surprise, the dream did come true. ⁴In fact, I had dreamt about travelling to Guam for many years. ⁵All of my friends had been there, and their high recommendations were really impressive. ⁶However, the high cost of the trip to Guam was always my concern. ⁷With the unexpected surprise, I could finally go to this heaven to go snorkelling, to go shopping, and just to relax. ⁸That night, I couldn't sleep because I was so excited. ⁹I thought I was really the luckiest person in the world.

中文翻譯 ❯ ●

1 我真是不敢相信！2 我渴望一次海外度假已經很長一段時間了。3 令我驚訝的是，這個夢想真的成真了。4 事實上，我已經夢想到關島旅遊很多年了。5 我所有的朋友們都已經去過那裡，而且他們的極力推薦實在令人印象深刻。6 然而，到關島旅行的高額費用總是讓我有所顧慮。7 有了這個意外的驚喜，我終於可以去這個天堂浮潛、購物或純粹放鬆一下。8 那天晚上我無法入睡，因為我實在太興奮了。9 我想我真的是世界上最幸運的人了。

範文句型解析

1

I just could not believe it!
我真是不敢相信！

解析 ▶ "I can't believe it!" 表示令人驚訝的、令人難以置信的事，因為是描述過去發生的事，所以這裡將助動詞改成過去式的 "could"，副詞 "just" 用來加強語氣，意思是「實在，真是」。

2

I had longed for an overseas vacation for a long time.
我渴望一次海外度假已經很長一段時間了。

解析 ▶ 發生在過去、已完成的動作，使用過去完成式句型 "S + had + Vpp + ... + for + 一段時間 ."。

3

To my surprise, the dream did come true.
令我驚訝的是，這個夢想真的成真了。

解析 ▶ "To + 所有格 + 表示情緒的名詞，+ 子句 ." 是用來表示情緒的慣用句型，例如："To my shame, ..." 或 "To his sadness, ..."。

4

In fact, I had dreamt about travelling to Guam for many years.
事實上，我已經夢想到關島旅遊很多年了。

解析 ▶ "In fact, + 子句 ." 也可以寫成 "Actually, + 子句 ."，是表示事實的常用句型。

5

All of my friends had been there, and their high recommendations were really impressive.
我所有的朋友們都已經去過那裡，而且他們的極力推薦實在令人印象深刻。

解析 ▶ 用對等連接詞 "and" 來連接兩個子句，前者表示過去已經完成的動作，因此使用過去完成式；後者表示過去的事實，使用過去簡單式。

PART 1 unit 2 英文作文

25

6

 However, the high cost of the trip to Guam was always my concern.

然而，到關島旅行的高額費用總是讓我有所顧慮。

解析 ▶ 轉折語 "however" 開頭的句子，其語氣會與前文完全不同。前面說的都是想要去關島旅行的內容，這邊卻提出了一個不能成行的顧慮，所以會使用這樣的轉折語來改變語氣。用法相似的還有 "nevertheless" 和 "nonetheless"，在文章之中適度使用轉折語，可讓文章結構更加清楚。

7

 With the unexpected surprise, I could finally go to this heaven **to** go snorkelling, **to** go shopping, **and** just **to** relax.

有了這個意外的驚喜，我終於可以去這個天堂浮潛、購物或純粹放鬆一下。

解析 ▶ 由介系詞開頭的條件句 "With ...,＋主要子句."，表示在有了某個條件之後，主要子句就可以成真。這裡主要子句的部分是用對等連接詞連接三個表目的的不定詞片語，其句型為 "to Vr, to Vr, and to Vr ..."。

8

That night, I couldn't sleep because I was so excited.

那天晚上我無法入睡，因為我實在太興奮了。

解析 ▶ 主要句型是 " 主要子句＋ because ＋從屬子句 ."，後面的子句修飾前面的子句，說明無法入睡的原因。

9

I thought I was really the luckiest person in the world.

我想我真的是世界上最幸運的人了。

解析 ▶ 用 "I thought ＋ (that) ＋子句 ." 的句型來表示想法，子句內使用的是最高級的句型，因此記得要加上定冠詞 "the"。

必備字彙 與片語整理

⇒ believe	[bɪ`liv]	v.	相信
⇒ concern	[kən`sɝn]	n.	擔心，顧慮
⇒ heaven	[`hɛvən]	n.	天堂
⇒ impressive	[ɪm`prɛsɪv]	adj.	令人印象深刻的
⇒ lucky	[`lʌkɪ]	adj.	幸運的
⇒ recommendation	[ˌrɛkəmɛn`deʃən]	n.	推薦
⇒ relax	[rɪ`læks]	v.	放鬆，休息
⇒ surprise	[sɚ`praɪz]	n.	驚訝
⇒ unexpected	[ˌʌnɪk`spɛktɪd]	adj.	意料之外的
⇒ come true		phr.	成真，實現
⇒ fall asleep		phr.	睡著
⇒ go shopping		phr.	去購物
⇒ go snorkelling		phr.	去浮潛
⇒ long for		phr.	渴望

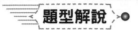

2-3 書信寫作

題型解說

「書信寫作」題型，會提示一種寫作背景主題情境，考生要針對這個情境寫一封信，提示也會提及信的內容要寫些什麼。信的上下款要符合一般的書信格式，如下所示：

December 23, 2022
Dear Mr. Chen,
Sincerely yours, Alice

信的一開始要先闡明這封信的主要目的是什麼。信的中段則應該談論內容細節，包括解釋寫信動機或提出要求等，而在最後則要寫出寫信者的期望或收信者應該對書信內容做出的回應，例如回信、補交資料或回電等。

示範例題

說明 請依照下面所提供的文字提示，寫一篇長度約 120 字（8 至 12 句）的英文書信，答案請寫在寫作能力測驗答案紙上。評分重點包括內容、組織、文法、用字遣詞、標點符號與大小寫。

寫作能力培養

28

提示 ▶ 上學期你參加了一週五天的密集式英文訓練課程，而你真的很喜歡那位外籍老師 Mr. Allan Smith。於是你代表你的同學寫一封信給他，表示你們對他課程的喜愛以及希望與他一起出遊或共進一餐。

___

参考範文 ►●

¹Dear Mr. Smith,

²I am one of your students who joined your class last semester. ³Our class was 231, and we took your English Intensive Course for the whole semester. ⁴In fact, we all like your courses and your teaching style. ⁵We have learned much more than in other English courses. ⁶Although we have our own business to take care of now, we still cannot forget the happy memories which you gave us.

⁷Recently, we have discussed about a date for a class reunion. ⁸And, we are looking forward to seeing you again. ⁹We do not know whether you are free on the 30th of June. ¹⁰However, we are meeting at Sunday's restaurant, and we are all excited about having a chance to meet you. ¹¹Please let me know whether you can come or not. ¹²We are expecting to hear from you soon.

Sincerely yours,
Angela Yang

1 親愛的史密斯先生：

　　2 我是參加你上期課程的學生之一。3 我們是 231 班，我們上了你一整期的英文密集課程。4 事實上，我們都很喜歡你的課程與教學方式。5 我們學到的比在其他英文課所學到的還要多得多。6 雖然我們現在都有自己的事要做，但是我們仍然無法忘記你帶給我們的美好回憶。

　　7 最近，我們討論了同學會的日期。8 而且，我們很期待能再見到你，9 我們不知道你在 6 月 30 日是否有空。10 不過，我們會在 Sunday's 餐廳見面，我們全都很期待能有機會見到你。11 請讓我知道你能不能來。12 我們期待很快收到你的回音。

你真誠的，

楊安琪拉

範文句型解析 ◦●

1

Dear Mr. Smith,

親愛的史密斯先生，

解析 ▶ 收信人的姓名是 "Allan Smith"，所以書信的開頭可以是 "Dear Mr. Smith," 或 "Dear Allan,"。

2

I am **one of** your students who joined your class last semester.

我是參加你上期課程的學生之一。

解析 ▶ 表示「其中之一」的句型是 "one of ＋複數名詞 "。此處還使用由關係代名詞 "who" 所引導的形容詞子句來修飾複數名詞 "students"。

3 Our class was 231 , and we took your English Intensive Course for the whole semester.
我們是 231 班，我們上了你一整期的英文密集課程。

解析 ▶ 使用對等連接詞 ", and" 來連接兩個句子，因為兩者都是過去發生的事實，因此使用過去簡單式。

4 In fact, we all like your course and your teaching style.
事實上，我們都很喜歡你的課程與教學方式。

解析 ▶ 表示「事實上」的 "In fact" 是非常常見的轉折語。類似的表達方式還有 "As a matter of fact"、"Actually" 等。

5 We have learned much more than in other English courses.
我們學到的比在其他英文課所學到的還要多得多。

解析 ▶ 以比較級句型構句，再以 "much" 修飾比較級，這是慣用的表達方式。

6 Although we have our own business to take care of now, we still cannot forget the happy memories **which you gave us**.
雖然我們現在都有自己的事要做，但是我們仍然無法忘記你帶給我們的美好回憶。

解析 ▶ 以連接詞 "although" 引導表示讓步的從屬子句，從屬子句和主要子句之間只要加上逗點就好，不可以再加 "but"。後面利用由關係代名詞 "which" 所引導的形容詞子句來修飾名詞 "memories"。

7 Recently, we have discussed about a date for a class reunion.
最近，我們討論了同學會的日期。

解析 ▶ 「討論」是一直持續到最近（Recently）的動作，因此使用現在完成式來表達。

8

And, we are **looking forward to** seeing you again.
而且，我們很期待能再見到你。

 解析 "look forward to + V-ing" 是固定的慣用表達句型，表示「期待做某事」，在書信類文章中經常會用到這個句型，務必要記下來。

9

We do not know whether you are free on the 30th of June.
我們不知道你在 6 月 30 日是否有空。

 解析 連接詞 "whether" 引導名詞子句來做為動詞 "know" 的受詞。

10

However, we are meeting at Sunday's restaurant, and we are all excited about having a chance to meet you.
不過，我們會在 Sunday's 餐廳見面，我們全都很期待能有機會見到你。

 解析 表示未來的計畫時，可以用現在進行式代替未來式。

11

Please let me know whether you can come or not.
請讓我知道你能不能來。

 解析 "whether you can come or not" 是名詞子句，這裡被當成動詞 "know" 的受詞。

12

We are expecting to hear from you soon.
我們期待很快收到你的回音。

 解析 expect 是「期待，期盼」的意思，常會以 "expect + to +原形動詞" 或 "expect that +子句" 的慣用句型出現。

必備字彙 與片語整理

⇒ business	[`bɪznɪs]	n.	事情；事業
⇒ course	[kors]	n.	課程
⇒ dear	[dɪr]	adj.	親愛的
⇒ forget	[fəˋgɛt]	v.	忘記
⇒ in fact		phr.	事實上
⇒ intensive	[ɪnˋtɛnsɪv]	adj.	密集的；加強的
⇒ join	[dʒɔɪn]	v.	參加
⇒ memory	[`mɛmərɪ]	n.	回憶
⇒ recently	[`risn̩tlɪ]	adv.	最近
⇒ semester	[səˋmɛstɚ]	n.	學期
⇒ sincerely	[sɪnˋsɪrlɪ]	adv.	真誠地
⇒ be looking forward to		phr.	期待做……
⇒ discuss about		phr.	討論
⇒ hear from		phr.	聽到……的回音
⇒ whether ... or not		phr.	是否……

英文書信實用例句 ⇒●

正式的書信開頭：

⇒ Many thanks for your letter dated August 3.
多謝您八月三日的來信。

⇒ We have acknowledged the receipt of your letter dated
March 5.
我們已確認收到您三月五日的來信。

33

➠ Your letter dated July 23 gave us much pleasure.

您在七月二十三日的來信讓我們很開心。

➠ We thank you very much for your inquiry dated October 7.

我們非常感謝您在十月七日的來信諮詢。

➠ We are honored to let you know ...

我們很榮幸通知您……

➠ We are pleased to inform you that ...

我們很高興通知您……

➠ The purpose of this letter is to inform you that ...

這封信的目的是通知您……

➠ We feel it our duty to inform you that/of ...

我們認為有義務通知您……

➠ Please allow us to call your attention to ...

請讓我們提醒您注意……

➠ We regret to inform you that/of ...

我們很遺憾要通知您……

➠ It's our pleasure to respond to your inquiry dated April 7.

我們很樂意回答您在四月七日所提出的問題。

➠ We are indeed sorry to hear that ...

我們真的很遺憾聽到……

➠ It gives us deep regret to announce to you that ...

我們非常遺憾要告知您……

➠ This letter is to inform you that ...

這封信是要通知您……

➠ We are pleased to acknowledge receipt of your inquiry dated July 2.

我們很高興收到您在七月二日所提出的問題。

正式的書信結尾：

➡ We hope to receive your letter at an early date.
我們希望早日收到你的回信。

➡ We would appreciate an early reply.
我們希望您能盡快回覆。

➡ Kindly reply at your earliest convenience.
請您盡快回覆。

➡ Please send us your reply by the earliest delivery.
請盡快給我們回覆。

➡ I believe that you will reply to us immediately.
我相信你會立刻回覆我們的。

➡ We look forward to receiving your early reply.
我們期待能盡早收到您的回覆。

➡ As the matter is urgent, an early reply will be appreciated.
由於情況緊急，希望能盡快收到回覆。

➡ We are anxiously awaiting your reply.
我們正急切地等待您的回應。

➡ I have to apologize to you for not answering your letter in time.
我必須為沒有及時回覆您的信件向您道歉。

➡ I hope you will forgive me for not having written to you for so long.
希望您能原諒我這麼久沒有寫信給您。

➡ We regret the trouble we are causing you.
我們很遺憾對您造成困擾。

➡ We hope you will pardon us for troubling you.
我們希望您能原諒我們所造成的困擾。

➡ I hope we may receive further information.
我希望我們可以獲得進一步的消息。

➡ Your early reply is definitely appreciated.
感謝您的盡早回覆。

➠ I expect to get your reply as soon as possible.
我期待能盡快收到你的回應。

➠ I'm glad to hear that you received a promotion.
我很高興聽說你獲得了升職。

其他書信常用句：

➠ I'm delighted to learn that you have passed the entrance exam.
我很高興得知你通過了入學考試。

➠ I'm sorry to hear that you failed your final exam.
我很遺憾聽到你的期末考不及格。

➠ I'm sad to learn that you did not get a raise this time.
我很遺憾得知你這次未能獲得加薪。

➠ I hope this letter finds you well.
收信愉快。

➠ How have you been doing?
你最近好嗎？

➠ Wishing you success.
希望你能成功。

➠ I'm thankful to you for your assistance.
我很感激你的協助。

➠ I appreciate very much your warm assistance.
我十分感激你的熱心協助。

➠ I'm so happy that you did a good job.
我很高興你的表現良好。

Part

寫作能力培養

2

「全民英檢中級寫作能力測驗」的考題重點，在於測驗考生建構文章的能力，其實追根究柢，文章是由一個個前後相關的句子按照邏輯組合起來的，建構文章的能力主要是建立在建構句子的能力之上。所以，想要寫出好文章，首先必須能寫出好句子，其要素包括：足夠的字彙、正確的文法、合乎語法的句型。本書第二部分特別為考生整理「必考文法句型解析」，並且透過「單句翻譯實力演練」，幫助考生擴充字彙、活用文法及句型。

Look Inside

寫作能力培養

必考文法句型解析

英文是相當重視句型結構的語言,而且句型的結構和文法觀念息息相關、相輔相成。五大句型是所有英文句子的骨架,不管是多麼複雜難懂的句子,只要掌握五大句型的構成方式,都能正確分析出句子的結構。

1-1 五大句型

五大句型公式

一、S(主詞)+ Vi(不及物動詞)

二、S(主詞)+ V(連綴動詞)+ SC(主詞補語)

三、S(主詞)+ Vt(及物動詞)+ O(受詞)

四、S(主詞)+ V(授與動詞)+ IO(間接受詞)+ DO(直接受詞)

S(主詞)+ V(授與動詞)+ DO(直接受詞)+ to/for + IO(間接受詞)

五、S(主詞)+ V(使役、感官、命名動詞)+ O(受詞)+ OC(受詞補語)

句型 一

S + Vi

解析 ▶ 這一類句型的動詞是不及物動詞,動詞後面不接受詞或補語就可以完整表達語意。必要時可以加上副詞來修飾動詞。

例句 ▶

⟹ I cry. 我哭。

⟹ They run in the park. 他們在公園裡跑。

⟹ Birds fly in the sky. 鳥在天上飛。

句型 二

S + V + SC

解析 ▶ 這一類句型中的動詞，本身的意義不完整，所以在動詞後面還必須接上補語來補充說明主詞，才能完整表達語意，所以這種動詞叫做「連綴」動詞：

連綴動詞的種類	
Be 動詞	is、am、are、was、were
表示狀態的改變	get、become、grow
表示狀態的持續	keep、stay
感官動詞	look（看起來）、sound（聽起來）、smell（聞起來）、taste（嚐起來）、feel（感覺起來）、seem（似乎）

例句 ▶

➡ The flower is red. 這花是紅的。

➡ The weather gets cold. 天氣變冷了。

句型 三

S + Vt + O

解析 ▶ 這一類句型的動詞是及物動詞，也就是在動詞後面一定要接受詞做為承受動作的對象。

例句 ▶

➡ I'm considering this plan. 我正在考慮這個計畫。

➡ I put off this trip. 我延後了這趟旅行。

➡ I quit smoking. 我戒菸了。

➡ I gave up this plan. 我放棄了這個計畫。

句型 四

S + V + IO + DO

解析 ▶ 這一類句型的動詞稱為授與動詞，動詞後面要接兩個受詞，來表示「將某物給某人」的意思，有以下兩種表達方式：

S	V（授與動詞）	IO（間接受詞：人）	DO（直接受詞：物）
I	sent	my friend	an e-mail.
我	寄了	我的朋友	一封電子郵件。

S	V（授與動詞）	DO（直接受詞：物）	for/to	IO（間接受詞：人）
I	sent	an e-mail	to	my friend.
我	寄了	一封電子郵件	給	我的朋友。

例句 ▶

➭ I brought my girlfriend a bunch of flowers. 我帶給了女友一束花。

➭ I gave my child $300 dollars. 我給了我的小孩 300 元。

➭ I sent an e-mail to my friend. 我寄了一封電子郵件給我的朋友。

➭ I bought a gift for my parents. 我買了一個禮物給我的父母。

句型 五

S + V + O + OC

解析 ▶ 這一類句型的動詞類型包括：使役動詞、感官動詞、命名動詞。動詞之後要接受詞和受詞補語，受詞補語可以是原形動詞、分詞、不定詞，用來說明受詞。這一類的動詞有以下四種分類：

使役V＋Vr	使役V＋to Vr	感官V＋Vr/V-ing	命名V＋N
make（使）	ask（要求）	hear（聽）	call（命名）
let（使）	command（命令）	see（看）	declare（宣稱）
have（使）	order（命令）	watch（觀看）	name（取名）
get（使）	require（要求）	look at（注視）	pronounce（宣稱）
	get（使）	notice（注意）	
	demand（要求）		

例句 ▶

➭ My mother makes me clean my room. 我母親要我清理房間。

【使役V＋Vr】

➭ My mother asks me to clean my room. 我母親要我清理房間。

【使役V＋to Vr】

➭ I see you run in the park. 我看見你在公園裡跑。　　【感官V＋Vr】

➭ He watches me doing this job. 他看著我做這份工作。【感官V＋V-ing】

➭ I named my dog "Happy". 我將我的狗命名為「Happy」。

【命名V＋N】

➭ I will have my hair cut next week. 下禮拜我會去剪頭髮。

【have＋O＋Vpp 表示由別人幫忙做的動作，是特殊的常考句型。】

五大句型綜合分析

分析 1

Money	talks.
S	Vi

有錢好辦事。

分析 2

An earthquake	happened.
S	Vi

地震發生了。

分析 3

The oranges on the table	aren't	mine.
S	V	SC

桌上的柳橙不是我的。

分析 4

My teacher	is	really handsome.
S	V	SC

我的老師真的很帥。

分析 5

They	read	magazines	everyday.
S	Vt	O	

他們每天都看雜誌。

分析 6

I	don't know	where I can buy this book.
S	Vt	O

我不知道在哪裡可以買到這本書。

分析 7

She	told	me	that she wants to learn English.
S	V	IO	DO

她告訴我她想學英文。

分析 8

Alice	bought	a bar of chocolate	for	me.
S	V	DO	to/for	IO

愛麗絲買了一條巧克力給我。

41

分析 ⑨

We	call	this fruit	a pineapple.
S	V	O	OC

我們稱這種水果是鳳梨。

分析 ⑩

The airplane to New York	crashed.
S	Vi

這架往紐約的飛機墜毀了。

分析 ⑪

Those flowers in the garden	are	beautiful.
S	V	SC

那些在花園裡的花很美。

分析 ⑫

He	looks for	a stable job	every day.
S	V	O	

他每天都在找一份穩定的工作。

分析 ⑬

I	saw	you	cry in the corner	last night.
S	V	O	OC	

昨天晚上我看見你在角落哭泣。

分析 ⑭

The doctor	declared	the girl	dead.
S	V	O	OC

醫生宣布這個女孩死亡了。

分析 ⑮

I	had	my car	fixed	yesterday.
S	V	O	OC	

昨天我去修理車子了。

1-2 主動與被動語態

常出現的被動語態時態

時態	主動	被動
現在簡單式	現在式動詞	is/am/are＋Vpp
現在進行式	be＋V-ing	is/am/are＋being＋Vpp
現在完成式	have/has＋Vpp	have/has＋been＋Vpp
現在完成進行式	have/has + been＋V-ing	X
過去簡單式	過去式動詞	was/were＋Vpp
過去進行式	was/were＋V-ing	was/were＋being＋Vpp
未來簡單式	will＋Vr	will＋be＋Vpp
	be going to＋Vr	be going to＋be＋Vpp
未來進行式	will＋be＋V-ing	X

現在簡單式
is/am/are＋Vpp

否定句 I don't like English grammar.
▶ English grammar isn't liked by me. 英文文法不被我喜歡。

疑問句 Do you like English grammar?
▶ Is English grammar liked by you? 英文文法被你喜歡嗎？

現在進行式
is/am/are＋being＋Vpp

否定句 Mary isn't drinking a cup of coffee now.
▶ A cup of coffee isn't being drunk by Mary now.
現在一杯咖啡沒正在被瑪麗喝。

疑 問句　Is Mary drinking a cup of coffee now?

▶ Is a cup of coffee being drunk by Mary now?

現在一杯咖啡正在被瑪麗喝嗎？

現在完成式

have/has＋been＋Vpp

否 定句　I haven't done my homework yet.

▶ My homework hasn't been done by me yet.

我的作業尚未被我做完。

疑 問句　Have you done your homework yet?

▶ Has your homework been done by you yet?

你的作業被你做完了嗎？

過去簡單式

was/were＋Vpp

否 定句　They didn't do their homework yesterday.

▶ Their homework wasn't done by them yesterday.

他們的作業昨天沒被他們做。

疑 問句　Did they do their homework yesterday?

▶ Was their homework done by them yesterday?

他們的作業昨天被他們做了嗎？

過去進行式

was/were＋being＋Vpp

否 定句　My mother wasn't planting a flower at 7:00 yesterday.

▶ A flower wasn't being planted by my mother at 7:00

yesterday. 昨天七點花沒正在被我母親種。

疑 問句　Was my mother planting a flower at 7:00 yesterday?

▶ Was a flower being planted by my mother at 7:00

yesterday? 昨天七點花正在被我母親種嗎？

未來簡單式

will＋be＋Vpp

be going to＋be＋Vpp

否定句 You won't see the dog next time.

▶ The dog won't be seen by you next time.

下回這隻狗將不會被你看到。

疑問句 Will you see the dog next time?

▶ Will the dog be seen by you next time?

下回這隻狗會被你看到嗎？

主動語態與被動語態的轉換 ▶

解析 ▶ 主動語態和被動語態的轉換，必須特別注意動詞及人稱的改變，如果主動語態的主詞是不確定或非特定的對象，則被動語態中的 "by somebody" 可以省略。另外要注意轉換主動與被動語態並不會影響句子原本的時態。

	主詞	動詞	受詞	
主動語態：	I	like	dogs.	現在簡單式
被動語態：	Dogs	are liked	by me.	現在簡單式

例句 ▶

➠ I study English every day.

➢ English is studied by me every day.

英文每天被我讀。

➠ Cats eat mice.

➢ Mice are eaten by cats.

老鼠被貓吃。

➠ She washes her car every week.

➢ Her car is washed by her every week.

她的車每個星期都被她洗。

45

主動與被動語態綜合練習

請以英文被動語態的表達方式,將下列中文句子翻譯為英文:

1. 這杯子每天被洗。

▶ _____

2. 這杯子五分鐘前被洗。

▶ _____

3. 這杯子現在正在被洗。

▶ _____

4. 這杯子昨晚八點正在被洗。

▶ _____

5. 這杯子明天將被洗。

▶ _____

6. 這杯子已經被洗好了。

▶ _____

7. 這杯子在你來之前已經被洗好了。

▶ _____

Answer

 解答

1. 這杯子每天被洗。

▶ *This cup is washed every day.*

2. 這杯子五分鐘前被洗。

▶ *This cup was washed 5 minutes ago.*

3. 這杯子現在正在被洗。

▶ *This cup is being washed now.*

4. 這杯子昨晚八點正在被洗。

▶ *This cup was being washed at 8 o'clock last night.*

5. 這杯子明天將被洗。

▶ *This cup will be washed tomorrow.*

6. 這杯子已經被洗好了。

▶ *This cup has been washed (already).*

7. 這杯子在你來之前已經被洗好了。

▶ *This cup had been washed before you came.*

名詞子句

名詞子句可以代替名詞做為主詞、受詞、補語、同位語,本書依其引導的連接詞將名詞子句分類為:「由 IF 引導的名詞子句」、「由疑問詞引導的名詞子句」、「由 THAT 引導的名詞子句」。

由 IF 引導的名詞子句

解析 ▶ 用 if/whether/whether or not 來引導 Yes/No 的一般疑問句,形成「由 IF 引導的名詞子句」,來代替句子中的名詞。if 不可省略,而且由連接詞所引導的子句必須改為直述句的呈現方式。

例句 ▶

➠ I wonder **this thing**. 我懷疑這件事。

Is Paul a handsome teacher? 保羅是一位很帥的老師嗎?

➢ I wonder <u>if Paul is a handsome teacher</u>.

➢ I wonder <u>whether Paul is a handsome teacher</u>.

➢ I wonder <u>whether or not Paul is a handsome teacher</u>.

➢ I wonder <u>whether Paul is a handsome teacher or not</u>.

我懷疑保羅是不是一位很帥的老師。

【用連接詞 if 或 whether (or not) 來引導 Yes/No 的一般疑問句 "Is Paul a handsome teacher?",形成「由 IF 引導的名詞子句」,用來代替句子中原本的名詞 "this thing"。】

➠ **This thing** is a question. 這件事是個問題。

Is Paul handsome? 保羅很帥嗎?

➢ <u>If Paul is handsome</u> is a question. 保羅帥不帥是個問題。

【直接用連接詞 if 或 whether (or not) 來引導 Yes/No 的一般疑問句 "Is Paul handsome?",形成「由 IF 引導的名詞子句」,用來代替原本句子中的名詞 "this thing"。】

➢ It is a question <u>if Paul is handsome</u>. 保羅帥不帥是個問題。

【用虛主詞 it 引導真正的主詞,這裡的主詞就是「由 IF 引導的名詞子句」。】

由疑問詞引導的名詞子句

用各種疑問詞來引導疑問詞疑問句，形成「由疑問詞引導的名詞子句」，來代替句子中的名詞。帶有不同意義的疑問詞無論是在句中還是句首都不可省略，而且還須注意，由疑問詞所引導的子句必須改為直述句的呈現方式。

例句

➡ I don't know **this thing**. 我不知道這件事。

How old is Alice? 愛麗絲幾歲？

➤ I don't know how old Alice is. 我不知道愛麗絲幾歲。

➡ I don't know **this thing**. 我不知道這件事。

Where did Christine go last night? 克莉絲汀昨晚去哪了？

➤ I don't know where Christine went last night.

我不知道克莉絲汀昨晚去哪了。

➡ I don't know **this thing**. 我不知道這件事。

How does Neal go to work? 尼爾是怎麼去上班的？

➤ I don't know how Neal goes to work.

我不知道尼爾是怎麼去上班的。

➡ I don't know **this thing**. 我不知道這件事。

What is William doing now? 威廉現在正在做什麼？

➤ I don't know what William is doing now.

我不知道威廉現在正在做什麼。

➡ I don't know **this thing**. 我不知道這件事。

What can Vivian do? 薇薇安能做什麼？

➤ I don't know what Vivian can do. 我不知道薇薇安能做什麼。

【這裡的 can 是有意義的助動詞，不可以省略。】

➡ I don't know **this thing**. 我不知道這件事。

Whose pen is this? 這枝筆是誰的？

➤ I don't know whose pen this is. 我不知道這枝筆是誰的。

PART 2 unit 1 必考文法句型解析

49

⟹ **This thing** is a secret. 這件事是一個秘密。

⟹ **Where did Steward go last night?** 史都華昨晚去哪裡了？

　➤ <u>Where Steward went last night</u> is a secret.

　➤ It is a secret <u>where Steward went last night</u>.

　　史都華昨晚去哪裡是一個祕密。

由 THAT 引導的名詞子句 ❯●

解析 ▶ 用 that 來引導直述句，形成「由 THAT 引導的名詞子句」，來代替句子中的名詞。that 若放在前後子句之間且無意義時可以省略，但若放在句首則不可省略。

例句 ▶

⟹ I believe **this thing**. 我相信這件事。

Ivan is a handsome teacher. 伊凡是一位很帥的老師。

　➤ I believe <u>(that) Ivan is a handsome teacher</u>.

　　我相信伊凡是一位很帥的老師。

　　【that 在句中是無意義的連接詞，可以省略。】

⟹ **This thing** is a fact. 這件事是個事實。

Frank is a liar. 法蘭克是一個騙子。

　➤ <u>That Frank is a liar</u> is a fact.

　　法蘭克是一個騙子（的這件事）是個事實。

　　【把 that 放在句首當連接詞，此時的 that 不可省略。】

　➤ It is a fact <u>(that) Frank is a liar</u>.

　　法蘭克是一個騙子（的這件事）是個事實。

　　【這裡的虛主詞 it 用來指稱「由 THAT 引導的名詞子句」，此時的 that 可省略。】

1-4 直接引用與間接引用

直接引用改寫成間接引用時，要根據直接引用的句型使用連接詞，還要注意人稱及動詞時態的變化。直接引用改寫成間接引用時，動詞的時態必須要配合主要子句的時態而變化，主要子句若為現在簡單式、未來簡單式、現在完成式，則引用句的時態不變；若主要子句的時態為過去簡單式，則引用句的時態必須改變。

間接引用的時態變化

解析 ▶ 主要子句是過去簡單式的時候，直接引用轉換成間接引用的過程中，必須特別注意其動詞時態必須隨之改變，其規則如下：

直接引用的動詞時態	間接引用的動詞時態
現在簡單式	過去簡單式
過去簡單式	過去完成式
現在完成式	過去完成式
現在進行式	過去進行式

例句 ▶

⟹ Tony said, "I am going to the movies."

　　湯尼說：「我要去看電彰。」

　➤ Tony said that **he was going** to the movies.

　　湯尼說他要去看電彰。

　　【主要子句為過去簡單式，引用句的動詞時態須由現在進行式變成過去進行式。】

⟹ Tony said, "They had no money." 湯尼說：「他們沒錢。」

　➤ Tony said **that they had had** no money. 湯尼說他們沒錢。

　　【主要子句為過去簡單式，引用句的動詞時態由過去簡單式變成過去完成式。】

⟹ She said, "I took your textbook by mistake."

　　她說：「我不小心拿了你的課本。」

> She said that **she had taken my** textbook by mistake.

她說她不小心拿了我的課本。

【主要子句為過去簡單式，引用句的動詞時態由過去簡單式變成過去完成式，所有格 your 要改成 my。】

➡ Mary said, "I will go to the movies." 瑪麗說：「我會去看電彰。」

> Mary said that she **would go** to the movies.

瑪麗說她會去看電彰。

【主要子句為過去簡單式，引用句的助動詞及動詞時態由現在簡單式變成過去簡單式。】

➡ Ann said, "I can't find a job." 安說：「我找不到工作。」

> Ann said that **she couldn't find** a job. 安說她找不到工作。

【主要子句為過去簡單式，引用句的助動詞及動詞時態由現在簡單式變成過去簡單式。】

➡ Angela said, "I don't like my job."

安琪拉說：「我不喜歡我的工作。」

> Angela said that **she didn't like her** job.

安琪拉說她不喜歡她的工作。

【主要子句為過去簡單式，引用句的助動詞及動詞時態由現在簡單式變成過去簡單式。】

➡ She said, "The Sun rises in the east." 她說：「太陽從東方升起。」

> She said that the Sun **rises** in the east. 她說太陽從東方升起。

【當引用句的內容是不變的真理時，動詞時態不做任何改變。】

問句型式的直接引用與間接引用

解析 ▶ 直接引用若為 Yes/No 的一般疑問句，則改成間接引用時的連接詞必須使用 if。直接引用若為疑問詞疑問句，間接引用則須用疑問詞相連接。直接引用若為請求疑問句，間接引用須用不定詞連接。

例句 ▶

➠ Mary said, "Are you hungry, Nancy?"

瑪麗說：「南西，妳很餓嗎？」

➤ Mary asked Nancy **if she was hungry**. 瑪麗問南西她是否很餓。

➠ Mary said, "Is Peter a good student?"

瑪麗說：「彼得是個好學生嗎？」

➤ Mary asked **if Peter was a good student**.

瑪麗問彼得是不是個好學生。

➠ Mother said to me, "Where have you been?"

母親跟我說：「你到哪裡去了？」

➤ Mother asked me **where I had been**. 母親問我到哪裡去了。

➠ Mary said, "Where were you last night?"

瑪麗說：「昨晚你在哪裡？」

➤ Mary asked **where I had been last night**.

瑪麗問我昨晚在哪裡。

➠ He asked me, "Will you give me a hand?"

他問我：「你願意幫我一個忙嗎？」

➤ He asked me **to give him a hand**. 他請我幫他的忙。

命令型式的直接引用與間接引用 ◦

解析 ▶ 直接引用若為命令口吻，則間接引用必須利用不定詞來引導。

例句 ▶

➠ Mary said, "Be a good student, Peter."

瑪麗說：「彼得，要做一個好學生。」

➤ Mary asked Peter **to be a good student**.

瑪麗要求彼得做一個好學生。

⟱ He said, "Come on in, George." 他說：「進來，喬治。」

➤ He required George **to come on in**. 他要求喬治進來。

⟱ He said, "Open your book, Billy." 他說：「打開你的書，比利。」

➤ He ordered Billy **to open his book**. 他命令比利打開他的書。

⟱ He said, "Don't open your book, George."

他說：「喬治，不要打開你的書。」

➤ He commanded George **not to open his book**.

他命令喬治不要打開他的書。

祈願型式的直接引用與間接引用

解析 ▶ 直接引用的句子若為 May 開頭的祈願句型，間接引用的句子必須
使用 that 當連接詞，句型為「S ＋ prayed ＋ that ... might ...」。

例句 ▶

⟱ Mary said, "May God bless you." 瑪麗說：「願上帝保佑你。」

➤ Mary prayed **that God might bless me**. 瑪麗祈禱願上帝保佑我。

⟱ Mary said, "May you have a Merry Christmas."

瑪麗說：「祝你聖誕快樂。」

➤ Mary prayed **that I might have a Merry Christmas**.

瑪麗祈禱祝我聖誕快樂。

⟱ Mary said, "May God forgive me." 瑪麗說：「願上帝寬恕我。」

➤ Mary prayed **that God might forgive her**.

瑪麗祈禱願上帝寬恕她。

建議型式的直接引用與間接引用 🔊

解析 🔊 直接引用的句子如果是用 Let's 開頭的建議句型，間接引用的句型為「S + suggested/recommended + that + S + should ...」。

例句 🔊

➠ Mary said, "Let's go shopping." 瑪麗說：「我們去購物吧。」

➢ Mary suggested **that we should go shopping**.
瑪麗建議我們去購物。

➠ Mary said, "Let's study English together."
瑪麗說：「我們一起念英文吧。」

➢ Mary recommended **that we should study English together**.
瑪麗建議我們一起念英文。

感嘆型式的直接引用與間接引用 🔊

解析 🔊 直接引用的句子如果是用 How/What 開頭，間接引用也同樣要用 How/What 連接。

例句 🔊

➠ Mary said, "How beautiful the girl is!"
瑪麗說：「這女孩多美呀！」

➢ Mary said **how beautiful the girl was**. 瑪麗說這女孩真是美。

➠ Mary said, "What a pretty girl Belle is!"
瑪麗說：「貝兒是一位多漂亮的女孩呀！」

➢ Mary said **what a pretty girl Belle was**.
瑪麗說貝兒真是一位漂亮的女孩。

1-5 形容詞子句

形容詞子句的形成

解析 形容詞子句的作用是代替形容詞來修飾名詞，所修飾的對象有可能會是「人」或「物」，依據修飾對象的不同，會使用不同的關係代名詞做引導。當關係代名詞為主格或受格時，無論修飾的是人還是物，都可以用 that 來引導。

	主格	受格	所有格
人	who/that	whom/that	whose
物	which/that	which/that	whose
人或物	that	that	X

例句

⟹ The woman is Canadian. 那個女人是加拿大人。

She is talking to your father. 她正在和你父親說話。

➢ The woman **who is talking to your father** is Canadian.
正在和你父親說話的那個女人是加拿大人。

【代表「人」的主格關係代名詞 who，引導形容詞子句修飾主詞 The woman。】

⟹ The man is over there. 那個男人在那裡。

You talked to the man yesterday. 你昨天跟那個男人說過話。

➢ The man **whom you talked to yesterday** is over there.
你昨天說過話的那個男人在那裡。

【代表「人」的受格關係代名詞 whom，引導形容詞子句修飾主詞 The man。】

⟹ The girl is my friend. 那個女孩是我的朋友。

The girl's father is a doctor. 那個女孩的父親是一個醫生。

➢ The girl **whose father is a doctor** is my friend.
父親是醫生的那個女孩是我的朋友。

【代表「人」的所有格關係代名詞 whose，引導形容詞子句修飾主詞 The girl。】

⟹ The cat is mine. 那隻貓是我的。

Its tail is crooked. 牠的尾巴彎彎曲曲的。

➢ The cat **whose tail is crooked** is mine.
那隻尾巴彎彎曲曲的貓是我的。

【代表「物」的所有格關係代名詞 whose，引導形容詞子句修飾主詞 The cat。】

⇒ The book is a bestseller. 那本書是一本暢銷書。
The book has many pictures. 那本書有很多圖片。

➢ The book **which has many pictures** is a bestseller.
有很多圖片的那本書是一本暢銷書。

【代表「物」的主格關係代名詞 which，引導形容詞子句修飾主詞 The book。】

⇒ The book is a bestseller. 那本書是一本暢銷書。
I bought the book yesterday. 我昨天買了那本書。

➢ The book **which I bought yesterday** is a bestseller.
我昨天買的那本書是一本暢銷書。

【代表「物」的受格關係代名詞 which，引導形容詞子句修飾主詞 The book。】

關係代名詞的省略

解析 ▶ 關係代名詞為受格時可以直接省略。關係代名詞為主格時，省略關係代名詞必須將形容詞子句改為分詞構句的型式。關係代名詞為所有格時不可省略。

例句 ▶

⇒ The girl **who lives** upstairs is my friend.
⇒ The girl **that lives** upstairs is my friend.
⇒ The girl **living** upstairs is my friend.
住在樓上的那個女孩是我的朋友。

【關係代名詞為代表「人」的主格，可以使用 who 或用 that 代替，也可以省略關係代名詞而採用分詞構句。】

⇒ The girl **whom you talked to** is my friend.
⇒ The girl **that you talked to** is my friend.
⇒ The girl **to whom you talked** is my friend.
和你說話的那個女孩是我的朋友。

【關係代名詞為代表「人」的受格，可以使用 whom 或用 that 代替，也可以直接省略關係代名詞。但要注意，若關係代名詞之前有介系詞，關係代名詞就不能用 that 代替，也不能省略。】

➠ The girl **whose father** is a doctor is my friend.

父親是醫生的那個女孩是我的朋友。

【關係代名詞是「人」的所有格，所以只能用 whose，而不能用 that 代替，也不能省略。】

➠ The book **which has** many pictures is a bestseller.

➠ The book **that has** many pictures is a bestseller.

➠ The book **having** many pictures is a bestseller.

有很多圖片的那本書是一本暢銷書。

【關係代名詞是代表「物」的主格，所以可以使用 which 或用 that 代替，也可以省略關係代名詞而採用分詞構句表達。】

➠ The book **which I talked about** yesterday is a bestseller.

➠ The book **that I talked about** yesterday is a bestseller.

➠ The book **about which I talked** yesterday is a bestseller.

我昨天談到的那本書是一本暢銷書。

【關係代名詞是代表「物」的受格，可以使用 which 或用 that 代替，也可以直接省略關係代名詞。但要注意，若關係代名詞之前出現介系詞，那麼關係代名詞就不能用 that 代替，也不能省略。】

➠ The book **whose cover** is yellow is a bestseller.

有黃色封面的那本書是一本暢銷書。

【關係代名詞是「物」的所有格，所以只能用 whose，而不能用 that 代替，也不能省略。】

一定要使用 THAT 的情況

情況❶ 當修飾的先行詞中同時出現「人」和「物」時

➠ **The boy and his cat that** were taken care of by their baby-sitter went to the park yesterday.

被保母照顧的那個男孩與他的貓昨天去了公園。

情況 2 當修飾的先行詞前面出現「最高級」時

➡ John is **the smartest student that** I have ever taught.
約翰是我指導過的學生之中最聰明的。

情況 3 當先行詞前面出現表示「唯一」的形容詞時

➡ He is **the only student that** finishes his homework on time.
他是唯一一位準時完成作業的學生。

情況 4 疑問詞與關係代名詞重複時

➡ **Who is the girl that** is singing in the forest?
正在森林裡唱歌的那個女孩是誰？

情況 5 先行詞中出現「序數」時

➡ He is **the first man that** told me the truth.
他是第一個告訴我事實的人。

情況 6 先行詞為 everything, anything, nothing, something 時

➡ I'll tell you **something that** you must be interested in.
我會告訴你一件你一定會感興趣的事。

不可以使用 THAT 的情況

情況 1 關係詞前面出現介系詞

➡ The girl **with whom** you talked yesterday is my sister.
昨天和你說話的女孩是我的妹妹。

情況 2 非限定用法

➡ Vincent, **who was a famous singer,** sang lots of touching songs.
文生，他以前是一位著名的歌手，唱過許多感人的歌曲。

情況❸ 關係代名詞是所有格的型式

➠ The house **whose** door is open is mine.
門開著的那間屋子是我的。

形容詞子句的變化用法

解析 ▶ 當形容詞子句帶有介系詞片語時，介系詞可放置在關係代名詞的前面，此時關係代名詞只能使用 whom 或 which，不可用 that 代替，亦不可以省略。將介系詞移到關係代名詞前面之後，還可依照以下表格所示，將原本「介系詞＋關係代名詞」的型式，簡化成一個表示「地點、時間、原因、方法」的關係副詞。

	表地點	表時間	表原因	表方法
關係副詞	where	when	why	how

例句 ▶

➠ The man **whom I talked to** is my teacher.

➠ The man **that I talked to** is my teacher.

➠ The man **I talked to** is my teacher.

➠ The man **to whom I talked** is my teacher.
和我說話的這個男子是我的老師。
【關係代名詞是代表「人」的受格，可以使用 whom 或用 that 代替，也可以直接省略關係代名詞。但要注意，若關係代名詞之前出現介系詞，那麼關係代名詞就不能用 that 代替，也不能省略。】

➠ The chair **which I am sitting on** is comfortable.

➠ The chair **that I am sitting on** is comfortable.

➠ The chair **I am sitting on** is comfortable.

➠ The chair **on which I am sitting** is comfortable.
我正在坐的這張椅子是舒服的。
【關係代名詞為代表「物」的受格，可以使用 which 或用 that 代替，也可以直接省略關係代名詞。但要注意，若關係代名詞之前出現介系詞，那麼關係代名詞就不能用 that 代替，也不能省略。】

➠ This is the house **in which I was born**.
➠ This is the house **where I was born**.

這是我出生的房子。

【in which = where，用來表示地點。】

➠ The beach was a place **to which she often went in the summer**.
➠ The beach was a place **where she often went in the summer**.

這個海灘是她以前夏天經常去的地方。

【to which = where，用來表示地點。】

➠ We visited a place in **which fruits abound**.
➠ We visited a place **where fruits abound**.

我們拜訪了一個盛產水果的地方。

【in which = where，用來表示地點。】

➠ Can you remember the day **on which we first met**?
➠ Can you remember the day **when we first met**?

你記得我們第一次見面的那天嗎？

【on which = when，用來表示時間。】

➠ This is **the reason for which he got mad**.
➠ This is **the reason why he got mad**.
➠ This is **why he got mad**.

這是他發火的原因。

【for which = why，用來表示原因。這裡使用 "This is ..." 的句型，後面接的主詞 the reason 和關係副詞 why 本身的意思一致，都是表示原因，所以這裡的 the reason 可省略。】

➠ This is **the way by which he made it**.
➠ This is **the way he made it**.
➠ This is **how he made it**.

這是他成功的方法。

【by which = how，用來表示方法。這裡使用 "This is ..." 的句型，後面接的主詞 the way 和關係副詞 how 本身的意思一致，都是表示方法，所以這裡的 the way 可省略。】

形容詞子句綜合練習

請以形容詞子句的表達方式合併下列句子：

1. I am not interested in the man.

The man is wearing blue pants.

▶ _____

2. The girl has long blond hair.

The girl looks beautiful.

▶ _____

3. The book has many pictures in it.

He bought the book yesterday.

▶ _____

4. The man is a PE teacher.

The man does exercises all the time.

▶ _____

5. The oranges are very fresh.

We made the orange juice this morning.

▶ _____

6. I want to make friends with the lovely girl.

You've known the lovely girl for five years.

▶ _____

7. The woman was sitting over there.

I like the woman.

▶ _____

8. I was awake all night because of the strong coffee.

My mom made the strong coffee.

▶ _____

9. I want a teacher.

The teacher gives us very few assignments.

▶ _____

10. The man needs a pair of glasses.

The man can't see very clearly.

▶ _____

11. The dog was not here.

I looked for the dog.

▶ _____

12. The girl is called Angela.

Peter loves the girl.

▶ _____

13. The woman is a popular eye doctor.

The woman has lived in Taiwan for years.

▶ _____

14. The man is an engineer.

His daughter is an astronaut.

▶ _____

15. I thanked the woman.

I borrowed her English dictionary.

▶ _____

16. The woman shouted "Stop! Thief!"

Her wallet was stolen.

▶ _____

17. The man is famous.

His picture is in the magazines.

▶ _____

18. The girl is my friend.

You met the girl yesterday.

 _____

19. The book is a bestseller.

The book's cover is purple.

 _____

20. The girl is my friend.

The girl lives upstairs.（省略關係代名詞）

 _____

Answer 解答

1. I am not interested in the man. 我對那個男人沒有興趣。
The man is wearing blue pants. 那個男人穿著藍色牛仔褲。

▶ *I am not interested in the man who is wearing blue pants.*
　　我對那個穿著藍色牛仔褲的男人沒興趣。

2. The girl has long blond hair. 那個女孩有一頭金色長髮。
The girl looks beautiful. 那個女孩看起來很漂亮。

▶ *The girl who looks beautiful has long blond hair.*
　　那個看起來很漂亮的女孩有一頭金色長髮。

3. The book has many pictures in it. 那本書裡面有很多圖片。
He bought the book yesterday. 他昨天買了那本書。

▶ *The book which he bought yesterday has many pictures in it.*
　　他昨天買的那本書裡面有很多圖片。

4. The man is a PE teacher. 那個男人是一位體育老師。
The man does exercises all the time. 那個男人總是在運動。

▶ *The man who does exercises all the time is a PE teacher.*
　　那個總是在運動的男人是位體育老師。

寫
作
能
力
培
養

5. The oranges are very fresh. 那些柳丁非常新鮮。

We made the orange juice this morning.

今天早上我們做了柳丁汁。

▶ *The oranges which we made juice this morning are very fresh.*

　　我們今天早上做果汁的那些柳丁非常新鮮。

6. I want to make friends with the lovely girl.

我想要跟那位可愛的女孩做朋友。

You've known the lovely girl for five years.

你已經認識那個可愛的女孩五年了。

▶ *I want to make friends with the lovely girl whom you've known for five years.*

　　我想和那個你已經認識五年的可愛女孩做朋友。

7. The woman was sitting over there. 那個女人之前坐在那裡。

I like the woman. 我喜歡那個女人。

▶ *The woman whom I like was sitting over there.*

　　我喜歡的那個女人之前坐在那裡。

8. I was awake all night because of the strong coffee.

我因為喝了很濃的咖啡而整夜睡不著。

My mom made the strong coffee. 我媽媽煮了很濃的咖啡。

▶ *I was awake all night because of the strong coffee which my mom made.*

　　我因為喝了媽媽煮的很濃的咖啡而整夜睡不著。

9. I want a teacher. 我想要一個老師。

The teacher gives us very few assignments.

那個老師給我們非常少的作業。

▶ *I want a teacher who gives us very few assignments.*

　　我想要一個給我們非常少作業的老師。

10. The man needs a pair of glasses. 那個男人需要一副眼鏡。
The man can't see very clearly. 那個男人看不清楚。

▶ *The man who can't see very clearly needs a pair of glasses.*

那個看不清楚的男人需要一副眼鏡。

11. The dog was not here. 那隻狗當時不在這裡。
I looked for the dog. 我找了那隻狗。

▶ *The dog which I looked for was not here.*

我找的狗當時不在這裡。

12. The girl is called Angela. 那個女孩叫做安琪拉。
Peter loves the girl. 彼得愛那個女孩。

▶ *The girl whom Peter loves is called Angela.*

彼得愛的女孩叫做安琪拉。

13. The woman is a popular eye doctor.

那個女人是一位受歡迎的眼科醫生。

The woman has lived in Taiwan for years.

那個女人已經住在台灣多年了。

▶ *The woman who has lived in Taiwan for years is a popular eye doctor.*

那個住在台灣多年的女人是一位受歡迎的眼科醫生。

14. The man is an engineer. 那個男人是一名工程師。
His daughter is an astronaut. 他的女兒是一名太空人。

▶ *The man whose daughter is an astronaut is an engineer.*

那個女兒是太空人的男子是一位工程師。

15. I thanked the woman. 我謝謝那位女子。
I borrowed her English dictionary. 我向她借英文字典。

▶ *I thanked the woman whose English dictionary I borrowed.*

我謝謝那位借我她的英文字典的女子。

16. The woman shouted "Stop! Thief!" 那個女人大喊：「站住！小偷！」
Her wallet was stolen. 她的皮夾被偷了。

▶ *The woman whose wallet was stolen shouted "Stop! Thief!"*

那個皮夾被偷了的女子大喊：「站住！小偷！」

17. The man is famous. 那個男人很有名。
His picture is in the magazines. 他的照片在雜誌裡。

▶ *The man whose picture is in the magazines is famous.*

那個照片在雜誌裡的男人很有名。

18. The girl is my friend. 那個女孩是我的朋友。
You met the girl yesterday. 你昨天遇到那個女孩。

▶ *The girl whom you met yesterday is my friend.*

昨天你遇到的那個女孩是我的朋友。

19. The book is a bestseller. 那本書是一本暢銷書。
The book's cover is purple. 那本書的封面是紫色的。

▶ *The book whose cover is purple is a bestseller.*

封面是紫色的那本書是一本暢銷書。

20. The girl is my friend. 那個女孩是我的朋友。
The girl lives upstairs. 那個女孩住在樓上。

▶ *The girl living upstairs is my friend.*（省略關係代名詞）

住在樓上的那個女孩是我的朋友。

形容詞子句翻譯練習

請將下列中文句子翻譯為含有形容詞子句的英文句子：

1. 克莉絲汀是一位在台灣教英文的老師。(Christine)

▶ _____

2. 這些正坐在教室裡的學生是我的。

▶ _____

3. 你在百貨公司買的那件背心是特價的。

▶ _____

4. 你有找到那本用英文寫的書嗎？

▶ _____

5. 你記得那位坐在角落的女孩嗎？

▶ _____

6. 這本粉紅色封面的書非常有趣。

▶ _____

7. 這首由莎拉・布萊曼演唱的歌曲非常感人。(Sarah Brightman)

▶ _____

8. 約翰是一個住在台北的醫生。

▶ _____

9. 我住在台南的妹妹真的是個很漂亮的女孩。

▶ _____

10. 這就是我出生和成長的地方。(where)

▶ _____

Answer

1. 克莉絲汀是一位在台灣教英文的老師。(Christine)

▶ *Christine is a teacher who teaches English in Taiwan.*

2. 這些正坐在教室裡的學生是我的。

▶ *These students who are sitting in the classroom are mine.*

3. 你在百貨公司買的那件背心是特價的。

▶ *That vest which you bought in the department store is on sale.*

4. 你有找到那本用英文寫的書嗎？

▶ *Did you find that book which is written in English?*

5. 你記得那位坐在角落的女孩嗎？

▶ *Do you remember that girl who is sitting in the corner?*

6. 這本粉紅色封面的書非常有趣。

▶ *This book whose cover is pink is very interesting.*

7. 這首由莎拉‧布萊曼演唱的歌曲非常感人。(Sarah Brightman)

▶ *The song which is sung by Sarah Brightman is very touching.*

8. 約翰是一個住在台北的醫生。

▶ *John is a doctor who lives in Taipei.*

9. 我住在台南的妹妹真的是個很漂亮的女孩。

▶ *My younger sister who lives in Tainan is really a pretty girl.*

10. 這就是我出生和成長的地方。(where)

▶ *This is where I was born and grew up.*

1-6 副詞子句

　　副詞子句是有副詞功能的子句，通常會被用來修飾動詞。副詞子句置於句末不必加逗號，至於句首則必須有逗號。副詞子句可依其作用區分為以下八大類：

表時間【可做分詞構句】	表地點	表原因【可做分詞構句】
表結果	表條件【可做分詞構句】	表狀態
表目的	表讓步【可做分詞構句】	

表時間的副詞子句

解析 ▶ 表時間的副詞子句是有著時間副詞功能的子句，通常用來修飾動詞。表時間的副詞子句經常會與下列連接詞相連接：when, whenever, while, as, as soon as, until, till, since, after, before, the moment, the minute 等。

句型比較 ▶

➡ I jog **every day**. 我每天慢跑。

　　【every day 是時間副詞片語】

➡ I jog **when I have free time**. 我有空閒時間就會慢跑。

　　【用 when 來連接表時間的副詞子句】

➡ **When I have free time**, I jog. 我有空閒時間就會慢跑。

　　【副詞子句置於句首，要加逗號】

例句 ▶

➡ **As soon as I see him**, I smile.

　　= I smile **as soon as I see him**.

　　我一看到他，我就微笑。

➡ **Whenever I see him**, he always eats.

　　= He always eats **whenever I see him**.

　　無論何時我看到他，他都在吃。

寫作能力培養

→ **Until you come back**, I won't leave.

= I won't leave **until you come back**.

直到你回來，我都不會離開。

→ **Since he left**, I have never seen him.

= I have never seen him **since he left**.

自從他離開，我就沒見過他了。

→ **While I am taking a shower**, he is watching TV.

= He is watching TV **while I am taking a shower**.

當我正在沖澡時，他正在看電視。

→ **When you come tomorrow**, I will be home.

= I will be home **when you come tomorrow**.

你明天來的時候，我將會在家。

表地點的副詞子句

解析 ▶ 表地點的副詞子句是有著地方副詞功能的子句，通常用來修飾動詞。表地點的副詞子句經常會與下列連接詞相連接：where, wherever 等。

句型比較 ▶

→ I jog **in the park**. 我在公園慢跑。【in the park 是地方副詞片語】

→ I jog **where there are many trees**.

我在有很多樹的地方慢跑。【用 where 來連接表地點的副詞子句】

表原因的副詞子句

解析 ▶ 表原因的副詞子句是用來說明動作發生原因的子句，經常會與下列連接詞一併使用：

表原因的連接詞	中文意義
because, since, as	因為
now that, seeing that, considering that	既然
due to the fact that, thanks to the fact that	由於

另外，以下三組表原因的副詞子句可以用「連接詞＋介系詞＋ N」的型式代替：

連接詞＋子句	連接詞＋介系詞＋ N	中文意義
because	because of	因為
due to the fact that	due to	由於
thanks to the fact that	thanks to	多虧

例句 ▶️

➡️ **Because I was sick**, I didn't go to school.
　因為我生病了，所以我沒有去上學。【連接詞＋子句】

➡️ **Because of my sickness**, I didn't go to school.
　因為我生病了，所以我沒有去上學。【連接詞＋介系詞＋N】

表結果的副詞子句 ▶️

解析 ▶️ 表結果的副詞子句是用來說明動作發生的結果，經常會利用下列連接詞連接兩個子句：

表結果的連接詞	句型	中文意義
.., so ...	子句＋,＋so＋子句.	……，所以……
.. so ... that ...	so＋adj＋that＋子句. so＋adj＋a/an＋N＋that＋子句.	如此……以致於……
... such ... that ...	such＋a/an＋adj＋N＋that＋子句.	如此……以致於……

例句 ▶️

➡️ We arrived very early, **so** we got good seats.
　我們非常早就到了，所以我們拿到了好位子。

➡️ She is **so** emotional **that** every little thing upsets her.
　她是如此情緒化，以致於任何小事都會惹她不高興。

⟹ She is **such** an emotional girl **that** every little thing upsets her.
她是一個如此情緒化的女孩，以致於任何小事都會惹她不高興。

⟹ It is **such** a loaf of stale bread **that** no one wants to eat it.
這塊麵包太不新鮮了，以致於沒有人想要吃。

表條件的副詞子句 ⟩•●

條件子句的六種句型：

類型	句型	例句
介系詞型	介系詞＋N ➤ with ➤ without	⟹ With pay, I'll buy you lunch. 　有拿到錢的話，我會請你吃午餐。 ⟹ Without pay, I won't buy you lunch. 　沒有拿到錢的話，我不會請你吃午餐。
介系詞片語型	介系詞片語＋N ➤ in case of ➤ on condition of ➤ in the event of ➤ subject to	⟹ In case of getting paid, I'll buy you lunch. 　萬一有拿到錢，我會請你吃午餐。 ⟹ On condition of getting paid, I'll buy you lunch. 　有拿到錢的情況下，我會請你吃午餐。
連接詞與連接詞片語型	連接詞＋子句 ➤ if ➤ once ➤ unless ➤ suppose/ 　supposing ➤ provided/ 　providing ➤ in case ➤ on condition that 　in the event that	⟹ If I get paid, I will buy you lunch. 　假如我有拿到錢，我會請你吃午餐。 ⟹ Once I get paid, I'll buy you lunch. 　一旦我拿到錢，我就請你吃午餐。 ⟹ Unless I get paid, I won't buy you lunch. 　除非我拿到錢，否則我不會請你吃午餐。 ⟹ Suppose I get paid, I'll buy you lunch. 　假設我有拿到錢，我會請你吃午餐。 ⟹ In case I get paid, I'll buy you lunch. 　萬一我拿到錢，我就請你吃午餐。 ⟹ On condition that I get paid, I'll buy you lunch. 　在我有拿到錢的情況下，我會請你吃午餐。

命令句型	Vr 開頭，主要子句前要加 "and"	➡ Get paid, and I'll buy you lunch. 我要先拿到錢，才會請你吃午餐。
不定詞構句型	To + Vr 開頭	➡ To get paid, I'll buy you lunch. 假如拿到錢，我會請你吃午餐。
分詞構句型	V-ing 開頭	➡ Having enough money, I will buy you a gift. 有足夠的錢的話，我會買禮物給你。

條件子句改寫練習

1. If there is no break in your life line, it means you'll have a happy life.（用 without 改寫）

   ▶ _____

2. Some people said that if your eyebrows grow together or your arms are hairy, you'll be very rich.（用 supposing 改寫）

   ▶ _____

3. It is said that if you sleep on a pillow with a mirror, you will see what your future husband looks like.（用 on condition of 改寫）

   ▶ _____

4. A myth said that if you walk under a ladder, you'll have bad luck.（用 in the event that 改寫）

   ▶ _____

5. If you are rich, she will marry you.（用 Unless 改寫）

   ▶ _____

Answer 解答

1. If there is no break in your life line, it means you'll have a happy life.（用 without 改寫）

   ▶ *Without a break in your life line, it means you'll have a happy life.*

寫作能力培養

74

2. Some people said that if your eyebrows grow together or your arms are hairy, you'll be very rich. （用 supposing 改寫）

▶ *Some people said that supposing your eyebrows grow together or your arms are hairy, you'll be very rich.*

3. It is said that if you sleep on a pillow with a mirror, you will see what your future husband looks like. （用 on condition of 改寫）

▶ *It is said that on condition of sleeping on a pillow with a mirror, you'll see what your future husband looks like.*

4. A myth said that if you walk under a ladder, you'll have bad luck. （用 in the event that 改寫）

▶ *A myth said that in the event that you walk under a ladder, you'll have bad luck.*

5. If you are rich, she will marry you. （用 Unless 改寫）

▶ *Unless you are rich, she will not marry you.*

條件子句翻譯練習

1. 假如你右耳癢，有人在說你好話。（使用 if）

▶ _____

2. 假如我搭計程車，我可以在七點前到達那裡。（使用命令句型）

▶ _____

3. 把那扇門打開，你就會看到許多樹。（on condition of）

▶ _____

4. 假如你用功讀書，你將會得到好成績。（用不定詞構句）

▶ _____

5. 假設他愛妳，他就不會傷害妳的感受。（supposing）

▶ _____

1. 假如你右耳癢,有人在說你好話。(使用 if)

▶ *If your right ear itches, somebody says something good about you.*

2. 假如我搭計程車,我可以在七點前到達那裡。(使用命令句型)

▶ *Take the taxi, and I'll arrive there by 7:00.*

3. 把那扇門打開,你就會看到許多樹。(on condition of)

▶ *On condition of opening the door, you'll see many trees.*

4. 假如你用功讀書,你將會得到好成績。(用不定詞構句)

▶ *To study hard, you'll get good grades.*

5. 假設他愛妳,他就不會傷害妳的感受。(supposing)

▶ *Supposing he loves you, he will not hurt your feelings.*

表狀態的副詞子句

> **解析** ▶ 表狀態的副詞子句是用子句來修飾動作的狀態,經常會由下列連接詞引導:as、just the way、as if、as though。

例句 ▶

⟶ The steak is cooked **as I like it.**
這牛排是按我喜歡的方式料理的。

⟶ The fish is cooked **just the way I like it.**
這條魚正是按我喜歡的方式來烹調的。

⟶ He made a speech to me **as if he was a hero.**
他對我訓話,就好像他是個英雄似的。

表目的的副詞子句

解析 ▶ 表目的的副詞子句是用子句來修飾所做動作的目的，句型有以下二種，中文意義都是「為了……」。

連接詞型	in order that＋子句
不定詞型	in order to＋Vr

例句 ▶

➡ I arrive early **in order that I can get a good view of the volcano**.
我早到是為了要得到一個觀賞火山的好視野。

➡ I arrive early **in order to get a good view of the volcano**.
我早到是為了要得到一個觀賞火山的好視野。

➡ They must wear gloves **in order not to leave any fingerprints**.
為了不留下任何指紋，他們必須要戴手套。

表讓步的副詞子句

解析 ▶ 表讓步的副詞子句是用子句來修飾所做動作的目的，句型有以下二種，中文意義都是「僅管……」、「無論……」。

類型	句型	常用範例
連接詞型	連接詞＋子句	although, though, even though, while, however＋adj
介系詞型	介系詞＋名詞	despite, in spite of, regardless of

例句 ▶

➡ **Although I am sick**, I still go to school.
僅管我生病了，我還是去上學。【although 和 but/yet 不能同時出現。】

➡ **In spite of many difficulties**, she still accomplished her work.
僅管有很多困難，她仍完成了她的工作。【介系詞 in spite of＋N】

> **Regardless of people's protests**, the president still changed the system.
>
> 不顧人們的抗議，總統仍改變了體制。【介系詞 regardless of＋N】
>
> **Despite danger**, he still went to Russia.
>
> 不顧危險，他仍然去了俄國。【介系詞 despite＋N】
>
> **However hard it is**, I'll still do it.
>
> 不管有多困難，我仍會去做。【however adj＋子句】

三大子句綜合練習

請判斷下列英文句子中不同顏色的部分為何種子句：

_____ 1. This is the day **when we first met**.

_____ 2. I ask **where Charles went last night**.

_____ 3. I don't remember the place **where we first met**.

_____ 4. I jog **where there are many trees**.

_____ 5. I don't know **when he died**.

_____ 6. Can you tell me the year **when the game is held**?

_____ 7. I usually watch TV **when I finish my homework**.

_____ 8. I doubt **when he will get married**.

_____ 9. **When I called you**, you were studying English.

_____ 10. That was the day **when you lent me some money**.

Answer 解答

形容詞子句　**1.** This is the day **when we first met**.

名詞子句　**2.** I ask **where Charles went last night**.

形容詞子句	**3.** I don't remember the place **where we first met**.
副詞子句	**4.** I jog **where there are many trees**.
名詞子句	**5.** I don't know **when he died**.
形容詞子句	**6.** Can you tell me the year **when the game is held**?
副詞子句	**7.** I usually watch TV **when I finish my homework**.
名詞子句	**8.** I doubt **when he will get married**.
副詞子句	**9. When I called you**, you were studying English.
形容詞子句	**10.** That was the day **when you lent me some money**.

分詞構句

解析 ▶ 表「時間」、「原因」、「條件」、「讓步」的副詞子句可以改為分詞構句的型式。所謂分詞構句就是以分詞為句子開頭的構句方式，是英檢考試中經常出現的考題型式。

分詞構句的形成有以下三個步驟：

簡易記憶 三大步驟	步驟說明	範例
Step 1 觀察主詞 是否一致	如果主要子句與副詞子句的主詞一致，就直接省略副詞子句的主詞；如果主詞不一致，就保留副詞子句的主詞。	When ~~I~~ entered the room, I found him sleeping. 【主詞一致，省略副詞子句中的主詞。】
Step 2 省略連接詞	直接將表示時間、原因、條件、讓步的連接詞省略。	~~When~~ entered the room, I found him sleeping. 【省略表時間的連接詞 when。】
Step 3 將動詞改成 分詞	不論原來的動詞時態為何，分詞構句一律以現在分詞表示主動，過去分詞表示被動。 【例外：完成式則會改為 "Having + Vpp"。】	Entering the room, I found him sleeping. 【enter（進入）是主動的動作，因此將動詞改為現在分詞，字首要大寫。】

PART 2 unit 1 必考文法句型解析

➠ While he was eating dinner, I was doing the shopping.

   ➤ **He eating** dinner, I was doing the shopping.

   他在吃晚餐的時候，我正在購物。

➠ Since my mother was ill, I couldn't go to the concert.

   ➤ **My mother being** ill, I couldn't go to the concert.

   因為我媽媽生病了，我不能去音樂會。

➠ When I knew he failed the test, I was secretly pleased that he had learned a lesson.

   ➤ **Knowing** he failed the test, I was secretly pleased that he had learned a lesson.

   知道他考試不及格的時候，我暗暗高興他學到了一次教訓。

➠ If I get paid, I'll buy you lunch.

   ➤ **Getting** paid, I'll buy you lunch.

   拿到錢的話，我會請你吃午餐。

分詞構句練習 ▶

1. After I had finished my work, I went to bed.

   ▶ _____

2. The old man looked very happy when he was surrounded by many children.

   ▶ _____

3. Since I had a slight cold, I went to bed early.

   ▶ _____

4. As I had nothing to do, I went downtown.

   ▶ _____

5. Because it was written in haste, her letter is very hard to read.

▶ _____

6. Although the book is written in Chinese, we can't understand it.

▶ _____

7. Although the book is written in Chinese, it can't be understood by us.

▶ _____

8. If I get good grades, my mother will buy me a cake.

▶ _____

9. While I disapprove of what you say, I would defend to the death your right to say it.

▶ _____

10. Because I didn't know what to do, I asked for her advice.

▶ _____

Answer ●●●●●●●●●●●●●●●●●●●●●●●●●●●●●● 解答

1. After I had finished my work, I went to bed.

▶ *Having finished my work, I went to bed.*
做完功課之後，我就去睡覺了。

2. The old man looked very happy when he was surrounded by many children.

▶ *Surrounded by many children, the old man looked very happy.*
被許多孩子圍繞時，那個老人看起來非常高興。

3. Since I had a slight cold, I went to bed early.

▶ *Having a slight cold, I went to bed early.*
因為有一點感冒，我早早就睡了。

4. As I had nothing to do, I went downtown.

▶ *Having nothing to do, I went downtown.*

因為沒事可做，我就去了市區。

5. Because it was written in haste, her letter is very hard to read.

▶ *Written in haste, her letter is very hard to read.*

因為寫得倉促，她的信很難辨識。

6. Although the book is written in Chinese, we can't understand it.

▶ *The book written in Chinese, we can't understand it.*

雖然那本書是用中文寫成的，我們卻看不懂。

7. Although the book is written in Chinese, it can't be understood by us.

▶ *Written in Chinese, the book can't be understood by us.*

雖然是用中文寫的，那本書我們看不懂。

8. If I get good grades, my mother will buy me a cake.

▶ *I getting good grades, my mother will buy me a cake.*

假如我得到好成績，我媽媽會買蛋糕給我。

9. While I disapprove of what you say, I would defend to the death your right to say it.

▶ *Disapproving of what you say, I would defend to the death your right to say it.*

雖然我不同意你所說的話，但是我會誓死維護你這麼說的權利。

10. Because I didn't know what to do, I asked for her advice.

▶ *Not knowing what to do, I asked for her advice.*

因為我不知道要做什麼，所以我問了她的建議。

1-7 假設語氣

假設語氣的四大句型

解析 ▶ 假設語氣所陳述的通常不是事實，而是個人主觀的願望或假想，常見的有以下四種句型：

可能實現的假設	If＋S＋現在式V ..., I will＋Vr ...
與現在事實相反的假設	If＋S＋were/Vpt ..., S＋would/could/should/might ＋Vr ...
與過去事實相反的假設	If＋S＋had＋Vpp ..., S＋would/could/should/might ＋have＋Vpp ...
幾乎不可能實現的假設	If＋S＋were to＋Vr ..., S＋would/could/should/ might＋Vr ...

例句 ▶

⟹ If I **have** enough money, I **will buy** that house.

假如我有足夠的錢，我會買那棟房子。

【可能實現的假設】

⟹ If I **had** enough money this year, I **would buy** that house.

假如我今年有足夠的錢，我就會買那棟房子了。

【與現在事實相反的假設】

⟹ If I **had had** enough money last year, I **would have bought** that house.

假如我去年有足夠的錢，我當時就會買那棟房子了。

【與過去事實相反的假設】

⟹ If I **were to have** enough money next year, I **would buy** that house.

假如我明年有足夠的錢，我就會買那棟房子。

【幾乎不可能實現的假設】

四大句型練習 ▶●

請依照指定的句型,將下列中文句子翻譯為正確的英文。

1. 假如我有空,我會洗衣服。

▶ _____

2. 假如我現在有空,我會洗衣服。

▶ _____

3. 如果我是你,我就會買那部車。

▶ _____

4. 假如我昨天有空,我就會洗衣服了。

▶ _____

5. 假如我之後有空,就會洗衣服。(之後不會有空)

▶ _____

Answer ▶● •

1. 假如我有空,我會洗衣服。

▶ *If I have time, I will do my laundry.*

【可能實現的假設】

2. 假如我現在有空,我會洗衣服。

▶ *If I had time now, I would do my laundry.*

【與現在事實相反的假設】

【In fact, I don't have time now, so I don't do my laundry.】

3. 如果我是你,我就會買那部車。

▶ *If I were you, I would buy that car.*

【與現在事實相反的假設】

【In fact, I am not you, so I do not buy that car.】

4. 假如我昨天有空,我就會洗衣服了。

▶ *If I had had time yesterday, I would have done my laundry.*

【與過去事實相反的假設】

【In fact, I didn't have time yesterday, so I didn't do my laundry.】

5. 假如我之後有空，就會洗衣服。（之後不會有空）

▶ *If I were to have time after, I would do my laundry.*

【幾乎不可能實現的假設】

【In fact, I won't have time after, so I won't do my laundry.】

比較as if的假設句型 ▶

⇒ I feel as if I am sick. 我覺得我好像生病了。

【as if / as though 後面加現在式子句，表示這是有可能發生的事實。】

⇒ I feel as if I were floating in the air. 我覺得我好像浮在空中似的。

【as if / as though 後面加過去式子句，表示發生機率非常小的事實。】

假設語氣倒裝句 ▶

解析 ▶ 假設語氣的倒裝句型，是把從屬子句中的 were 或 had 移到句首，再將 if 刪除。特別要注意的是可能實現的假設句，因為從屬子句的部分沒有用到這些詞，所以不能使用倒裝句型。

假設語氣倒裝句的構成有以下三大步驟：

簡易記憶 三大步驟	步驟說明	範例
Step 1 找出關鍵字	找出關鍵字 were 或 had。	If I were you, I would be annoyed. 【找出關鍵字為 were。】
Step 2 刪除連接詞	刪除假設語氣的連接詞 if。	If I were you, I would be annoyed. 【刪除連接詞 if。】
Step 3 將關鍵字 移至句首	將關鍵字 were 或 had 移到句首大寫。	Were I you, I would be annoyed. 【將關鍵字 were 移到句首，記得第一個字母要大寫。】

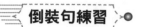

請將下列假設語氣的句子改寫成倒裝句型：

1. If I have time, I will do my laundry.

   ▶ _____

2. If I had time, I would do my laundry.

   ▶ _____

3. If I had had time, I would have done my laundry.

   ▶ _____

4. If the clock hadn't rung this morning, I would have been late to school.

   ▶ _____

5. If I were to have time after, I would do my laundry.

   ▶ _____

 **Answer** 解答

1. If I have time, I will do my laundry.

   ▶【這一句是可能實現的假設語氣的句子，無倒裝句。】

    假如我有空，我會洗衣服。

2. If I had time, I would do my laundry.

   ▶ *Had I time, I would do my laundry.*

    假如我有空，我就會洗衣服了。

3. If I had had time, I would have done my laundry.

   ▶ *Had I had time, I would have done my laundry.*

    假如我那時有空，我就會洗衣服了。

4. If the clock hadn't rung this morning, I would have been late to school.

▶ *Had the clock not rung this morning, I would have been late to school.*

假如今天早上鬧鐘沒響，我上學就會遲到了。

5. If I were to have time after, I would do my laundry.

▶ *Were I to have time after, I would do my laundry.*

假如我之後有空，我會洗衣服。

比較級與最高級

比較級與最高級的變化規則

解析 ▶ 形容詞和副詞有原級、比較級和最高級三種變化，詳細變化規則如下表所示：

原級 (base word)	比較級 (comparative)	最高級 (superlative)
一般字尾	**+ -er**	**+ -est**
long	longer	the longest
short	shorter	the shortest
clever	cleverer	the cleverest
hard	harder	the hardest
字尾為 e	**+ -r**	**+ -st**
wise	wiser	the wisest
wide	wider	the widest
發音為「子母子」	**重複字尾 + -er**	**重複字尾 + -est**
big	bigger	the biggest
hot	hotter	the hottest
sad	sadder	the saddest
字尾為 y **【ly 結尾的副詞必須改成「more + 原級」及「the most + 原級」】**	**去 y + -ier**	**去 y + -iest**
crazy	crazier	the craziest
lazy	lazier	the laziest
healthy	healthier	the healthiest
slowly	more slowly	the most slowly
quickly	more quickly	the most quickly
多音節	**more + 原級**	**the most + 原級**
expensive	more expensive	the most expensive
comfortable	more comfortable	the most comfortable
handsome	more handsome	the most handsome
famous	more famous	the most famous
不規則變化		
good、well	better	the best
bad、badly	worse	the worst
many、much	more	the most
little	less	the least
far（指距離）	farther	the farthest
far（指程度）	further	the furthest

比較級的基本句型

句型

A＋V（一般動詞）＋adv（比較級）＋than＋B

A＋beV＋adj（比較級）＋than＋B

例句

➡ I walk more slowly than he (does). 我走得比他慢。

【句尾的助動詞通常省略。】

＝ I walk more slowly than him.【口語用法】

➡ I am taller than he (is). 我比他高。

【句尾的 beV 通常省略。】

＝ I am taller than him.【口語用法】

同級比較句型

基本句型

	be 動詞句型	一般動詞句型
肯定句	A＋beV＋as＋adj＋as＋B	A＋V＋as＋adv＋as＋B
否定句	A＋beV＋not＋so＋adj＋as＋B	A＋助動詞＋not＋V＋so＋adv＋as＋B

例句

➡ This city is as crowded as that one.

這個城市跟那個一樣擁擠。

➡ My English grades are as good as theirs.

我的英文分數和他們的一樣好。

➡ This bag isn't so heavy as that one.

這個袋子不像那個那麼重。

➡ She isn't so jealous as her sister.

她不像她姐姐那麼忌妒。

➡ I walk as slowly as he (does). 我走路和他一樣慢。

I don't walk so slowly as he (does). 我走路不像他那麼慢。

活用句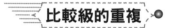

➡ She is **as intelligent as** beautiful. 她才貌雙全。

➡ I like **as coffee as** tea. 咖啡和茶我都喜歡。

➡ I am nearly **as old as** he. 我幾乎和他一樣老。

➡ I am **not** quite **so** old **as** he. 我沒有他那麼老。

➡ I will come there **as soon as possible**. 我會盡快到那裡。

➡ I will finish my homework **as soon as I could**. 我會盡快做完功課。

比較級的重複

句型 ▶

「比較級＋ and ＋比較級」，表示「越來越……」。

例句 ▶

➡ The weather gets colder and colder. 天氣越來越冷。

➡ I become fatter and fatter. 我變得越來越胖。

➡ My salary is more and more. 我的薪水越來越多。

➡ I'm busier and busier. 我越來越忙。

➡ The price is more and more expensive. 價格越來越貴。

相對比較句

句型 ▶

「the 比較級＋ S ＋ V ..., the 比較級＋ S ＋ V ...」表示
「越……，越……」。

例句 ▶

➡ The higher the mountain (is), the deeper the water (is).
山越高，水越深。

⟹ The more I know him, the more I like him.

我越認識他，我就越喜歡他。

⟹ The more products you sell, the more money you make.

你賣越多產品，錢就賺越多。

⟹ The harder you study, the better grades you get.

你念得越認真，成績就越好。

利用片語來比較

句型 ▶

A＋be superior to＋B（比較好）	A＋be equal to＋B（相等的）
A＋be inferior to＋B（比較差）	A＋be similar to＋B（相似的）
A＋be senior to＋B（比較資深、年長）	A＋be the same as＋B（相同的）
A＋be junior to＋B（比較資淺、年幼）	A＋be different from＋B（不同的）

例句 ▶

⟹ He is superior to me in English. 他在英文上優於我。

⟹ He is inferior to me in work ability. 他在工作能力上輸我。

其他比較句型

句型 ▶

句型	中文意義
S＋V＋more than＋數字＋N	超過
S＋V＋less than＋數字＋N	少於
S＋V＋no more than＋數字＋N	只有
S＋V＋not more than＋數字＋N	頂多

例句 ▶

⟹ I have no more than a baby. 我只有一個小孩。

⟹ He works not more than 3 days in this company.

他在這家公司頂多工作了三天。

最高級的基本句型

句型 ▶

A＋beV＋the 最高級＋(N)＋of all
A＋beV＋the 最高級＋of＋all＋複數名詞
A＋beV＋the 最高級＋N＋介系詞＋地點
A＋beV＋the 最高級＋N＋that＋完成式子句

例句 ▶

➡ Jack is the laziest student of all. 傑克是所有學生當中最懶惰的。

【A＋beV＋the 最高級＋(N)＋of all】

➡ Jack is the laziest of all students. 傑克是所有學生當中最懶惰的。

【A＋beV＋the 最高級＋of all＋複數名詞】

➡ Jack is the laziest student in the world.

傑克是世界上最懶惰的學生。【A＋beV＋the 最高級＋N＋介系詞＋地點】

➡ Jack is the laziest student that I have ever taught.

傑克是我教過最懶惰的學生。

【A＋beV＋the 最高級＋N＋that＋完成式子句】

以比較級表達最高級

句型 ▶

be 動詞句型	A＋beV＋形容詞比較級＋than any other＋單數名詞
	A＋beV＋形容詞比較級＋than all the other＋複數名詞
	No＋N＋beV＋形容詞比較級＋than＋N
一般動詞句型	A＋V＋副詞比較級＋than any other＋單數名詞
	A＋V＋副詞比較級＋than all the other＋複數名詞
	No＋N＋V＋副詞比較級＋than＋N

例句 ▶

➠ Jack is taller than all the other students.

傑克比其他所有學生都高。

➠ No students are lazier than Jeff.

沒有學生比傑夫更懶惰了。

➠ Nothing else is more important than love.

沒有其他束西比愛更重要。

➠ I type more quickly than any other student in our class.

我打字比我們班其他任何一位學生都要快。

➠ Ariel sings better than all the other sisters in her family.

愛莉兒比家中其他姊妹唱得還好。

➠ No man in the world earns more money than Bill.

世界上沒有人賺得比比爾多。

比較級與最高級綜合練習 ▶

請將下列中文句子翻譯為正確的英文句子。

1. 這個袋子比那個貴。

▶ _____

2. 我有超過三個袋子。

▶ _____

3. 我只有三個好朋友。

▶ _____

4. 他們頂多有一百萬。

▶ _____

5. 我了解他和你一樣多。

▶ _____

6. 我會盡快回信給你。

▶ _____

7. 天色越來越暗。

▶ _____

8. 這袋子似乎越來越重。

▶ _____

9. 施比受更有福。

▶ _____

10. 你越富有，你就變得越貪心。

▶ _____

11. 今天的天氣比昨天好多了。

▶ _____

12. 她是我認識最聰明的女孩。

▶ _____

Answer 解答

1. 這個袋子比那個貴。

▶ _This bag is more expensive than that._

2. 我有超過三個袋子。

▶ _I have more than three bags._

3. 我只有三個好朋友。

▶ _I have no more than three good friends._

4. 他們頂多有一百萬。

▶ _They have not more than one million._

5. 我了解他和你一樣多。

▶ *I see him as much as you do.*

6. 我會盡快回信給你。

▶ *I will write back to you as soon as possible.*

7. 天色越來越暗。

▶ *It gets darker and darker.*

8. 這袋子似乎越來越重。

▶ *This bag seems heavier and heavier.*

9. 施比受更有福。

▶ *It's better to give than to take.*

10. 你越富有，你就變得越貪心。

▶ *The richer you are, the greedier you become.*

11. 今天的天氣比昨天好多了。

▶ *The weather today is much better than yesterday.*

12. 她是我認識最聰明的女孩。

▶ *She is the most intelligent girl that I have ever known.*

介系詞句型

---

with（由於；有……）▶

➠ **With** your assistance, I will probably finish my teacher's assignment in a few days.

有你的協助，我有可能可以在幾天後完成老師指派的作業。

about（關於）▶

➠ **About** your credibility, the manager in City Bank wants something more detailed.

關於你的信用，City 銀行的經理想知道更多細節。

despite（儘管；不顧）▶

➠ **Despite** complaints, the boss still fired some staff in his office.

不顧有抱怨，老闆仍開除了一些他辦公室的員工。

without（沒有）▶

➠ **Without** a doubt, she is the right person for this position.

毫無疑問，她是這個職位的適當人選。

regardless of（不管；不顧）▶

➠ **Regardless of** danger, I still went for an adventure in the jungle.

不顧危險，我仍然到叢林去探險了。

thanks to（多虧）▶

➠ **Thanks to** your help, I did it without trouble.

多虧你的協助，我沒遇到麻煩就完成了。

for the sake of（看在……的份上）▶

➠ **For the sake of** your heart, you should work out every day in the gym.

看在你心臟的份上，你應該每天去健身房運動。

副詞句型

moreover（此外；尤有甚者）▶

⇒ **Moreover**, he stole my new watch.

此外，他偷了我的新手錶。

as a matter of fact（事實上）▶

⇒ **As a matter of fact**, I have had a girlfriend for three months.

事實上，我有女朋友三個月了。

basically（基本上）▶

⇒ **Basically**, male customers are not the same as female ones.

基本上，男性顧客與女性顧客不同。

on the contrary（相反地）▶

⇒ **On the contrary**, I asked my best friend to leave me alone.

相反地，我要我最好的朋友別管我。

By contrast（相反地）▶

⇒ **By contrast**, I wish I had never known her.

相反地，我真希望從沒認識她。

虛主詞的句型 ▶

It is＋adj＋to＋Vr ...（某件事是……的）▶

⇒ **It is difficult to** practice English writing without a good book.

= <u>To practice English writing without a good book</u> is difficult.

沒有一本好書要練習英文寫作是很困難的。

【It 是虛主詞，畫線的不定詞片語才是真正的主詞。】

It is＋adj＋that ...（某件事是……的）▶

⇒ **It is vital that** pollution should be controlled.

= <u>That pollution should be controlled</u> is vital.

控制污染應該是很重要的。

【It 是虛主詞，畫線的 that 子句才是真正的主詞。】

There is/are ... （有……）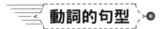

➠ **There are** several people in the park.

= Several people are in the park.

有幾個人在公園裡。

【There 是虛主詞，畫線的名詞片語才是真正的主詞。】

I believe it＋adj ... （我相信……）

➠ **I believe it possible** to travel to Mars one day.

= I believe that it is possible to travel to Mars one day.

我相信有天可能可以到火星上旅行。

【it 是虛主詞，畫線的不定詞片語才是真正的主詞。】

動詞的句型

祈使句

➠ **Look** on the bright side of everything. 凡事往好處看。

感官動詞接原形動詞

➠ I **saw him cheat** on the test. 我看見他考試作弊。

V＋V-ing 的句型

➠ I **enjoy viewing** sea in the sunset. 我喜歡在夕陽中看海。

V＋N＋V-ing 的句型

➠ I **found a few boys sleeping** in the bed.

我發現一些男孩在床上睡覺。

suggest 的用法

➠ The doctor **suggested that** she **(should)** have an operation.

醫師建議她要動手術。

【S＋suggest＋that＋S＋(should)＋Vr】

insist 的用法

➠ My mother **insists that** I **(should)** go to bed by midnight.

我母親堅持我在午夜以前要上床睡覺。

【S＋insist＋that＋S＋(should)＋Vr】

demand 的用法 ▶

➡ The professor **demanded that** we **(should)** be on time for every class.

教授要求我們每一堂課都要準時。

【S＋demand＋that＋S＋(should)＋Vr】

表示習慣的用法 ◦

used to＋Vr（過去曾經……）▶

➡ There **used to** be a river nearby.

這附近以前有河。

be used to＋V-ing（習慣於……）▶

➡ He **is used to** getting up late.

他習慣晚起。

get used to＋V-ing／名詞（漸漸習慣於……）▶

➡ I **get used to** new surroundings.

我漸漸習慣於新的環境。

分詞構句 ◦

現在分詞構句 ▶

➡ **Finishing** my work, I walked out of the office and got some fresh air.

完成工作之後，我走出辦公室來呼吸一些新鮮空氣。

【V-ing 在句首，表示主動。】

➡ The plane crashed thunderously, **killing** all people on it.

飛機雷鳴般地墜毀了，造成機上所有人都死了。

【V-ing 在主句之後，表示主動的結果。】

⇒ **Blamed** by his teacher, he cried loudly.

被老師責備後，他放聲大哭。

【Vpp 在句首，表示被動。】

⇒ The visitors arrived finally, warmly **greeted** by local officials.

參訪者終於抵達，被當地官員熱情接待。

【Vpp 在主句之後，表示被動的結果。】

再怎麼長的文章都是由一個一個句子組合起來的。學習連貫式翻譯的第一步，就是要學會單句翻譯。只要掌握了單句翻譯的技巧，一整篇的連貫式翻譯也就難不倒你了。

2-1 中翻英的藝術

　　基本上，中文與英文在表達方式、文法結構等方面，與其他語言相比已算是十分接近，可是因為文化差異或是生活思考方式的不同，總是會造成些許的落差，這也是學生有時一不小心就會寫出中式英文的原因。

　　翻譯雖重逐字推敲，但是否能忠實去精譯及反映作者的原意，將會是中翻英能否得高分的關鍵。全民英檢中級中翻英的考題，計分著重於用字遣詞、文法結構、傳達題意。句與句之間非獨立的個體，所以句與句之間應有連接詞與轉折語來連結與修飾。當然文法結構的完整度是必要的，標點符號的使用亦要注意。

　　例如，「我吃了一些東西，然後喝了一杯咖啡。」不可以譯成 "I ate something, then drank a cup of coffee."。雖然中文裡沒有像英文一樣有所謂的連接詞，不管要一連使用幾個動詞都沒關係，但是在用英文表達時，如果要一連使用兩個以上的動詞，一定要有連接詞才行。所以本句的正確譯法為 "I ate something and then drank a cup of coffee."

　　翻譯最難的地方就在於，語言的轉換並沒有一定的公式可用，也沒有標準答案，而只有較恰當或正確的翻譯方式，雖然，或許會有一些規則可循，但是終究不能夠像科學定律一樣加以套用。也就是因為如此，電腦翻譯軟體即使再進步，卻始終無法得出能媲美人工翻譯的質感。因此，想要寫出好翻譯，絕對不是光憑沙盤推演就能夠做得到的，唯一的方法就是實際從練習的過程中磨練自己的翻譯功力。

　　以下先針對單句中翻英進行演練，在接下來的章節之中也會提供連貫式翻譯的模擬練習題供考生增進翻譯實力。

▶ **休閒與娛樂** ●

1. 今晚去看場電影如何？

▶ _____

2. 我們何不明天舉辦一場烤肉派對？

▶ _____

3. 今天下午何不玩牌或下棋？

▶ _____

4. 為何不在墾丁國家公園（Kenting National Park）野餐？

▶ _____

5. 這真是令人難忘的經驗！

▶ _____

6. 那麼，祝你明天看球愉快！

▶ _____

7. 祝你一路順風！

▶ _____

8. 祝你有個愉快的聖誕節。

▶ _____

9. 祝你新年快樂。

▶ _____

10. 我不認為他的年紀足以進入夜店。

▶ _____

11. 你昨晚在 Den 的派對愉快嗎？

▶ _____

12. 這些小孩兩天前有去打棒球嗎？

▶ _____

13. 這女人允許她的兒子去 KTV 了嗎？

▶ _____

14. Charles 前天有去看電影嗎？

▶ _____

15. 你昨天和你朋友們去慢跑了嗎？

▶ _____

16. 去年你有去泰國嗎？

▶ _____

17. 你可以給我一些去加拿大旅遊的資訊嗎？

▶ _____

18. 你最近有沒有去中國？

▶ _____

19. 這星期你有做什麼有趣的事嗎？

▶ _____

20. 你的荷蘭之旅如何？

▶ _____

21. 去看電影如何？

▶ _____

22. 你何不休一天假，休息一下？

▶ _____

23. 你為何不出去？

▶ _____

24. 我們今晚何不去看場電影？

▶ _____

25. 到底誰會來參加派對？

▶ _____

26. 誰昨天和 Smith 先生打了棒球？

▶ _____

27. 你何時要去健行？

▶ _____

28. 今天下課後你會去哪裡？

▶ _____

29. 你星期天通常會去哪裡？

▶ _____

30. 這些女孩去了哪裡玩？

▶ _____

31. 他們最後去了哪裡？

▶ _____

32. 在台灣最受歡迎的運動是什麼？

▶ _____

33. 今晚你們會做什麼？

▶ _____

34. 他想去哪個國家？中國還是加拿大？

▶ _____

35. 他說他從未去過倫敦。

▶ _____

Answer ●●●●●●●●●●●●●●●●●●●●●●●●●●●●●● 解答

1. 今晚去看場電影如何？

▶ _What about seeing a movie tonight?_

2. 我們何不明天舉辦一場烤肉派對？

▶ *Why don't we have a BBQ party tomorrow?*

3. 今天下午何不玩牌或下棋？

▶ *Why not play cards or chess this afternoon?*

4. 為何不在墾丁國家公園（Kenting National Park）野餐？

▶ *Why not have a picnic in Kenting National Park?*

5. 這真是令人難忘的經驗！

▶ *What an unforgettable experience it is!*

6. 那麼，祝你明天看球愉快！

▶ *So, have a great time at the baseball game tomorrow!*

7. 祝你一路順風！

▶ *Have a nice trip!*

8. 祝你有個愉快的聖誕節。

▶ *May you have a Merry Christmas.*

9. 祝你新年快樂。

▶ *May you have a Happy New Year.*

10. 我不認為他的年紀足以進入夜店。

▶ *I don't think that he is old enough to enter the nightclub.*

11. 你昨晚在 Den 的派對愉快嗎？

▶ *Did you enjoy Den's party last night?*

12. 這些小孩兩天前有去打棒球嗎？

▶ *Did the children play baseball two days ago?*

13. 這女人允許她的兒子去 KTV 了嗎？

▶ *Did the woman permit her son to go to a karaoke bar?*

14. Charles 前天有去看電影嗎？

▶ *Did Charles go to the movies the day before yesterday?*

15. 你昨天和你朋友們去慢跑了嗎？

▶ *Did you go jogging with your friends yesterday?*

16. 去年你有去泰國嗎？

▶ *Did you go to Thailand last year?*

17. 你可以給我一些去加拿大旅遊的資訊嗎？

▶ *Can you give me some information about Canada tour?*

18. 你最近有沒有去中國？

▶ *Have you been to China lately?*

19. 這星期你有做什麼有趣的事嗎？

▶ *Have you done anything interesting this week?*

20. 你的荷蘭之旅如何？

▶ *How was your trip to the Netherlands?*

21. 去看電影如何？

▶ *How about going to the cinema?*

22. 你何不休一天假，休息一下？

▶ *Why don't you take a day off and get some rest?*

23. 你為何不出去？

▶ *Why don't you go out?*

24. 我們今晚何不去看場電影？

▶ *Why don't we see a movie tonight?*

25. 到底誰會來參加派對？

▶ *Who will come to the party actually?*

26. 誰昨天和 Smith 先生打了棒球？

▶ *Who played baseball with Mr. Smith yesterday?*

27. 你何時要去健行？

▶ *When do you go hiking?*

28. 今天下課後你會去哪裡？

▶ *Where will you go after class today?*

29. 你星期天通常會去哪裡？

▶ *Where do you usually go on Sundays?*

30. 這些女孩去了哪裡玩？

▶ *Where did the girls play?*

31. 他們最後去了哪裡？

▶ *Where did they go finally?*

32. 在台灣最受歡迎的運動是什麼？

▶ *What's the most popular sport in Taiwan?*

33. 今晚你們會做什麼？

▶ *What are you going to do tonight?*

34. 他想去哪個國家？中國還是加拿大？

▶ *Which country does he want to visit, China or Canada?*

35. 他說他從未去過倫敦。

▶ *He said that he had never come to London before.*

氣候與地理 ▶

1. 紐約是一座迷人的城市。

▶ _____

2. 現在雨下得好大！

▶ _____

3. 我討厭夏天。天氣太熱了。

▶ _____

4. 地球繞著太陽轉是一個事實。

⏵ _____

5. 要下雨了。我想我需要一件雨衣。

⏵ _____

6. 你有聽說在土耳其發生了大地震嗎？

⏵ _____

7. 當你在東京時天氣好嗎？

⏵ _____

8. 台北的天氣如何？

⏵ _____

9. 一陣雨剛過，美麗的彩虹便出現在天上。

⏵ _____

10. 那場暴風雨造成嚴重的農業損失。

⏵ _____

Answer 解答

1. 紐約是一座迷人的城市。

⏵ _New York is a fascinating city._

2. 現在雨下得好大！

⏵ _It's raining cats and dogs!_

3. 我討厭夏天。天氣太熱了。

⏵ _I hate summer days. It is too hot._

4. 地球繞著太陽轉是一個事實。

⏵ _That the Earth goes around the Sun is a fact._

5. 要下雨了。我想我需要一件雨衣。

⏵ _It's going to rain. I think I need a raincoat._

6. 你有聽說在土耳其發生了大地震嗎？

▶ *Did you hear about the big earthquake in Turkey?*

7. 當你在東京時天氣好嗎？

▶ *Was the weather nice when you were in Tokyo?*

8. 台北的天氣如何？

▶ *What's the weather like in Taipei?*

9. 一陣雨剛過，美麗的彩虹便出現在天上。

▶ *As soon as the shower gone, a beautiful rainbow appeared in the sky.*

10. 那場暴風雨造成嚴重的農業損失。

▶ *The storm caused serious agricultural damage.*

交通與安全 ●

1. 你有聽說 John 昨晚出車禍受傷了嗎？真可怕！

▶ _____

2. 不要隨意穿越馬路。太危險了！

▶ _____

3. 注意！梯子倒下了。

▶ _____

4. Doris 今天上午在往台北的路上被開了一張超速罰單。

▶ _____

5. 我們的油快用完了！

▶ _____

6. 萬一有緊急事件，請按警鈴。

▶ _____

7. 向右轉，你就可以看到有一棟房子在便利商店旁。

▶ _____

8. 我剛加滿油。

▶ _____

9. 在起風的日子航行太危險了。

▶ _____

10. 你可以告訴我怎麼去嗎？

▶ _____

11. 你能不能載我去上學？

▶ _____

12. 當你明天去搭車時會需要什麼嗎？

▶ _____

13. 579 號公車多久一班？

▶ _____

14. 從這裡到車站有多遠？

▶ _____

15. 誰的護照不見了？

▶ _____

16. 你家在哪裡？

▶ _____

17. Tanya 住在哪裡？

▶ _____

18. 高速公路的交通狀況怎麼樣？

▶ _____

19. 地圖上面說什麼？

▶ _____

20. 警察正在指揮交通嗎？

▶ _____

Answer ●●●●●●●●●●●●●●●●●●●●●●●●●●●●●●●●●● 解答

1. 你有聽說 John 昨晚出車禍受傷了嗎？真可怕！

▶ *Have you heard that John was injured by a car accident last night? It was awful!*

2. 不要隨意穿越馬路。太危險了！

▶ *Don't jaywalk. It's dangerous!*

3. 注意！梯子倒下了。

▶ *Look out! The ladder is falling down.*

4. Doris 今天上午在往台北的路上被開了一張超速罰單。

▶ *Doris got a ticket for speeding on her way to Taipei this morning.*

5. 我們的油快用完了！

▶ *We are running out of gas!*

6. 萬一有緊急事件，請按警鈴。

▶ *If there's an emergency, please press the panic button.*

7. 向右轉，你就可以看到有一棟房子在便利商店旁。

▶ *Turn right, then you will see a house next to a convenience store.*

8. 我剛加滿油。

▶ *I just filled up the tank.*

9. 在起風的日子航行太危險了。

▶ *It's too dangerous to sail a boat on a windy day.*

10. 你可以告訴我怎麼去嗎？

▶ *Can you show me how to get there?*

11. 你能不能載我去上學？

▶ *Will you give me a ride to school?*

12. 當你明天去搭車時會需要什麼嗎？

▶ *Will you need anything when you are waiting in the station tomorrow?*

13. 579 號公車多久一班？

▶ *How often does the No. 579 bus run?*

14. 從這裡到車站有多遠？

▶ *How far is it from here to the station?*

15. 誰的護照不見了？

▶ *Whose passport is missing?*

16. 你家在哪裡？

▶ *Where is your place?*

17. Tanya 住在哪裡？

▶ *Where does Tanya live?*

18. 高速公路的交通狀況怎麼樣？

▶ *What's the traffic situation on the freeway?*

19. 地圖上面說什麼？

▶ *What does the map show?*

20. 警察正在指揮交通嗎？

▶ *Is the policeman directing the traffic?*

教育與學習

1. 我們去考全民英檢中級測驗吧！

▶ _____

2. 安靜點！否則你會被你的老師罵。

▶ _____

3. Daniel，要當一位好學生。

▶ _____

4. 你的英文說得很好。

▶ _____

5. 她是我們班上最聰明的學生。

▶ _____

6. 他稱讚 Charles 聰明。

▶ _____

7. 哇！你的英文真強。

▶ _____

8. 希望你能通過入學考試。

▶ _____

9. Harrison 出了什麼事？他這次考得很差。

▶ _____

10. 你的報告遲交了。

▶ _____

11. Lee 博士今晚有一場演講。你要來嗎？

▶ _____

12. 假如我有時間，我就會把功課做完。

▶ _____

13. 我偶爾會因為考試而熬夜。

▶ _____

14. 活到老學到老。

▶ _____

15. 他和你一樣聰明。

▶ _____

16. 我很確定英文是相當重要的。

▶ _____

17. 說到英文,沒有人比 John 更好。

▶ _____

18. 我已經學英文十年了。

▶ _____

19. 這間圖書館是念書的好地方。

▶ _____

20. Kim 不但用功,還很聰明。

▶ _____

21. 他的老師一直都認真教英文嗎?

▶ _____

22. 你昨晚有做功課嗎?

▶ _____

23. 你念英文已經念超過三小時了嗎?

▶ _____

24. 王先生已經上完寫作課了嗎?

▶ _____

25. 在 2020 年之前你就已經學德文學三年了嗎?

▶ _____

26. 你的朋友是大學生嗎?

▶ _____

27. 你昨天來的時候,有很多學生嗎?

▶ _____

28. 在你的課堂上有多少學生？

▶ _____

29. 你為什麼轉系了？

▶ _____

30. 你何不休息一下？

▶ _____

31. 誰得到最高分？

▶ _____

32. 你的作業何時會寫完？

▶ _____

33. 我們應該何時交作業？

▶ _____

34. 你在哪裡上學？

▶ _____

35. 哪本書是 Tommy 的？

▶ _____

36. 我需要一本可以教我寫作的書。

▶ _____

37. 我知道的英文字彙很少。

▶ _____

38. 接近期中考的時候，圖書館總是很擁擠。

▶ _____

39. 我擅長讀跟寫，不擅長聽跟說。

▶ _____

40. 傑夫平時從不念書，所以他總是得在考試前夕熬夜念書。

▶ _____

Answer 解答

1. 我們去考全民英檢中級測驗吧！

▶ *Let's take a GEPT Intermediate Test!*

2. 安靜點！否則你會被你的老師罵。

▶ *Be quiet! Or you'll be scolded by your teacher.*

3. Daniel，要當一位好學生。

▶ *Be a good student, Daniel.*

4. 你的英文說得很好。

▶ *You speak English beautifully.*

5. 她是我們班上最聰明的學生。

▶ *She is the smartest student in our class.*

6. 他稱讚 Charles 聰明。

▶ *He praised Charles for his cleverness.*

7. 哇！你的英文真強。

▶ *Wow! Your English ability is really impressive.*

8. 希望你能通過入學考試。

▶ *Hope you can pass the entrance examination.*

9. Harrison 出了什麼事？他這次考得很差。

▶ *What's wrong with Harrison? He got really bad grades this time.*

10. 你的報告遲交了。

▶ *Your report is late.*

11. Lee 博士今晚有一場演講。你要來嗎？

▶ *Dr. Lee is giving a lecture tonight. Are you coming?*

12. 假如我有時間，我就會把功課做完。

▶ *If I had time, I would finish my homework.*

13. 我偶爾會因為考試而熬夜。

▶ *I occasionally burn the midnight oil for a test.*

14. 活到老學到老。

▶ *It's never too late to learn.*

15. 他和你一樣聰明。

▶ *He is as smart as you are.*

16. 我很確定英文是相當重要的。

▶ *I'm sure that English is pretty important.*

17. 說到英文，沒有人比 John 更好。

▶ *When it comes to English, no one is better than John.*

18. 我已經學英文十年了。

▶ *I have learned English for 10 years.*

19. 這間圖書館是念書的好地方。

▶ *This library is a good place for studying.*

20. Kim 不但用功，還很聰明。

▶ *Kim is not only hardworking but also smart.*

21. 他的老師一直都認真教英文嗎？

▶ *Does his teacher always teach English wholeheartedly?*

22. 你昨晚有做功課嗎？

▶ *Did you do your homework last night?*

23. 你念英文已經念超過三小時了嗎？

▶ *Have you studied English for more than 3 hours?*

24. 王先生已經上完寫作課了嗎？

▶ *Has Mr. Wang finished his writing class?*

25. 在 2020 年之前你就已經學德文學三年了嗎？

▶ *Had you learned German for 3 years by 2020?*

26. 你的朋友是大學生嗎？

▶ *Is your friend a university student?*

27. 你昨天來的時候，有很多學生嗎？

▶ *Were there many students when you came yesterday?*

28. 在你的課堂上有多少學生？

▶ *How many students are there in your class?*

29. 你為什麼轉系了？

▶ *Why did you change your major?*

30. 你何不休息一下？

▶ *Why don't you take a break?*

31. 誰得到最高分？

▶ *Who got the highest score?*

32. 你的作業何時會寫完？

▶ *When will you finish your homework?*

33. 我們應該何時交作業？

▶ *When should we hand our homework in?*

34. 你在哪裡上學？

▶ *Where is your school?*

35. 哪本書是 Tommy 的？

▶ *Which book belongs to Tommy?*

36. 我需要一本可以教我寫作的書。

▶ *I need a book which can teach me how to write.*

37. 我知道的英文字彙很少。

▶ *My English vocabulary bank is small.*

38. 接近期中考的時候，圖書館總是很擁擠。

▶ *When midterm tests are approaching, the library is always crowded.*

39. 我擅長讀跟寫，不擅長聽跟說。

▶ *I am good at reading and writing but poor in listening and speaking.*

40. 傑夫平時從不念書，所以他總是得在考試前夕熬夜念書。

▶ *Jeff never studies at normal times, so he has to stay up late before taking tests all the time.*

工作與職場

1. 你有什麼建議？

▶ _____

2. 很抱歉回覆晚了。你的訂單已經準備好了。

▶ _____

3. 我聽說 John 因為工作態度不良而被開除了。

▶ _____

4. 我必須為我打錯字道歉。

▶ _____

5. 很抱歉犯下這麼嚴重的錯誤。我會立即更正。

▶ _____

6. 你的表現令人印象深刻。

▶ _____

7. 我對你的絕佳表現感到印象深刻。

▶ _____

8. 我希望你能很快拿到加薪。

▶ _____

9. 我希望你能很快升遷。

▶ _____

10. 希望我能盡快再見到你。
　　▶ _____

11. 期待你能盡快回覆，謝謝。
　　▶ _____

12. 不要對我擺臉色，這不是我的錯。
　　▶ _____

13. 你的進度已經落後四天了。
　　▶ _____

14. 我以在幼稚園工作維生。
　　▶ _____

15. 我一直很認真工作。
　　▶ _____

16. 你很容易生氣嗎？
　　▶ _____

17. 在你去日本前曾經當過店員嗎？
　　▶ _____

18. 你在這家公司工作多久了？
　　▶ _____

19. 你怎麼把機器打開的？
　　▶ _____

20. 你何時會結束你的工作？
　　▶ _____

21. 這個男人的工作是什麼？
　　▶ _____

22. 他期望的待遇是什麼？
　　▶ _____

23. 因為他不在，所以主管取消了會議。

▶ _____

24. 假如他被開除，我就會辭職。

▶ _____

25. 你想要應徵行銷的職位嗎？

▶ _____

Answer 解答

1. 你有什麼建議？

▶ _What do you recommend?_

2. 很抱歉回覆晚了。你的訂單已經準備好了。

▶ _Sorry for the late reply. Your order is ready._

3. 我聽說 John 因為工作態度不良而被開除了。

▶ _I have heard that John had been fired because of his bad working attitude._

4. 我必須為我打錯字道歉。

▶ _I have to apologize for my typing mistakes._

5. 很抱歉犯下這麼嚴重的錯誤。我會立即更正。

▶ _Sorry for the terrible mistakes. I'll correct them right away._

6. 你的表現令人印象深刻。

▶ _Your performance is really impressive._

7. 我對你的絕佳表現感到印象深刻。

▶ _I'm so impressed by your excellent performance._

8. 我希望你能很快拿到加薪。

▶ _I hope you get a raise soon._

9. 我希望你能很快升遷。

▶ *I hope you get a promotion soon.*

10. 希望我能盡快再見到你。

▶ *Hope I can see you again as soon as possible.*

11. 期待你能盡快回覆，謝謝。

▶ *Look forward to your fast reply, thanks.*

12. 不要對我擺臉色，這不是我的錯。

▶ *Don't give me that attitude, it's not my fault.*

13. 你的進度已經落後四天了。

▶ *You're 4 days behind your schedule.*

14. 我以在幼稚園工作維生。

▶ *I work in a kindergarten for a living.*

15. 我一直很認真工作。

▶ *I have been working so hard.*

16. 你很容易生氣嗎？

▶ *Do you get angry easily?*

17. 在你去日本前曾經當過店員嗎？

▶ *Were you a store clerk before you went to Japan?*

18. 你在這家公司工作多久了？

▶ *How long have you been working in this company?*

19. 你怎麼把機器打開的？

▶ *How do you turn on the machine?*

20. 你何時會結束你的工作？

▶ *When will you finish your work?*

21. 這個男人的工作是什麼？

▶ *What's the man's occupation?*

22. 他期望的待遇是什麼？

▶ *What's his expected salary?*

23. 因為他不在，所以主管取消了會議。

▶ *The supervisor cancelled the meeting since he was not here.*

24. 假如他被開除，我就會辭職。

▶ *If he is fired, I'll quit.*

25. 你想要應徵行銷的職位嗎？

▶ *Do you want to apply for the marketing position?*

餐飲與購物 ▶

1. 你覺得我們去一家很棒的餐廳約會如何？

▶ _____

2. 我們吃一些巧克力冰淇淋吧！

▶ _____

3. 這件尺寸不對。我需要試另一件。

▶ _____

4. 我想要試穿這個。更衣室在哪裡？

▶ _____

5. 一共是五百二十元。付現還是刷卡？

▶ _____

6. 我沒辦法讓你殺價，這已經是最便宜的價格了。

▶ _____

7. 我通常會在週末時去百貨公司購物。

▶ _____

8. 這本有很多照片的書是暢銷書。
▶ _____

9. 我們待會去買東西吧。
▶ _____

10. 你想要在超市裡買什麼東西嗎？
▶ _____

11. 你認為我應該買這雙短襪嗎？
▶ _____

12. 這個男人喜歡披薩嗎？
▶ _____

13. 你也想要點飲料嗎？
▶ _____

14. 她等會會買麵包嗎？
▶ _____

15. 你昨晚到的時候，他們正要去購物嗎？
▶ _____

16. 你花了多少錢？
▶ _____

17. 待會要不要去購物？
▶ _____

18. 要不要去書店買些書？
▶ _____

19. 是誰決定要去牛排館吃晚餐的？
▶ _____

20. 誰拿了蘋果汁？
▶ _____

21. 我打算要去買要穿去參加貝蒂生日派對的衣服。

▶ _____

22. 那家新的購物中心在哪裡？

▶ _____

23. 老實說，你去哪裡吃大餐了？

▶ _____

24. 你喜歡哪種沙拉醬？

▶ _____

25. 哪個最便宜 ？

▶ _____

Answer ●●●●●●●●●●●●●●●●●●●●●●●●●●●●● 解答

1. 你覺得我們去一家很棒的餐廳約會如何？

▶ *What would you say if we date in a nice restaurant?*

2. 我們吃一些巧克力冰淇淋吧！

▶ *Let's have some chocolate ice cream!*

3. 這件尺寸不對。我需要試另一件。

▶ *It's the wrong size. I need to try on another one.*

4. 我想要試穿這個。更衣室在哪裡？

▶ *I want to try it on. Where's the fitting room?*

5. 一共是五百二十元。付現還是刷卡？

▶ *The total amount is $520. Cash or credit cards?*

6. 我沒辦法讓你殺價，這已經是最便宜的價格了。

▶ *Please don't bargain with me. It's the lowest price.*

7. 我通常會在週末時去百貨公司購物。

▶ *I usually go shopping in the department stores on weekends.*

8. 這本有很多照片的書是暢銷書。

▶ *The book which has lots of pictures is a bestseller.*

9. 我們待會去買東西吧。

▶ *Let's go shopping later.*

10. 你想要在超市裡買什麼東西嗎？

▶ *Do you want to buy anything from the supermarket?*

11. 你認為我應該買這雙短襪嗎？

▶ *Do you think I should buy these socks?*

12. 這個男人喜歡披薩嗎？

▶ *Does the man like pizza?*

13. 你也想要點飲料嗎？

▶ *Would you like to order a drink too?*

14. 她等會會買麵包嗎？

▶ *Is she going to buy some bread later?*

15. 你昨晚到的時候，他們正要去購物嗎？

▶ *Were they about to go shopping when you arrived last night?*

16. 你花了多少錢？

▶ *How much did you spend?*

17. 待會要不要去購物？

▶ *Why not go shopping later?*

18. 要不要去書店買些書？

▶ *Why not go to a bookstore and buy some books?*

19. 是誰決定要去牛排館吃晚餐的？

▶ *Who decided to have dinner in a steakhouse?*

20. 誰拿了蘋果汁？

▶ *Who has the apple juice?*

21. 我打算要去買要穿去參加貝蒂生日派對的衣服。

▶ *I'm planning to shop for my clothes for Betty's birthday party.*

22. 那家新的購物中心在哪裡？

▶ *Where's the new shopping mall?*

23. 老實說，你去哪裡吃大餐了？

▶ *Tell me the truth, where did you have the feast?*

24. 你喜歡哪種沙拉醬？

▶ *Which salad dressing would you like?*

25. 哪個最便宜 ？

▶ *Which one is the cheapest?*

1. Gloria，妳最好不要打擾 Wang 先生。他正在睡覺。

▶ _____

2. 離我遠一點。我現在不想和你說話。

▶ _____

3. 你不可以那樣做！

▶ _____

4. 因為我正在念書，所以沒辦法出門。

▶ _____

5. 我很抱歉。電話收訊很差。你可以再說一次嗎？

▶ _____

6. 你是我見過最帥的人。

▶ _____

7. Sue 好美啊！真希望我能和她結婚。

▶ _____

127

8. 祝你們幸福美滿。

▶ _____

9. 願你有個美夢。

▶ _____

10. 他到底為何不寫信給我？

▶ _____

11. 我已經等很久了，Maria 總是遲到。

▶ _____

12. 你不該那麼說的，這樣說並不公平。

▶ _____

13. 你真不該這麼做！

▶ _____

14. 你怎麼可以對我做這種事？

▶ _____

15. 我從未想過你會對我說謊。

▶ _____

16. Mark 到底在廚房裡做了什麼？這裡一團糟。

▶ _____

17. 到底為什麼 Nancy 會這麼生氣？她今天早上吃錯藥了嗎？

▶ _____

18. 那是誰做的？

▶ _____

19. 他究竟為何不幫我？

▶ _____

20. 當你見到 Jena，告訴她我想她。

▶ _____

21. 我住在六樓，而且這棟大樓的電梯壞了。
▶ _____

22. 噢，糟糕，我忘了放錢在皮夾裡。
▶ _____

23. Lee 先生，請允許我先說幾句話。
▶ _____

24. Rupert，我們不是好朋友嗎？
▶ _____

25. 我不喜歡住在樓上的那個女孩。
▶ _____

26. 在談完政治情勢後，總統繼續談論經濟相關問題。
▶ _____

27. Mary 問我昨晚是否有睡好。
▶ _____

28. 我沒有我哥哥高。
▶ _____

29. 我們有的越多，想要的就越多。
▶ _____

30. 他足夠強壯，可以舉起很多重物。
▶ _____

31. 這是我出生的房子。
▶ _____

32. 油比水輕是一個事實。
▶ _____

33. 能與你見面是我的榮幸。
▶ _____

34. 明天兩點如何？
▶ _____

35. 你介意我借用你的筆嗎？
▶ _____

36. 你介意把音樂關小聲一點嗎？
▶ _____

37. 你爸爸每天早上七點起床嗎？
▶ _____

38. 昨晚你有看見那個警察在大廳裡嗎？
▶ _____

39. 你昨晚又熬夜了嗎？
▶ _____

40. 這男人有拿到錢了嗎？
▶ _____

41. 我可以晚點回電給你嗎？
▶ _____

42. 你可以告訴我帳單是否已經到期了嗎？
▶ _____

43. 你介意我坐在這裡嗎？
▶ _____

44. 可以請你幫我修理水槽嗎？
▶ _____

45. 你可以告訴我怎麼做嗎？
▶ _____

46. 你最近有見到我的堂兄 Charles 嗎？
▶ _____

47. 你已經洗過澡了嗎？

▶ _____

48. 你母親以前有見過 Mary 嗎？

▶ _____

49. 他到這裡的時候，你已經吃完蘋果了嗎？

▶ _____

50. 在她先生回來之前，Brooke 太太油漆完牆壁了嗎？

▶ _____

51. 當我回來時，已經有人整理了房間嗎？

▶ _____

52. Alice 與 Tim 仍住在紐約嗎？

▶ _____

53. 我的身高足以碰到天花板了嗎？

▶ _____

54. 你的父母正在照顧他們的狗嗎？

▶ _____

55. 昨晚你的父親很生氣嗎？

▶ _____

56. 昨晚九點時你正在睡覺嗎？

▶ _____

57. 一切都好嗎？

▶ _____

58. 你今天為何這麼早起？

▶ _____

59. 那個男人多高？

▶ _____

60. 你的袋子多重？
⏵ _____

61. 為何 Mary 如此難過？
⏵ _____

62. 為何那個女孩不能和 Joe 說話？
⏵ _____

63. 為何 Jeff 要和 Lisa 說話？
⏵ _____

64. 為何 Tom 要那樣做？
⏵ _____

65. Helen 正在和誰說話？
⏵ _____

66. 照片裡的男人是誰？
⏵ _____

67. 說話的人是誰？
⏵ _____

68. 誰做了那件事？
⏵ _____

69. 誰是最高的？
⏵ _____

70. 誰是 Jane 的姊姊？
⏵ _____

71. 誰是班上最聰明的？
⏵ _____

72. 在 Peter 桌上的是誰的書？
⏵ _____

73. 誰的手機在響？

▶ _____

74. 誰的電腦壞了？

▶ _____

75. 誰的狗正在前院奔跑？

▶ _____

76. 誰的相機被偷了？

▶ _____

77. 誰的課本放在講台上？

▶ _____

78. 誰的杯子是乾淨的？

▶ _____

79. 在牆上的月曆是誰的？

▶ _____

80. 你的午休時間是什麼時候？

▶ _____

81. Mary 的父親何時回來？

▶ _____

82. 你每天早上通常幾點起床？

▶ _____

83. 你們老師的生日是什麼時候？

▶ _____

84. 你通常什麼時候洗澡？

▶ _____

85. 你何時能回家煮晚飯？

▶ _____

86. 她有說過實話嗎？
▶ _____

87. 最近你到哪裡去了？
▶ _____

88. 這兩個女生在哪裡？
▶ _____

89. Charles 明天的早餐會吃什麼？
▶ _____

90. 哪台電腦的品質最好？
▶ _____

91. 他生病的這件事似乎很可疑。
▶ _____

92. 這個得到第一名的男孩是我的哥哥。
▶ _____

93. 不論他們去了哪裡，他們發現大家都很窮。
▶ _____

94. Ben 昨晚摔斷了手臂。
▶ _____

95. 我聽說 John 昨天生病了。
▶ _____

96. 抱歉讓你久等。剛剛有急診，所以醫生要到四點才會有空。
▶ _____

97. 我聽說 John 今天好多了。
▶ _____

98. 噢，我的背痛死了！
▶ _____

99. 你在早上感覺比較好嗎？

▶ _____

100. 當我去看醫生時，你能幫我看小孩嗎？

▶ _____

Answer 解答

1. Gloria，妳最好不要打擾 Wang 先生。他正在睡覺。

▶ *Gloria, you'd better not disturb Mr. Wang. He's sleeping.*

2. 離我遠一點。我現在不想和你說話。

▶ *Leave me alone. I don't want to talk to you now.*

3. 你不可以那樣做！

▶ *You can't do that!*

4. 因為我正在念書，所以沒辦法出門。

▶ *As I am studying, I can't go outside.*

5. 我很抱歉。電話收訊很差。你可以再說一次嗎？

▶ *I'm so sorry. The reception is bad. Can you say that again?*

6. 你是我見過最帥的人。

▶ *You are the most handsome guy that I've ever seen.*

7. Sue 好美啊！真希望我能和她結婚。

▶ *How beautiful Sue is!I wish I could marry her.*

8. 祝你們幸福美滿。

▶ *Wish you a happy marriage.*

9. 願你有個美夢。

▶ *May you have a nice dream.*

10. 他到底為何不寫信給我？

▶ *Why in the world doesn't he write to me?*

11. 我已經等很久了，Maria 總是遲到。

▶ *I've been waiting for a long time. Maria is always late.*

12. 你不該那麼說的，這樣說並不公平。

▶ *You shouldn't say that, it's unfair to say so.*

13. 你真不該這麼做！

▶ *You shouldn't have done something like that!*

14. 你怎麼可以對我做這種事？

▶ *How could you do this to me?*

15. 我從未想過你會對我說謊。

▶ *I have never thought that you would lie to me.*

16. Mark 到底在廚房裡做了什麼？這裡一團糟。

▶ *What on earth has Mark done in the kitchen? It's a mess.*

17. 到底為什麼 Nancy 會這麼生氣？她今天早上吃錯藥了嗎？

▶ *What on earth makes Nancy so angry? Did she get up on the wrong side of bed this morning?*

18. 那是誰做的？

▶ *Who did that?*

19. 他究竟為何不幫我？

▶ *Why on earth doesn't he give me a hand?*

20. 當你見到 Jena，告訴她我想她。

▶ *When you see Jena, tell her l miss her.*

21. 我住在六樓，而且這棟大樓的電梯壞了。

▶ *I live on the sixth floor, and the elevators in the building are not working properly.*

22. 噢，糟糕，我忘了放錢在皮夾裡。

▶ *Oh, no, I forgot to put money in my wallet.*

23. Lee 先生，請允許我先說幾句話。

▶ *Mr. Lee, please let me say a few words first.*

24. Rupert，我們不是好朋友嗎？

▶ *Rupert, we are good friends, aren't we?*

25. 我不喜歡住在樓上的那個女孩。

▶ *I don't like the girl who lives upstairs.*

26. 在談完政治情勢後，總統繼續談論經濟相關問題。

▶ *After talking about politics, the president continued to talk about economic issues.*

27. Mary 問我昨晚是否有睡好。

▶ *Mary asked me if I had a good sleep last night.*

28. 我沒有我哥哥高。

▶ *I am not so tall as my brother.*

29. 我們有的越多，想要的就越多。

▶ *The more we have , the more we want.*

30. 他足夠強壯，可以舉起很多重物。

▶ *He is strong enough to lift many heavy things up.*

31. 這是我出生的房子。

▶ *This is the house where I was born.*

32. 油比水輕是一個事實。

▶ *It's a fact that oil is lighter than water.*

33. 能與你見面是我的榮幸。

▶ *It's my pleasure meeting you here.*

34. 明天兩點如何？

▶ *How about two o'clock tomorrow?*

35. 你介意我借用你的筆嗎？

▶ *Do you mind if I borrow your pen?*

36. 你介意把音樂關小聲一點嗎？

▶ *Do you mind turning down the music?*

37. 你爸爸每天早上七點起床嗎？

▶ *Does your father get up at 7 every morning?*

38. 昨晚你有看見那個警察在大廳裡嗎？

▶ *Did you see the police officer in the lobby last night?*

39. 你昨晚又熬夜了嗎？

▶ *Did you stay up again last night?*

40. 這男人有拿到錢了嗎？

▶ *Did the man get the money?*

41. 我可以晚點回電給你嗎？

▶ *May I call you back later?*

42. 你可以告訴我帳單是否已經到期了嗎？

▶ *Could you tell me if my bill was due?*

43. 你介意我坐在這裡嗎？

▶ *Would you mind if I sit here?*

44. 可以請你幫我修理水槽嗎？

▶ *Could you please help me fix my sink?*

45. 你可以告訴我怎麼做嗎？

▶ *Can you show me how to do it?*

46. 你最近有見到我的堂兄 Charles 嗎？

▶ *Have you seen my cousin Charles recently?*

47. 你已經洗過澡了嗎？

▶ *Have you already had a bath?*

48. 你母親以前有見過 Mary 嗎？

▶ *Has your mother ever seen Mary before?*

49. 他到這裡的時候,你已經吃完蘋果了嗎?

▶ *Had you eaten up an apple when he came here?*

50. 在她先生回來之前,Brooke 太太油漆完牆壁了嗎?

▶ *Had Mrs. Brooke finished painting the wall before her husband was back?*

51. 當我回來時,已經有人整理了房間嗎?

▶ *Had anyone cleaned the room already when I was back?*

52. Alice 與 Tim 仍住在紐約嗎?

▶ *Are Alice and Tim still living in New York?*

53. 我的身高足以碰到天花板了嗎?

▶ *Am I tall enough to reach the ceiling?*

54. 你的父母正在照顧他們的狗嗎?

▶ *Are your parents taking care of their dog now?*

55. 昨晚你的父親很生氣嗎?

▶ *Was your father very angry last night?*

56. 昨晚九點時你正在睡覺嗎?

▶ *Were you sleeping at 9 last night?*

57. 一切都好嗎?

▶ *How's everything going?*

58. 你今天為何這麼早起?

▶ *How come you got up so early today?*

59. 那個男人多高?

▶ *How tall is the man?*

60. 你的袋子多重?

▶ *How heavy is your bag?*

61. 為何 Mary 如此難過?

▶ *Why is Mary so sad?*

62. 為何那個女孩不能和 Joe 說話？

▶ *Why couldn't the girl talk to Joe?*

63. 為何 Jeff 要和 Lisa 說話？

▶ *Why did Jeff talk to Lisa?*

64. 為何 Tom 要那樣做？

▶ *Why did Tom do things like that?*

65. Helen 正在和誰說話？

▶ *Who's Helen talking to?*

66. 照片裡的男人是誰？

▶ *Who is the man in the picture?*

67. 說話的人是誰？

▶ *Who is the speaker?*

68. 誰做了那件事？

▶ *Who did that thing?*

69. 誰是最高的？

▶ *Who is the tallest?*

70. 誰是 Jane 的姊姊？

▶ *Who is Jane's sister?*

71. 誰是班上最聰明的？

▶ *Who is the smartest in the class?*

72. 在 Peter 桌上的是誰的書？

▶ *Whose book is on Peter's desk?*

73. 誰的手機在響？

▶ *Whose cell phone is ringing?*

74. 誰的電腦壞了？

▶ *Whose computer is out of order?*

75. 誰的狗正在前院奔跑？

▶ *Whose dog is running in the yard?*

76. 誰的相機被偷了？

▶ *Whose camera has been stolen?*

77. 誰的課本放在講台上？

▶ *Whose textbook is on the podium?*

78. 誰的杯子是乾淨的？

▶ *Whose cups are clean?*

79. 在牆上的月曆是誰的？

▶ *Whose calendar is on the wall?*

80. 你的午休時間是什麼時候？

▶ *When do you have your lunch break?*

81. Mary 的父親何時回來？

▶ *When did Mary's father come back?*

82. 你每天早上通常幾點起床？

▶ *What time do you usually get up every morning?*

83. 你們老師的生日是什麼時候？

▶ *When is your teacher's birthday?*

84. 你通常什麼時候洗澡？

▶ *When do you usually take a shower?*

85. 你何時能回家煮晚飯？

▶ *When can you back home and cook dinner?*

86. 她有說過實話嗎？

▶ *Has she ever told the truth?*

87. 最近你到哪裡去了？

▶ *Where have you been recently?*

88. 這兩個女生在哪裡？

▶ *Where are these two girls?*

89. Charles 明天的早餐會吃什麼？

▶ *What will Charles have for tomorrow's breakfast?*

90. 哪台電腦的品質最好？

▶ *Which computer has the best quality?*

91. 他生病的這件事似乎很可疑。

▶ *That he was sick seemed doubtful.*

92. 這個得到第一名的男孩是我的哥哥。

▶ *The boy who won the first prize is my brother.*

93. 不論他們去了哪裡，他們發現大家都很窮。

▶ *Wherever they went, they found everyone was poor.*

94. Ben 昨晚摔斷了手臂。

▶ *Ben fell and broke his arm last night.*

95. 我聽說 John 昨天生病了。

▶ *I have heard John was sick yesterday.*

96. 抱歉讓你久等。剛剛有急診，所以醫生要到四點才會有空。

▶ *Sorry to keep you waiting. There's been an emergency and the doctor won't be available until four.*

97. 我聽說 John 今天好多了。

▶ *I have been told that John is feeling better today.*

98. 噢，我的背痛死了！

▶ *Ouch, my back is really killing me!*

99. 你在早上感覺比較好嗎？

▶ *Do you feel better in the morning?*

100. 當我去看醫生時，你能幫我看小孩嗎？

▶ *Can you baby-sit for me when I go to the doctor's?*

Part
精選模擬試題

3

全民英檢的中級寫作測驗分為「中譯英」與「英文作文」二個部分，兩個部分各考一個題目。第一部分「中譯英」的考題類型是連貫式翻譯，題目會提供一篇長度約四到六句的中文短文，考生需將其翻譯成恰當的英文；第二部分「英文作文」則有三種可能會出現的題型，分別是「看圖寫作」、「故事接龍」與「書信寫作」。

Look Inside

精選
模擬試題

1-1 模擬試題篇

TEST 1 感冒篇

請將下列中文敘述翻譯為正確的英文，將答案寫在答案欄中。

　　我是一個經常感冒的人。昨天早上我離開家的時候，天氣十分暖和。所以我沒有穿夾克，只穿了一件襯衫與短褲。但是到了傍晚，氣溫卻急速下降。雖然晚上我很早就回家，但我還是覺得有點不舒服。今天我不但打噴嚏還頭昏，我想我最好馬上去診所看醫生。

字彙篇

中翻英

請將下列中文敘述翻譯為正確的英文，將答案寫在答案欄中。

許多人認為背英文單字是件困難的事。我每天會試著記一些新的單字。當我在讀英文雜誌的時候，我會把我不認識的字記在我的筆記本上。然後我會試著將這些新字用在日常會話之中。雖然有時仍會用錯，但我覺得進步很多。

郵差篇

請將下列中文敘述翻譯為正確的英文，將答案寫在答案欄中。

我認識一位每天穿著綠色制服的郵差。每天早上他會把信件送到我們社區來。如果有掛號信要送給我們，他就會在門口按一下門鈴，然後要我們拿印章來蓋章。他認識附近的每一個人，而我們每一個人也都認識他。他真是一位認真的郵差。

145

請將下列中文敘述翻譯為正確的英文,將答案寫在答案欄中。

　　英文是一種重要的語言,所以很多人都正在學習。許多學生認為學會用英文聽和說都很困難。但是只要不斷練習,任何困難皆可克服。也許犯錯會讓你覺得不好意思。但是每個人都會犯錯。最重要的是,要能開口大聲說英文。

_____

_____

_____

請將下列中文敘述翻譯為正確的英文,將答案寫在答案欄中。

　　不用說,每天運動是非常重要的。當我還是小孩子時,我的身體很虛弱,並且經常感冒。自從上了高中之後,我就盡量找機會打籃球。雖然功課一直很多,我還是每天花一小時來運動。三年來持續不斷的運動,使我不但變強壯也更健康了。現在大家都說我和以前完全不一樣了。

_____

_____

_____

鄉村生活篇

請將下列中文敘述翻譯為正確的英文，將答案寫在答案欄中。

你比較喜歡住在哪裡？是城市還是鄉下？我生長在鄉下的一個小村落。那時我家的附近有一條清澈的小溪。我們常在夏天到那裡游泳與釣魚。那時候我們非常快樂。現在的我住在大城市裡，雖然生活方便許多，但是那種悠閒的生活已經不再。

_____

_____

_____

_____

小學同學篇

請將下列中文敘述翻譯為正確的英文，將答案寫在答案欄中。

那是一個沒有預料到、且令人吃驚的事件。上星期一，我在公園慢跑時，一位小姐上前來叫我的名字。原來她是我的小學同學。真是令人驚訝！我們已經五年沒有見面了。現在她比以前胖上許多，難怪我那時沒一下子認出她來。她現在已經是兩個孩子的媽了。

_____

_____

_____

_____

8

請將下列中文敘述翻譯為正確的英文，將答案寫在答案欄中。

學英文需要花我很多時間與耐性，但這是絕對值得的。如今我們學英文，不僅是為了要具備競爭力，也是為了要更加了解這個世界。我每天至少花二個小時閱讀英文。藉著閱讀英文，我可以學到更多新的單字與句型，因此我覺得我的英文能力每天都更進步了一點。你呢？你也正在學這全球性的語言嗎？

_____

_____

_____

9

請將下列中文敘述翻譯為正確的英文，將答案寫在答案欄中。

你有試過色彩測驗嗎？色彩測驗可以告訴你你的性格如何。舉例來說，如果你喜歡藍色，你可能傾向於沉靜而執著。如果紅色是你最愛的顏色，那麼你可能喜歡冒險。如果你喜歡綠色，表示你渴望和平。如果你喜歡棕色，表示你是成熟且仔細的。不管你相不相信，它都是一個參考。

_____

_____

_____

TEST 10　籃球運動篇

請將下列中文敘述翻譯為正確的英文,將答案寫在答案欄中。

除了游泳外,我最喜歡的運動是籃球。每當我有空的時侯,我會邀請一些朋友組成兩隊彼此比賽。由於我們的球打得比另一隊更好,所以我們常常贏球。因為經常打球,我不但變得健康許多,而且也交到了更多朋友。最重要的是,我也長得越來越高了。

_____

_____

_____

TEST 11　交通運輸篇

請將下列中文敘述翻譯為正確的英文,將答案寫在答案欄中。

發展高效率的運輸工具是非當必要的。沒有高效率的運輸工具,我們根本不可能在短時間內從台灣到美國,或是從歐洲到亞洲。另外,也不可能可以環遊世界或是互相傳遞訊息。一般來說,運輸工具指的是汽車、火車、飛機等等交通工具。不過,電報、電話、網際網路系統也都算是運輸工具的一種。

_____

_____

_____

請將下列中文敘述翻譯為正確的英文,將答案寫在答案欄中。

　　美國人和台灣人在約定時間上非常不一樣。當美國人準備拜訪他們的親朋好友的時候,會事先打電話預約。時間一旦確定,除非情況緊急,否則不會輕易改變。相反地,我的台灣朋友卻常在沒有先通知我的情況下,半夜來敲我的門。除此之外,他們常常只因為心情不好就取消約會。所以,我覺得他們應該學習如何尊重別人的時間。

_____

_____

_____

_____

_____

請將下列中文敘述翻譯為正確的英文,將答案寫在答案欄中。

　　我已經學了十幾年的英文。雖然我每天都讀英文書籍和看英文電視節目,但我對自己的英文沒信心。上個月我和太太參加旅行團到洛杉磯度蜜月,那次的旅行讓我對自己的英文產生信心。我太太在買一只昂貴的戒指時想殺價,可是她不會用英文說。我幫她殺價,結果,她以半價買到了那只戒指。

_____

_____

_____

_____

 音樂藝術篇

請將下列中文敘述翻譯為正確的英文,將答案寫在答案欄中。

　　學習音樂的好處,在於表演者可以盡情表現他們的情感和音樂技巧;聆聽者可以發現音樂的美與藝術性。不同音樂類型,代表不同文化和世代的演變。舉例來說,年輕人喜歡嘻哈和饒舌音樂,老一輩的人則偏愛藍調和爵士。不管何種音樂,都可找到熱愛它的人。

_____

_____

_____

_____

 皮包失竊篇

請將下列中文敘述翻譯為正確的英文,將答案寫在答案欄中。

　　星期天下午我和朋友有約,我們決定下午三點在電影院門口碰面。我在買電影票的時候,發現皮夾被偷了。裡頭有我的身分證、幾張信用卡、提款卡和一些錢。我的朋友立刻幫我打電話報警。我想,大概是剛才坐公車時在和朋友聊天,扒手就趁機偷走了我的錢包。

_____

_____

_____

_____

白淨肌膚篇

請將下列中文敘述翻譯為正確的英文，將答案寫在答案欄中。

　　越來越多的亞洲女人偏好白淨的肌膚。她們傾向認為白皮膚才是美麗而吸引人的。因此，她們會購買大量能夠美白肌膚的產品。此外，讓肌膚變黑的正是紫外線。因此，預防紫外線對皮膚的傷害就很重要了。

_____

_____

_____

_____

運動休閒篇

請將下列中文敘述翻譯為正確的英文，將答案寫在答案欄中。

　　運動是很好的休閒活動。它可以減輕心理壓力，還可以消除疲勞。規律的運動可以幫助肥胖的人減肥。不過，都市人常常工作忙碌且找不到適合的運動場所。他們只能到健身房健身，進而逐漸遠離了大自然。

_____

_____

_____

新聞閱讀篇

請將下列中文敘述翻譯為正確的英文，將答案寫在答案欄中。

大多數人喜歡看新聞，而我也是。每天的新聞中都有著大量的資訊。不同的人喜歡看不同種類的新聞。有些人喜歡看運動新聞，有些人只看頭條新聞，有些人則喜歡娛樂新聞。我最喜歡看頭條，因為頭條有最重要的國內外新聞。如果你沒有太多時間可以看完所有的新聞，頭條新聞毫無疑問是你最好的選擇。

棄貓篇

請將下列中文敘述翻譯為正確的英文，將答案寫在答案欄中。

上個月，我在回家途中看見一個大箱子。我打開箱子，發現裡面有好幾隻小貓。牠們幾乎快要餓死了；我想不透是誰會對牠們這麼狠心。我一衝動就把牠們帶回家了，可是我媽媽從來就不喜歡貓。很幸運地，有兩個鄰居喜歡貓，收養了牠們。

陳年舊物篇

請將下列中文敘述翻譯為正確的英文,將答案寫在答案欄中。

很多人喜歡老舊的東西。老音樂和老電影既感人又浪漫。老古董是無價之寶,而且充滿回憶。陳年老酒香醇可口。老人仁慈而有智慧。這些人事物越老就越珍貴。

1-2 試題解析篇

TEST 1　感冒篇

解析篇

題目敘述

　　1 我是一個經常感冒的人。2 昨天早上我離開家的時候，天氣十分暖和。3 所以我沒有穿夾克，只穿了一件襯衫與短褲。4 但是到了傍晚，氣溫卻急速下降。5 雖然晚上我很早就回家，但我還是覺得有點不舒服。6 今天我不但打噴嚏還頭昏，我想我最好馬上去診所看醫生。

參考範文

　　1I am a person who often catches colds. 2When I left home yesterday morning, it was quite warm. 3Therefore, I didn't wear a jacket but just a shirt and a pair of shorts. 4However, in the evening, the temperature dropped sharply. 5Although I went home early at night, I still felt a little bit uncomfortable. 6Today I not only sneezed but also felt dizzy, so I think I'd better go to the clinic and see a doctor right away.

範文句型解析

我是一個經常感冒的人。

➡ I am a person who often catches colds.

解析 ▶ 本句利用 who 引導的形容詞子句來修飾前面的 "a person"。

155

昨天早上我離開家的時候，天氣十分暖和。

⟹ **When** I left home yesterday morning, it was quite warm.

解析 ▶ 本句以疑問詞 when 來構成表時間的副詞子句，昨天發生的動作會使用過去簡單式來表達。

所以我沒有穿夾克，只穿了一件襯衫與短褲。

⟹ **Therefore**, I didn't wear a jacket but just a shirt and a pair of shorts.

解析 ▶ "so" 通常不會直接出現在句子的開頭，這裡的「所以」翻譯成較適合放在句首的 "therefore" 或 "thus" 會更恰當。

但是到了傍晚，氣溫卻急速下降。

⟹ **However**, in the evening, the temperature dropped sharply.

解析 ▶ "but" 通常不會直接出現在句子的開頭，因此這裡把「但是」翻譯成較適合放在句首的 "however" 或 "nevertheless"。

雖然晚上我很早就回家，但我還是覺得有點不舒服。

⟹ **Although** I went home early at night, I still felt a little bit uncomfortable.

解析 ▶ 以 although 引導表讓步的副詞子句，要注意 "although" 不可以和 "but" 出現在同一個句子裡。時態依然要和前文一致，使用過去簡單式。

今天我不但打噴嚏還頭昏，我想我最好馬上去診所看醫生。

➠ Today I **not only** sneezed **but also** felt dizzy, so I think I'd better go to the clinic and see a doctor right away.

6

解析 本句使用了 "not only A but also B" 的句型，在這裡用來連接兩個過去簡單式動詞。逗點前後的兩個句子表達的是因果關係，所以不可將兩個句子並置，因此雖然中文原文沒有「所以」兩個字，還是要加上連接詞 "so"，使句子合乎英文文法。

 必備字彙 與片語整理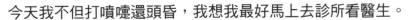

➠ clinic	[`klɪnɪk]	n.	診所
➠ dizzy	[`dɪzɪ]	adj.	頭暈的
➠ leave	[liv]	v.	離開
➠ quite	[kwaɪt]	adv.	十分，相當
➠ sneeze	[sniz]	v.	打噴嚏
➠ temperature	[`tɛmprətʃɚ]	n.	溫度
➠ uncomfortable	[ʌn`kʌmfɚtəbl̩]	adj	不舒服的
➠ wear	[wɛr]	v.	穿
➠ a little bit		phr.	一點點
➠ a pair of shorts		phr.	一條短褲
➠ catch a cold		phr.	得到感冒
➠ drop down sharply		phr.	快速下降
➠ had better		phr.	最好
➠ right away		phr.	立刻

題目敘述

1 許多人認為背英文單字是件困難的事。2 我每天會試著記一些新的單字。3 當我在讀英文雜誌的時候，我會把我不認識的字記在我的筆記本上。4 然後我會試著將這些新字用在日常會話之中。5 雖然有時仍會用錯，但我覺得進步很多。

參考範文

1Many people think that it's difficult to memorize English words. 2Every day I try to learn some new English words. 3When I read an English magazine, I write down the words I am not familiar with on my notebook. 4Then I try to use these new words in my everyday conversation. 5Although sometimes I still use them in the wrong way, I think that I have improved a lot.

範文句型解析

1

許多人認為背英文單字是件困難的事。

➡ Many people think that **it's** difficult **to** memorize English words.

解析 ▶ 本句用 "it is＋adj＋to＋Vr" 的句型。本句亦可寫成 "Many people think it difficult to memorize English words."

2

我每天會試著記一些新的單字。

➡ Every day I **try to** learn some new English words.

解析 ▶ 每天的動作會用現在簡單式來表達。"try to＋Vr" 表示「試著做某事」。

3

當我在讀英文雜誌的時候,我會把我不認識的字記在我的筆記本上。

➠ **When** I read an English magazine, I write down the words I am not familiar with on my notebook.

解析 ▶ 本句以 when 引導時間副詞子句,說明寫下筆記的時間。

4

然後我會試著將這些新字用在日常會話之中。

➠ Then I **try to** use these new words in my everyday conversation.

解析 ▶ "try to＋Vr" 表示「試著做某事」。

5

雖然有時仍會用錯,但我覺得進步很多。

➠ **Although** sometimes I still use them in the wrong way, I think that I have improved a lot.

解析 ▶ 本句以 although(=though)引導表讓步的副詞子句。

 必備字彙 與片語整理

➠ although	[ɔl`ðo]	conj.	雖然,儘管
➠ conversation	[ˌkɑnvɚ`seʃən]	n.	會話
➠ difficult	[`dɪfəˌkəlt]	adj.	困難的
➠ improve	[ɪm`pruv]	v.	改善
➠ magazine	[ˌmægə`zin]	n.	雜誌
➠ memorize	[`mɛməˌraɪz]	v.	記憶
➠ notebook	[`notˌbuk]	n.	筆記本
➠ be familiar with		phr.	熟悉
➠ improve a lot		phr.	進步很多
➠ write down		phr.	寫下

題目敘述

¹我認識一位每天穿著綠色制服的郵差。²每天早上他會把信件送到我們社區來。³如果有掛號信要送給我們,他就會在門口按一下門鈴,然後要我們拿印章來蓋章。⁴他認識附近的每一個人,而我們每一個人也都認識他。⁵他真是一位認真的郵差。

參考範文

¹I know a mail carrier wearing a green uniform every day. ²Every morning he delivers letters to our community. ³If there are any registered letters for us, he will ring the doorbell, and ask for our stamps to sign for the letter. ⁴He knows everyone in our neighborhood, and everyone also knows him. ⁵He is really a hardworking mail carrier.

範文句型解析

我認識一位每天穿著綠色制服的郵差。

➡ I know a mail carrier **wearing** a green uniform every day.

1

解析 ▶ 本句也可使用以關係代名詞 who 引導的形容詞子句修飾先行詞 "mail carrier",也就是寫成 "I know a mail carrier who is wearing a green uniform every day.",但也可以簡化成如同範文中的這種分詞構句。

每天早上他會把信件送到我們社區來。

➡ Every morning he **delivers** letters to our community.

2

解析 ▶ 每天會進行的動作應該使用現在簡單式來表達。

3

如果有掛號信要送給我們，他就會在門口按一下門鈴，然後要我們拿印章來蓋章。

➠ If there **are** any registered letters for us, he will ring the doorbell, and ask for our stamps to sign for the letter.

解析 ▶ 本句以連接詞 If 引導條件從屬子句，時態必須配合前文，使用現在簡單式。

4

他認識附近的每一個人，而我們每一個人也都認識他。

➠ He knows everyone in our neighborhood, and everyone also knows him.

解析 ▶ 使用對等連接詞 "and" 來連接前後兩個句子，"and" 前面要加逗點。

5

他真是一位認真的郵差。

➠ He is **really** a hardworking mail carrier.

解析 ▶ 本句型為五大句型中典型的 "S＋V＋SC"，"a hardworking mail carrier" 是主詞補語，用來說明主詞 "he"。"really" 是副詞，用來強調句子的語氣。

 必備字彙 與片語整理

➠ community	[kə`mjunətı]	n.	社區
➠ doorbell	[`dor‚bɛl]	n.	門鈴
➠ hardworking	[‚hɑrd`wɝkıŋ]	adj.	努力的
➠ neighborhood	[`nebɚ‚hud]	n.	鄰近地區，鄰里
➠ ring	[rıŋ]	v.	按鈴
➠ stamp	[stæmp]	n.	印章
➠ uniform	[`junə‚fɔrm]	n.	制服
➠ deliver letter		phr.	送信
➠ in our neighborhood		phr.	在我們附近
➠ registered letter		phr.	掛號信
➠ sign for		phr.	簽收

題目敘述

1 英文是一種重要的語言，所以很多人都正在學習。2 許多學生認為學會用英文聽和說都很困難。3 但是只要不斷練習，任何困難皆可克服。4 也許犯錯會讓你覺得不好意思。5 但是每個人都會犯錯。6 最重要的是，要能開口大聲說英文。

參考範文

1English is an important language, so many people are learning it. 2Many students think that it is hard to learn listening and speaking English. 3However, as long as you practice it constantly, you will be able to overcome any difficulty. 4Maybe making mistakes makes you feel embarrassed . 5Nonetheless, everyone makes mistakes. 6Above all, you should be able to speak out loud in English.

範文句型解析

英文是一種重要的語言，所以很多人都正在學習。

➡ English is an important language, so many people are learning it.

解析 ▶ 本句以 "so" 引導表結果的副詞子句。"are learning" 是現在進行式，表示「正在學習」的意思。

許多學生認為學會用英文聽和說都很困難。

➠ Many students think that it is hard to learn listening and speaking English.

解析 ▶ 本句以 that 引導名詞子句做為動詞 "think" 的受詞。子句的結構為 "it＋beV＋adj.＋to＋Vr"。

但是只要不斷練習，任何困難皆可克服。

➠ However, as long as you practice it constantly, you will be able to overcome any difficulty.

解析 ▶ 連接詞 "as long as" 引導條件從屬子句，用以說明主要子句內容的發生條件。

也許犯錯會讓你覺得不好意思。

➠ Maybe making mistakes makes you feel embarrassed.

解析 ▶ 以動名詞片語當作主詞，本句基本結構為 "S＋make＋O＋Vr ..."，在這個句子中，原形動詞使用的是感官動詞 "feel"，在動詞後面必須再加上形容詞做為受詞補語。

但是每個人都會犯錯。

➠ Nonetheless, everyone makes mistakes.

解析 ▶ "nonetheless" 通常會放在句首，相當於 "nevertheless"、"however"，表示「然而，但是」的意思。

最重要的是，要能開口大聲說英文。

➠ Above all, you should be able to speak out loud in English.

解析 ▶ "Above all, ＋主要子句 ." 的句型表示「最重要的是，……」的意思，也可以使用 "What is more important is that ＋主要子句 ." 的句型來表達，表示「更重要的是，……」。

163

 必備字彙 與片語整理

⟹ constantly	[ˋkɑnstəntlɪ]	adv.	不斷地
⟹ difficulty	[ˋdɪfəˏkʌltɪ]	n.	困難
⟹ embarrassed	[ɪmˋbærəst]	adj.	難為情的，尷尬的
⟹ important	[ɪmˋpɔrtn̩t]	adj.	重要的
⟹ nonetheless	[ˏnʌnðəˋlɛs]	adv.	但是，然而
⟹ overcome	[ˏovəˋkʌm]	v.	克服
⟹ loud	[laʊd]	adj./adv.	大聲的；大聲地
⟹ above all		phr.	最重要的是
⟹ as long as		phr.	只要
⟹ be able to		phr.	能夠
⟹ make mistakes		phr.	犯錯
⟹ speak out		phr.	說出

題目敘述

　　1 不用說，每天運動是非常重要的。2 當我還是小孩子時，我的身體很虛弱，並且經常感冒。3 自從上了高中之後，我就盡量找機會打籃球。4 雖然功課一直很多，我還是每天花一小時來運動。5 三年來持續不斷的運動，使我不但變強壯也更健康了。6 現在大家都說我和以前完全不一樣了。

參考範文

　　1 It goes without saying that doing exercises everyday is extremely important. 2 When I was still a kid, my body was very weak, and I caught colds frequently. 3 After I attended senior high school, I continuously looked for opportunities to play basketball. 4 Although my studies took me a great deal of time, I still spent one hour exercising every day. 5 Three years of nonstop physical activities have made me not only stronger but also healthier. 6 Now, people say that I am a totally different person from what I was before.

範文句型解析

不用說，每天運動是非常重要的。

➡ **It goes without saying that** doing exercises everyday is extremely important.

> **解析** ▶ "It goes without saying that＋主要子句." 是時常用到的重要句型，表示「不用說，理所當然」。主要子句的結構是 "S＋beV＋SC."，因為主詞是動名詞片語，所以要使用單數的 "is"。

當我還是小孩子時，我的身體很虛弱，並且經常感冒。

➡ **When** I was still a kid, my body was very weak, **and** I caught colds frequently.

> **解析** ▶ 過去發生的事，使用過去簡單式描述，這裡以 "when" 引導表時間的副詞子句，說明主要子句發生的時間點是在小時候。主要子句的部分以連接詞 "and" 連接兩個過去簡單式的句子。

自從上了高中之後，我就盡量找機會打籃球。

➡ **After** I attended senior high school, I continuously looked for **opportunities to play** basketball.

> **解析** ▶ 過去發生的事，會使用過去簡單式來表達，這裡以 "after" 引導時間副詞子句，修飾主要子句。"opportunity＋of＋Ving" 或 "opportunity＋(for sb)＋to＋Vr" 是固定的表達句型，表示「做某事的機會」。

雖然功課一直很多，我還是每天花一小時來運動。

➡ **Although** my studies took me a great deal of time, I still **spent** one hour exercising every day.

> **解析** ▶ 連接詞 "although" 引導表示讓步的副詞子句，修飾後面的主要子句。因為整篇文章都是在說過去發生的事，所以雖然句尾出現了頻率副詞 "every day"，但所說的是「過去的每一天」，時態應是過去簡單式。"My studies took me a great deal of time." 也可以使用 "It took me a geat deal of time to study." 或 "I spent a great deal of time (in) studying." 或 "I spent a great deal of time on study." 等句子來表達。

5

三年來持續不斷的運動，使我不但變強壯也更健康了。

➦ **Three years of nonstop physical activities** have made me **not only** stronger **but also** healthier.

解析 本句主詞為 "three years of nonstop physical activities"，所以這裡的助動詞使用複數形態的 "have"。接著出現的是 "make＋sb＋adj." 句型，並用 "not only A but also B" 的句型來連接兩個比較級的形容詞。

6

現在大家都說我和以前完全不一樣了。

➦ **Now**, people say that I **am** a totally **different** person **from** what I was before.

解析 本句以時間副詞 "now" 開頭，強調時間，將過去和現在相比較，"A＋beV＋different＋from＋B" 是「A 和 B 不同」的意思，"A＋beV＋the same＋as＋B" 則是「A 和 B 相同」。這裡必須特別注意介系詞的使用時機。

 必備字彙 與片語整理

➦ continuously	[kən`tɪnjʊəslɪ]	adv.	持續不斷地
➦ extremely	[ɪk`strimlɪ]	adv.	非常地
➦ frequently	[`frikwəntlɪ]	adv.	經常地
➦ healthy	[`hɛlθɪ]	adj.	健康的
➦ kid	[kɪd]	n.	小孩
➦ strong	[strɔŋ]	adj.	強壯的
➦ totally	[`totl̩ɪ]	adv.	完全地
➦ weak	[wik]	adj.	虛弱的
➦ be different from		phr.	和……不同
➦ look for		phr.	尋找
➦ play basketball		phr.	打籃球
➦ senior high school		phr.	高中

題目敘述

　　1 你比較喜歡住在哪裡？是城市還是鄉下？**2** 我生長在鄉下的一個小村落。**3** 那時我家的附近有一條清澈的小溪。**4** 我們常在夏天到那裡游泳與釣魚。**5** 那時候我們非常快樂。**6** 現在的我住在大城市裡，雖然生活方便許多，但是那種悠閒的生活已經不再。

參考範文

　　1Which place do you prefer to live, in the city or in the countryside? **2**I grew up in a small village in the countryside. **3**At that time, there was a clear stream near our house. **4**We used to swim and fish there during the summer. **5**We were very happy then. **6**Now I live in a big city. Though the life here is more convenient, that kind of relaxation no longer exists.

範文句型解析

1

你比較喜歡住在哪裡？是城市或鄉下？

➡ Which place do you prefer to live, in the city **or** in the countryside?

解析 ▶ 用 "which place" 這種選擇疑問句開頭，後面則用連接詞 "or" 提出兩個選項供選擇。

我生長在鄉下的一個小村落。

➠ **I grew up** in a small village in the countryside.

解析 ▶ 過去發生的事用過去簡單式來表達。

 那時我家的附近有一條清澈的小溪。

➠ At that time, **there was** a clear stream near our house.

解析 ▶ 本句以時間副詞 "at that time" 開頭，強調所敘述的事情是發生在過去。"there was" 的意思是「以前有」，類似於 "there used to be"。

 我們常在夏天到那裡游泳與釣魚。

➠ **We used to** swim and fish there during the summer.

解析 ▶ "used to + Vr" 表示「過去經常做某事」。這裡使用 "and" 連接兩個原形動詞 swim 和 fish。

 那時候我們非常快樂。

➠ We were very happy **then**.

解析 ▶ "then = at that time"，在寫作時會盡量避免重複使用前文使用過的詞語，因此此處改用 "then"。

 現在的我住在大城市裡，雖然生活方便許多，但是那種悠閒的生活已經不再。

➠ **Now** I live in a big city. Though the life here is more convenient, that kind of relaxation **no longer** exists.

解析 ▶ 以時間副詞 "now" 開頭，強調現在的情形，和前文提及於過去發生的事相比較。"convenient" 是多音節的形容詞，因此比較級的形態是 "more convenient"。"no longer" 表示「不再」的意思。

 **必備字彙** 與片語整理

➡ city	[`sɪtɪ]	n.	城市，都會
➡ convenient	[kən`vinjənt]	adj.	便利的
➡ countryside	[`kʌntrɪ͵saɪd]	n.	鄉間，郊區
➡ exist	[ɪg`zɪst]	v.	存在；生存
➡ prefer	[prɪ`fɝ]	v.	偏愛，更喜歡
➡ relaxation	[rilæks`eʃən]	n.	悠閒放鬆
➡ stream	[strim]	n.	小溪
➡ then	[ðɛn]	adv.	那時候
➡ village	[`vɪlɪdʒ]	n.	村莊
➡ grow up		phr.	長大
➡ at that time		phr.	那時候
➡ no longer		phr.	不再

小學同學篇

題目敘述

　　1 那是一個沒有預料到、且令人吃驚的事件。**2** 上星期一，我在公園慢跑時，一位小姐上前來叫我的名字。**3** 原來她是我的小學同學。**4** 真是令人驚訝！我們已經五年沒有見面了。**5** 現在她比以前胖上許多，難怪我那時沒一下子認出她來。**6** 她現在已經是兩個孩子的媽了。

參考範文

　　1That was an unexpected and amazing incident. **2**Last Monday, while I was going jogging in the park, a lady came over and called my name. **3**It turned out that she was my elementary school classmate. **4**What a surprise! We had not seen each other for five years. **5**Now she is much heavier than before. It was no wonder I didn't recognize her immediately. **6**She is now a mother who has already had two children.

範文句型解析

那是一個沒有預料到、且令人吃驚的事件。

➠ That was an unexpected and amazing incident.

解析 表示在過去發生的一個事件，因此使用過去式來表達。

171

上星期一，我在公園慢跑時，一位小姐上前來叫我的名字。
➠ Last Monday, while I **was going** jogging in the park, a lady **came** over and **called** my name.

解析 ▶ 這裡的 "while" 引導表時間的副詞子句，基本句型為 "While ＋進行式子句，＋簡單式子句."。因為這整篇描述的事件都是過去事實，所以句型變化為 "While ＋過去進行式子句，＋過去簡單式子句."。

原來她是我的小學同學。
➠ It turned out that she was my elementary school classmate.

解析 ▶ turn out 的意思是「結果～」，通常會以 "It turns out that ＋子句" 的句型來使用。

真是令人驚訝！我們已經五年沒有見面了。
➠ What a surprise! I We **had not seen** each other **for** five years.

解析 ▶ "What a surprise!" = "What a surprise it is!" = "How surprising it is!" = "It is so surprising!"。因為通篇翻譯都是過去簡單式，所以當要使用完成式時，必須使用過去完成式句型 "S＋had＋Vpp ...＋for＋一段時間."。

現在她比以前胖上許多，難怪我那時沒一下子認出她來。
➠ Now she is **much** heavier than before. **It was no wonder** I didn't recognize her immediately.

解析 ▶ 這裡利用 "much" 來強調比較級以加強語氣。"It is no wonder (＋that)＋子句." 的句型，表示「難怪」的意思，可以簡化成 "No wonder＋子句."。

她現在已經是兩個孩子的媽了。

➡ She is now a mother who has already had two children.

6

解析 ▶ 表達的是會對現在造成影響的過去經驗，因此會使用現在完成式。
這裡利用由關係代名詞 "who" 引導的形容詞子句修飾名詞
"mother"。

 必備字彙 與片語整理

➡ already	[ɔl`rɛdɪ]	adv.	已經
➡ amazing	[ə`mezɪŋ]	adj.	令人吃驚的
➡ children	[`tʃɪldrən]	n.	小孩（複數）
➡ incident	[`ɪnsədənt]	n.	事件；插曲
➡ immediately	[ɪ`midɪətlɪ]	adv.	立刻，馬上
➡ recognize	[`rɛkəg͵naɪz]	v.	認出
➡ unexpected	[͵ʌnɪk`spɛktɪd]	adj.	出乎意料的
➡ while	[hwaɪl]	conj.	正當……的時候
➡ each other		phr.	彼此
➡ elementary school classmate		phr.	國小同學
➡ go jogging		phr.	慢跑
➡ turn out		phr.	結果……

173

題目敘述

　　1 學英文需要花我很多時間與耐性，但這是絕對值得的。**2** 如今我們學英文，不僅是為了要具備競爭力，也是為了要更加了解這個世界。**3** 我每天至少花二個小時閱讀英文。**4** 藉著閱讀英文，我可以學到更多新的單字與句型，因此我覺得我的英文能力每天都更進步了一點。**5** 你呢？你也正在學這全球性的語言嗎？

參考範文

　　1Studying English takes me lots of time and patience, but it is definitely rewarding. **2**Nowadays, we need to learn English not just to be competitive, but to learn more about the world. **3**I spend at least two hours on English reading every day. **4**By reading English, I can learn more new words and sentence patterns; therefore, I think my English ability improves a little bit every day. **5**How about you? Are you learning this universal language now?

學英文需要花我很多時間與耐性，但這是絕對值得的。

➡ Studying English **takes me** lots of time and patience, but it is definitely rewarding.

解析 ▶ 本句以動名詞 "Studying English" 做為主詞。這裡的 "take" 是「花費」的意思，這邊使用的句型是 "S takes sb sth ..."，如果所花費的是金錢，則動詞通常會使用 "cost "。句中的 "definitely" 也可以使用 "certainly" 或 "absolutely" 代替。

如今我們學英文，不僅是為了要具備競爭力，也是為了要更加了解這個世界。

➡ Nowadays, we need to learn English not just **to be** competitive, but **to learn** more about the world.

解析 ▶ 本句是 "not only ... but also ..." 的變化句型，將 "only" 以字義相似的 "just" 代換，並把 "also" 省略，連接兩個表目的的不定詞。

我每天至少花二個小時閱讀英文。

➡ I spend at least two hours on English reading every day.

解析 ▶ spend 之後要接 "on"，再接上名詞或動名詞，表示「把……花費在……上」。

藉著閱讀英文，我可以學到更多新的單字與句型，因此我覺得我的英文能力每天都更進步了一點。

➡ By reading English, I can learn more new words and sentence patterns; **therefore**, I think my English ability improves a little bit every day.

解析 ▶ "By + Ving ..." 表示「藉著……」，用來表達方法。"I can learn more new words and sentence patterns; therefore, I think my English ability improves a little bit every day" 也可以寫成 "I can learn more new words and sentence patterns, so I think my English ability improves a little bit every day"，要注意句子裡的 "so" 是連接詞，但是 "therefore" 只是副詞，不能用來連接兩個句子，所以必須用分號來連接兩個句子。

175

5

你呢？你也正在學這全球性的語言嗎？

➥ **How about you?** Are you learning this universal language now?

解析 "How about you?" 可以用在多種情境之下，用來詢問對方的狀況、意見等資訊。

 必備字彙 與片語整理

➥ by	[baɪ]	prep.	藉著
➥ competitive	[kəm`pɛtətɪv]	adj.	有競爭力的
➥ definitely	[`dɛfənɪtlɪ]	adv.	絕對地
➥ improve	[ɪm`pruv]	v.	改善；進步
➥ language	[`læŋɡwɪdʒ]	n.	語言
➥ nowadays	[`naʊə‚dez]	adv.	現今
➥ patience	[`peʃəns]	n.	耐心
➥ rewarding	[rɪ`wɔrdɪŋ]	adj.	有報酬的；有益的
➥ study	[`stʌdɪ]	v.	研讀
➥ therefore	[`ðɛr‚for]	adv.	因此
➥ universal	[‚junə`vɝsl̩]	adj.	世界性的
➥ world	[wɝld]	n.	世界
➥ at least		phr.	至少
➥ every day		phr.	每天
➥ sentence pattern		phr.	句型

色彩測驗篇

解析篇

P
A
R
T
3

unit 1
中譯英

題目敘述

1 你有試過色彩測驗嗎？ **2** 色彩測驗可以告訴你你的性格如何。 **3** 舉例來說，如果你喜歡藍色，你可能傾向於沉靜而執著。 **4** 如果紅色是你最愛的顏色，那麼你可能喜歡冒險。 **5** 如果你喜歡綠色，表示你渴望和平。如果你喜歡棕色，表示你是成熟且仔細的。 **6** 不管你相不相信，它都是一個參考。

參考範文

1Have you ever tried a color test? **2**A color test can tell you about your personality. **3**For example, if you like blue, you probably tend to be calm and loyal. **4**If red is your favorite color, then you might like to take risks. **5**If you like green, that means you long for peace. If you like brown, you are mature and careful. **6**Whether you believe it or not, it is a reference.

範文句型解析

你有試過色彩測驗嗎？
➡ Have you ever tried a color test?

解析 "color test" 是「色彩測驗」的意思。本句以現在完成式來詢問「人生當中曾經遭遇過的經驗」。

177

2

色彩測驗可以告訴你你的性格如何。

➡ A color test can **tell you about** your personality.

解析 ▶ " tell sb about sth" 意為「告訴某人關於某事的資訊」，這裡的介系詞會固定使用 "about"。類似的句型還有 "inform sb of sth"，對別人提出警告時則可以用 "warn sb of/against sth"，這類句型在寫作測驗中經常會派上用場，請務必記住。

3

舉例來說，如果你喜歡藍色，你可能傾向於沉靜而執著。

➡ **For example**, if you like blue, you probably **tend to** be calm and loyal.

解析 ▶ "for example" 是用來「舉例」的轉折語。本句以 if 引導條件從屬子句。 "tend to" 表示「傾向於～」的意思。

4

如果紅色是你最愛的顏色，那麼你可能喜歡冒險。

➡ **If** red is your favorite color, then you **might** like to take risks.

解析 ▶ 以 if 引導條件從屬子句，修飾主要子句 "you might like to take risks."。"might" 和 "may" 的差別在於事情發生的可能性大小，"might" 之後出現的事項的發生可能性較小。

5

如果你喜歡綠色，表示你渴望和平。如果你喜歡棕色，表示你是成熟且仔細的。

➡ **If** you like green, that means you long for peace. **If** you like brown, you are mature and careful.

解析 ▶ 前一句以 if 引導條件從屬子句 "If you like green,"，修飾主要子句 "that means you long for peace."。後一句則以 if 引導條件從屬子句 "If you like brown,"，修飾主要子句 "you are mature and careful."。

不管你相不相信，它都是一個參考。

6 ⟹ Whether you believe it or not, it is a reference.

解析 ▶ "whether you believe it or not" 表示「不管你是否相信它」的意思，可以簡化成 "believe it or not"（信不信由你）。

 必備字彙 與片語整理

⟹ calm	[kɑm]	adj.	冷靜的
⟹ favorite	[`fevərɪt]	adj.	最愛的
⟹ mature	[mə`tjʊr]	adj.	成熟的
⟹ personality	[ˌpɝsn̩`ælətɪ]	n.	人格
⟹ reference	[`rɛfərəns]	n.	參考
⟹ try	[traɪ]	v.	嘗試
⟹ color test		phr.	色彩測驗
⟹ long for		phr.	渴望
⟹ take risks		phr.	冒險
⟹ tend to		phr.	傾向於
⟹ whether ... or not		phr.	不論是否……

題目敘述

1 除了游泳外，我最喜歡的運動是籃球。2 每當我有空的時候，我會邀請一些朋友組成兩隊彼此比賽。3 由於我們的球打得比另一隊更好，所以我們常常贏球。4 因為經常打球，我不但變得健康許多，而且也交到了更多朋友。5 最重要的是，我也長得越來越高了。

參考範文

1Besides swimimg, my favorite sport is playing basketball. 2Whenever I have free time, I invite some friends to make two teams to compete with each other. 3Our team often wins because we play better than the other team. 4Due to the fact that I play basketball frequently, I get much healthier and make more friends. 5Most important of all, I am getting taller and taller.

範文句型解析

1

除了游泳外，我最喜歡的運動是籃球。
➡ Besides swimimg, my favorite sport is playing basketball.

解析 ▶ "besides＋N" 是「除了……之外」的意思，也可以用 "in addition to＋N" 代替。

2

每當我有空的時候，我會邀請一些朋友組成兩隊彼此比賽。

➠ Whenever I have free time, I invite some friends to make two teams to compete with each other.

解析 ▶ "Whenever ...,＋主要子句 ."，由連接詞 "whenever" 引導表示時間的副詞子句來修飾主要子句。

3

由於我們的球打得比另一隊更好，所以我們常常贏球。

➠ Our team often wins **because** we **play better than** the other team.

解析 ▶ 從屬連接詞 "because" 引導表示原因的副詞子句，修飾後面的主要子句。這裡的主要子句，使用的是比較級的句型 "S＋V＋副詞比較級＋than ..."。

4

因為經常打球，我不但變得健康許多，而且也交到了更多朋友。

➠ **Due to the fact that** I play basketball frequently, I get much healthier and make more friends.

解析 ▶ 表原因的副詞子句中使用了 "due to the fact that＋子句," 的句型，這個表達方式相當於 "because＋子句"，"due to" 的意義相似於 "because of, thanks to, owing to, on account of" 等介系詞片語，因為是介系詞片語，所以不能和連接詞一樣直接接子句，要先接上名詞，再用關係代名詞引導子句修飾前面的名詞 "fact"。

5

最重要的是，我也長得越來越高了。

➠ Most important of all, I am getting **taller and taller**.

解析 ▶ 「最重要的是……」的句型是 "Most important of all, ..."，也可以用 "What is the most important is that＋主要子句." 來表示。本句為比較級重複的句型，以 "比較級＋比較級" 的句型表示「越來越……」的意思。

181

 必備字彙 與片語整理

➡ besides	[bɪˋsaɪdz]	adv.	此外；
		prep.	除了……之外
➡ favorite	[ˋfevərɪt]	adj.	最愛的
➡ frequently	[ˋfrɪkwəntlɪ]	adv.	經常地
➡ invite	[ɪnˋvaɪt]	v.	邀請
➡ sport	[sport]	n.	運動
➡ tall	[tɔl]	adj.	高的
➡ team	[tim]	n.	隊伍
➡ whenever	[hwɛnˋɛvɚ]	conj.	每當；無論何時
➡ win	[wɪn]	v.	贏
➡ compete with		phr.	與……競爭
➡ due to the fact that		phr.	由於，因為
➡ make friends		phr.	交朋友
➡ most important of all		phr.	最重要的是……
➡ play basketball		phr.	打籃球

交通運輸篇

題目敘述

1 發展高效率的運輸工具是非常必要的。**2** 沒有高效率的運輸工具，我們根本不可能在短時間內從台灣到美國，或是從歐洲到亞洲。**3** 另外，也不可能可以環遊世界或是互相傳遞訊息。**4** 一般來說，運輸工具指的是汽車、火車、飛機。**5** 不過，電報、電話、網際網路系統也都算是運輸工具的一種。

參考範文

1 It is very necessary to develop efficient transportation. **2** Without efficient transportation, it is impossible for us to travel in a very short time from Taiwan to the US, or from Europe to Asia. **3** In addition, we are not able to travel around the world, or deliver information to each other. **4** Generally speaking, the word transportation means car, train, or airplane. **5** However, telegraph, telephone, and the Internet system can also be regarded as a part of transportation.

範文句型解析

發展高效率的運輸工具是非常必要的。

➡ It is very necessary **to develop efficient transportation**.

解析 ▶ "It ... to Vr ..." 是英文寫作時常用的重要句型。原來的句子是 "To develop efficient transportation is very necessary."，主詞太長會讓句子顯得失去焦點，所以使用虛主詞 "it" 代替不定詞片語，使句子的結構不會頭重腳輕。

沒有高效率的運輸工具，我們根本不可能在短時間內從台灣到美國，或是從歐洲到亞洲。

➡ Without efficient transportation, it is impossible for us **to travel** in a very short time from Taiwan to the US, or from Europe to Asia.

2

解析 ▶ "Without ..." 開頭的句型意為「沒有……」；相對的，"With ..." 的句型意為「有……；伴隨」。這一句的主詞是 "to travel in a very short time from Taiwan to the US, or from Europe to Asia"，句子裡的主詞太長會顯得失去焦點，於是這裡又用了一次 "It ... to Vr ..." 的句型。

另外，也不可能可以環遊世界或是互相傳遞訊息。

➡ In addition, we are not able **to travel** around the world, **or deliver** information to each other.

3

解析 ▶ "In addition, ..." 相當於 "Additionally, ..."，意為「另外……，除此之外」，在文章中常被用來做補充說明。後面的句子看起來很長，不過在結構上其實只是利用對等連接詞 "or" 連接不定詞片語中的兩個原形動詞 "travel ..." 和 "deliver ..."。

一般來說，運輸工具指的是汽車、火車、飛機。

➡ Generally speaking, the word transportation means car, train, or airplane.

4

解析 ▶ "Generally speaking, ..." 相當於 "Generally, ..."，意為「一般來說，……」，在文章中用來說明廣泛被人接受或為人所知的言論或思想。

5 不過，電報、電話、網際網路系統也都算是運輸工具的一種。

➡ 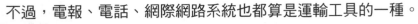 However, telegraph, telephone, and the Internet system can also be regarded as a part of transportation.

解析 ▶ "However, ..."除了「然而……」的意思之外，也有「但，不過……」的意思。

 必備字彙 與片語整理

➡ airplane	[`ɛr͵plen]	n.	飛機
➡ allow	[ə`laʊ]	v.	允許
➡ deliver	[dɪ`lɪvɚ]	v.	傳遞
➡ develop	[dɪ`vɛləp]	v.	發展
➡ efficient	[ɪ`fɪʃnt]	adj.	有效率的
➡ impossible	[ɪm`pɑsəbḷ]	adj.	不可能的
➡ necessary	[`nɛsə͵sɛrɪ]	adj.	必須的
➡ short	[ʃɔrt]	adj.	短的
➡ telegraph	[`tɛlə͵græf]	n.	電報
➡ telephone	[`tɛlə͵fon]	n.	電話
➡ train	[tren]	n.	火車
➡ transportation	[͵trænspɚ`teʃən]	n.	運輸工具
➡ travel	[`trævḷ]	v.	旅行
➡ without	[wɪ`ðaʊt]	prep.	沒有
➡ world	[wɝld]	n.	世界
➡ be regarded as		phr.	被視為
➡ in addition		phr.	另外
➡ generally speaking		phr.	一般而言
➡ Internet system		phr.	網路系統

 時間觀念篇

題目敘述

　¹美國人和台灣人在約定時間上非常不一樣。²當美國人準備拜訪他們的親朋好友的時候，會事先打電話預約。³時間一旦確定，除非情況緊急，否則不會輕易改變。⁴相反地，我的台灣朋友卻常在沒有先通知我的情況下，半夜來敲我的門。⁵除此之外，他們常常只因為心情不好就取消約會。⁶所以，我覺得他們應該學習如何尊重別人的時間。

參考範文

　¹There are many differences between Americans and Taiwanese in making an appointment with others. ²When Americans decide to visit their friends or relatives, they make a call in advance to make an appointment. ³Once the time is fixed, it takes almost an emergency to change it. ⁴On the contrary, my Taiwanese friends often knock on my door at midnight without notifying me first. ⁵Additionally, they often cancel dates just because they are in a bad mood. ⁶Therefore, I think they should learn how to respect the time of others.

範文句型解析

1

美國人和台灣人在約定時間上非常不一樣。

➠ There are many differences between Americans and Taiwanese **in** making an appointment with others.

解析 ▶ "There are many differences between A and B" 是寫作時常用到的重要句型，意為「A 和 B 有許多不同之處」，後面可以再接上 "in ..." 說明是在哪個方面的不同。

2

當美國人準備拜訪他們的親朋好友的時候，會事先打電話預約。

➠ When Americans decide to visit their friends or relatives, they make a call in advance to make an appointment.

解析 ▶ 這是 "When＋從屬子句,＋主要子句." 的句型。雖然中文並沒有寫出主要子句的主詞是「他們」，但在英文句子中，主要子句的主詞卻是不可省略的。不過，可以把句子寫成省略從屬子句主詞的句型 "Americans make a call in advance to make an appointment when deciding to visit their friends or relatives."。

3

時間一旦確定，除非情況緊急，否則不會輕易改變。

➠ Once the time is fixed, **it takes** almost an emergency **to** change it.

解析 ▶ "Once＋從屬子句,＋主要子句." 的句型，意為「一旦……，就……」。後面還用了 "it takes ... to ..." 的句型，這邊的 "take" 意為「花費；需要」，例如 "It took me one month to finish reading the book."（我花了一個月的時間讀完那本書。）。

相反地，我的台灣朋友卻常在沒有先通知我的情況下，半夜來敲我的門。

➠ On the contrary, my Taiwanese friends often knock on my door at midnight without notifying me first.

解析 ▶ "without + N/V-ing" 的句型，意為「沒有……」，可視使用情境置於句首或句尾。

 除此之外，他們常常只因為心情不好就取消約會。

➠ Additionally, they often cancel dates just because they are in a bad mood.

解析 ▶ "主要子句 , + just because +附屬子句 ." 的句型，意為「……，只因為……」。

 所以，我覺得他們應該學習如何尊重別人的時間。

➠ Therefore, I think they should **learn** how to respect the time of others.

解析 ▶ 這裡的 "how to respect the time of others" 是名詞子句，做為動詞 "learn" 的受詞。

 必備字彙 與片語整理

➠ additionally	[əˋdɪʃənˌlɪ]	adv.	除此之外
➠ almost	[ˋɔlˌmost]	adv.	幾乎
➠ between	[bɪˋtwin]	prep.	在兩者之間
➠ cancel	[ˋkænsl̩]	v.	取消
➠ change	[tʃændʒ]	v.	改變

⟱ decide	[dɪ`saɪd]	v.	決定
⟱ difference	[`dɪfərəns]	n.	不同，差異
⟱ emergency	[ɪ`mɝˌdʒənsɪ]	n.	緊急情況
⟱ fix	[fɪks]	v.	固定
⟱ knock	[nɑk]	v.	敲
⟱ learn	[lɝn]	v.	學習
⟱ once	[wʌns]	conj.	一旦
⟱ respect	[rɪ`spɛkt]	v.	尊重
⟱ take	[tek]	v.	花費；需要
⟱ without	[wɪ`ðaʊt]	prep.	沒有
⟱ in a bad mood		phr.	心情不好
⟱ in advance		phr.	事先
⟱ at midnight		phr.	半夜
⟱ just because		phr.	只因為
⟱ make a call		phr.	打電話
⟱ make an appointment		phr.	約定時間

蜜月旅行篇

題目敘述

1 我已經學了十幾年的英文。2 雖然我每天都讀英文書籍和看英文電視節目，但我對自己的英文沒信心。3 上個月我和太太參加旅行團到洛杉磯度蜜月，那次的旅行讓我對自己的英文產生信心。4 我太太在買一只昂貴的戒指時想殺價，可是她不會用英文說。5 因此我幫她殺價，結果她以半價買到了那只戒指。

參考範文

1I have been studying English for more than ten years. 2Although I read English books and watch English TV programs every day, I have no confidence in my ability of speaking English. 3Last month, my wife and I joined a package tour to Los Angeles for our honeymoon, and I am now more confident in speaking English after that journey. 4My wife wanted to bargain while she was trying to buy an expensive ring, but she didn't know how to express herself in English. 5Therefore, I bargained with the salesperson on her behalf, and she bought that ring at half price.

範文句型解析

1

我已經學了十幾年的英文。

➠ I have been studying English for more than ten years.

解析 ▶ 從過去一直持續到現在的動作，而且會持續進行下去，因此使用「現在完成進行式」來表達。

2

雖然我每天都讀英文書籍和看英文電視節目，但我對自己的英文沒信心。

➠ Although I read English books and watch English TV programs every day, I **have no confidence in** my ability of speaking English.

解析 ▶ 主要句型是 "Although＋附屬子句,＋主要子句."，其中，主要子句使用了 "have no confidence in N/V-ing"（對……沒信心）的句型。

3

上個月我和太太參加旅行團到洛杉磯度蜜月，那次的旅行讓我對自己的英文產生信心。

➠ Last month my wife and I joined a package tour to Los Angeles for our honeymoon, and I **am now** more **confident in** speaking English after that journey.

解析 ▶ 使用對等連接詞 "and" 連接兩個簡單式的句子，表達事件發生的先後順序，後面的句子使用了 "be confident in N/V-ing"（對……有信心）的句型。

4

我太太在買一只昂貴的戒指時想殺價，可是她不會用英文說。

➠ My wife wanted to bargain **while she was trying to buy an expensive ring**, but she didn't know **how to express herself in English**.

解析 ▶ 使用對等連接詞 "but" 連接兩個過去簡單式句子，其中，前面的句子含有從屬子句 "while she was trying to buy an expensive ring"。後面的句子則使用 "how to Vr ..." 的句型，做為動詞 "know" 的受詞。

191

因此我幫她殺價，結果她以半價買到了那只戒指。

➟ Therefore, I bargained with the salesperson on her behalf, **and** she bought that ring at half price.

解析 前後是兩個完整的句子，如果不要分開寫成兩個獨立的句子，就必須以連接詞相連接。這裡的 Therefore 也可以用 "consequently" 和 "in consequence" 替換，表示「結果～」。

 必備字彙 與片語整理

➟ ability	[əˋbɪlətɪ]	n.	能力
➟ bargain	[ˋbɑrgɪn]	v.	殺價
➟ consequently	[ˋkɑnsəˏkwɛntlɪ]	n.	結果，因此
➟ honeymoon	[ˋhʌnɪˏmun]	n.	蜜月
➟ journey	[ˋdʒɝnɪ]	n.	旅行
➟ ring	[rɪŋ]	n.	戒指
➟ speak	[spik]	v.	說（語言）
➟ study	[ˋstʌdɪ]	v.	學習
➟ a package tour		phr.	旅行團
➟ be confident in		phr.	對……有信心
➟ have confidence in		phr.	對……有信心
➟ at/for half price		phr.	以半價
➟ Los Angeles		phr.	洛杉磯
➟ more than		phr.	超過
➟ on behalf of		phr.	代表

題目敘述

1 學習音樂的好處，在於表演者可以盡情表現他們的情感和音樂技巧；聆聽者可以發現音樂的美與藝術性。2 不同音樂類型，代表不同文化和世代的演變。3 舉例來說，年輕人喜歡嘻哈和饒舌音樂，老一輩的人則偏愛藍調和爵士。4 不管何種音樂，都可找到熱愛它的人。

參考範文

1The benefit of learning music is that performers can freely express their emotions and show their music skills, and that listeners can find out the beauty and art of music. 2Different types of music represent the evolution of different cultures and generations. 3For example, young men like hip-hop and rap music; older generations prefer blues and jazz. 4No matter what type of music it is, it attracts people who love it.

範文句型解析

學習音樂的好處，在於表演者可以盡情表現他們的情感和音樂技巧；聆聽者可以發現音樂的美與藝術性。

➡ The benefit of learning music is that performers can freely express their emotions and show their music skills, and that listeners can find out the beauty and art of music.

解析 ▶ 這個句子使用的主要是 "S＋beV＋that" 所引導的名詞子句的句型，"that" 所引導的名詞子句，在這裡是主詞補語，補充說明主詞的相關資訊。"and" 則連接兩個以 "that" 引導的名詞子句。

2 不同音樂類型，代表不同文化和世代的演變。

➠ Different types of music **represent** the evolution of different cultures and generations.

解析 主詞是 "different types of music"，音樂是不可數名詞，但是音樂的種類是可數的，所以句中要用複數的 "types" 配合複數的動詞 "represent"。

3 舉例來說，年輕人喜歡嘻哈和饒舌音樂，老一輩的人則偏愛藍調和爵士。

➠ For example, young men like hip-hop and rap music; older generations prefer blues and jazz.

解析 "For example, ..." 和 "For instance, ..." 是在舉例說明時最常使用的表達方式。兩個完整的句子可以用分號區隔，或以 "and" 相連接，也可以用句號直接切分成兩個獨立的句子。

4 不管何種音樂，都可找到熱愛它的人。

➠ No matter what type of music it is, it attracts people **who love it**.

解析 "no matter what ..." 的意思是「無論，不管」，例如 "no matter what you say"（不論你說什麼）。類似的表達方式還有 "no matter who you are"（不論你是誰）、"no matter where you go"（不論你去哪裡）、"no matter how hard they tried"（不論他們多麼努力嘗試）等。這裡的 "who love it" 是形容詞子句，修飾先行詞的 "people"。

必備字彙 與片語整理

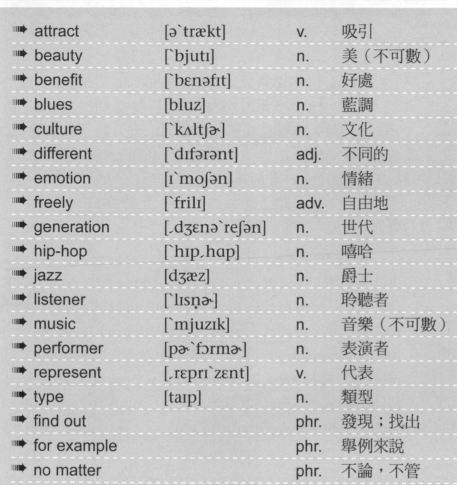

⇒ attract	[ə`trækt]	v.	吸引
⇒ beauty	[`bjutɪ]	n.	美（不可數）
⇒ benefit	[`bɛnəfɪt]	n.	好處
⇒ blues	[bluz]	n.	藍調
⇒ culture	[`kʌltʃɚ]	n.	文化
⇒ different	[`dɪfərənt]	adj.	不同的
⇒ emotion	[ɪ`moʃən]	n.	情緒
⇒ freely	[`frilɪ]	adv.	自由地
⇒ generation	[͵dʒɛnə`reʃən]	n.	世代
⇒ hip-hop	[`hɪp͵hɑp]	n.	嘻哈
⇒ jazz	[dʒæz]	n.	爵士
⇒ listener	[`lɪsn̩ɚ]	n.	聆聽者
⇒ music	[`mjuzɪk]	n.	音樂（不可數）
⇒ performer	[pɚ`fɔrmɚ]	n.	表演者
⇒ represent	[͵rɛprɪ`zɛnt]	v.	代表
⇒ type	[taɪp]	n.	類型
⇒ find out		phr.	發現；找出
⇒ for example		phr.	舉例來說
⇒ no matter		phr.	不論，不管
⇒ rap music		phr.	饒舌音樂

題目敘述

1 星期天下午我和朋友有約，我們決定下午三點在電影院門口碰面。2 我在買電影票的時候，發現皮夾被偷了。3 裡頭有我的身分證、幾張信用卡、提款卡和一些錢。4 我的朋友立刻幫我打電話報警。5 我想，大概是剛才坐公車時在和朋友聊天，扒手就趁機偷走了我的錢包。

參考範文

1I had a date with my friends on Sunday afternoon, and we decided to meet each other at three o'clock in front of a movie theater. 2When I was buying tickets, I realised my wallet stolen. 3In my wallet there were my identity card, several credit cards, bank cards, and some money. 4My friend helped me report to the police by his phone. 5I guess a pickpocket might have stolen my wallet while I was chatting with my friends on the bus.

範文句型解析

1

星期天下午我和朋友有約,我們決定下午三點在電影院門口碰面。

➠ I **had a date with** my friends on Sunday afternoon, and we decided to meet each other at three o'clock **in front of** a movie theater.

解析 ▶ 連接詞 "and" 連接兩個句子。前者使用 "have a date with＋sb"(與某人有約)的句型。後者使用 "in front of＋N"(在……前面)的句型。

2

我在買電影票的時候,發現皮夾被偷了。

➠ **When** I was buying tickets, I **realised my wallet stolen**.

解析 ▶ 主要句型為 "When＋從屬子句,＋主要子句."。後面的句子中使用了 "realise＋N＋Vpp" 的句型,意為「發現某人事物處在某狀態之中」,這裡的過去分詞表示被動語態,例如 "I realised her injured."(我發現她受傷了。)

3

裡頭有我的身分證、幾張信用卡、提款卡和一些錢。

➠ **In my wallet** there were **my identity card, several credit cards, bank cards, and some money**.

解析 ▶ 主要句型為 "There＋beV＋...＋in my wallet."。刪節號的部分使用了 "A, B, and C" 的句型,因為這部分的長度稍微長了一點,所以放在後面的 "in my wallet" 會使句子容易失焦,因此可以將其改放置在句首,讓句子的結構看起來更清楚。

4

我的朋友立刻幫我打電話報警。

➠ My friend **helped me report** to the police by his phone.

解析 ▶ "help＋sb＋Vr ..." 的句型,意為「幫助某人做某事」。

197

5

我想，大概是剛才坐公車時在和朋友聊天，扒手就趁機偷走了我的錢包。

➡ I **guess** a pickpocket **might have stolen** my wallet while I was chatting with my friends on the bus.

解析 ▶ 主要句型為 "主要子句＋while＋從屬子句."。主要子句使用了 "I guess (＋that)＋子句" 的句型，表示「我想……」的推論。另外 "may/might＋have＋Vpp" 的句型，是用來推測過去可能發生過的事情，但在語氣上並不是非常肯定。

 必備字彙 與片語整理

➡ bus	[bʌs]	n.	公車；巴士
➡ chat	[tʃæt]	v.	聊天
➡ decide	[dɪˋsaɪd]	v.	決定
➡ guess	[gɛs]	v.	猜想
➡ pickpocket	[ˋpɪk͵pɑkɪt]	n.	扒手
➡ steal	[stil]	v.	偷
➡ ticket	[ˋtɪkɪt]	n.	票
➡ wallet	[ˋwɑlɪt]	n.	皮夾
➡ bank card		phr.	提款卡
➡ credit card		phr.	信用卡
➡ have a date with		phr.	與……有約
➡ identity card		phr.	身分證
➡ Sunday afternoon		phr.	星期天下午

TEST 16　白淨肌膚篇

題目敘述

　　¹ 越來越多的亞洲女人偏好白淨的肌膚。² 她們傾向認為白皮膚才是美麗而吸引人的。³ 因此,她們會購買大量能夠美白肌膚的產品。⁴ 此外,讓肌膚變黑的正是紫外線。⁵ 因此,預防紫外線對皮膚的傷害就很重要了。

參考範文

　　¹More and more Asian women prefer fair skin. ²They tend to think that having fair skin means beauty and attractiveness. ³Therefore, they buy lots of products that can whiten their skin. ⁴Furthermore, it is ultraviolet rays that tan our skin. ⁵As a result, it is very important to prevent ultraviolet rays from damaging our skin.

範文句型解析

越來越多的亞洲女人偏好白淨的肌膚。

➡ More and more Asian women **prefer** fair skin.

1

解析 ▶ 這裡使用了比較級的重複句型,除此之外,膚色白皙中的「白」,不可以使用表示顏色的 white,而是必須使用特指「膚色白皙」的 fair。"more and more ..." 以及 "prefer＋N" 的句型,表示「越來越多……」及「比較喜歡……」。

199

2

她們傾向認為白皮膚才是美麗而吸引人的。

➠ They **tend to** think **that having fair skin means beauty and attractiveness**.

解析 "tend to ＋ Vr ..." 的句型指「傾向於做……」。這裡 "that" 引導的名詞子句是動詞 "think" 的受詞，其中，動名詞片語 "having fair skin" 是子句的主詞。

3

因此，她們會購買大量能夠美白肌膚的產品。

➠ Therefore, they buy **lots** of products **that can whiten their skin**.

解析 "lots of" 等於 "a lot of"，意為「大量的、許多的」，後面可以接可數或不可數名詞。"that" 引導的形容詞子句修飾先行詞 "products"。

4

此外，讓肌膚變黑的正是紫外線。

➠ Furthermore, **it is** ultraviolet rays **that** tan our skin.

解析 "It is ... that ..." 的句型又稱為強調句型，在使用這個句型時，會將想要強調的部分放在 that 之前，像這裡的這個句子，想要強調的是 ultraviolet rays，所以會將 ultraviolet rays 放在 that 之前，而像 "It is you that make her cry."（正是你讓她哭的。）這個句子，要強調的部分是 you，因此會將 you 放在 that 之前。

5

因此，預防紫外線對皮膚的傷害就很重要了。

➠ As a result, **it** is very important **to prevent** ultraviolet rays **from** damaging our skin.

解析 這是以 "it" 虛主詞開頭的句子，真正的主詞是後面的不定詞片語 "to prevent ultraviolet rays from damaging our skin"，其中 "prevent ... from ..." 是很重要的句型，意為「防止；阻礙」。類似的句型還有 "stop ... from ..."、"prohibit ... from ..."、"keep ... from ..."、"protect ... from ..."，在作答寫作測驗時經常會用到，務必要記下來。

 必備字彙 與片語整理

⇢ Asian	[`eʃən]	adj.	亞洲的
⇢ attractiveness	[ə`træktɪvnɪs]	n.	吸引力
⇢ beauty	[`bjutɪ]	n.	美麗
⇢ damage	[`dæmɪdʒ]	v.	破壞
⇢ mean	[min]	v.	意味著
⇢ more	[mor]	adj.	更多的
⇢ prefer	[prɪ`fɝ]	v.	比較喜歡
⇢ skin	[skɪn]	n.	皮膚
⇢ tan	[tæn]	v.	使曬黑
⇢ whiten	[`hwaɪtn̩]	v.	使變白
⇢ lots of		phr.	大量的
⇢ prevent from		phr.	防止
⇢ tend to		phr.	傾向於
⇢ ultraviolet rays		phr.	紫外線

PART 3

unit 1
中譯英

201

題目敘述

1 運動是很好的休閒活動。**2** 它可以減輕心理壓力，還可以消除疲勞。**3** 規律的運動可以幫助肥胖的人減肥。**4** 不過，都市人常常工作忙碌且找不到適合的運動場所。**5** 他們只能到健身房健身，進而逐漸遠離了大自然。

參考範文

1 Exercise is a very good recreational activity. **2** It can reduce our psychological stress and relieve fatigue. **3** Regular exercise can help obese people lose weight. **4** However, people living in big cities are busy at work and cannot find suitable places to exercise. **5** They can only go to gyms to do exercise, and they are becoming distant from the Mother Nature.

範文句型解析

1

運動是很好的休閒活動。

➡ **Exercise** is a very good recreational activity.

解析 ▶ 這個句子是 "S＋V＋SC." 的基本句型。要注意 "exercise" 是不可數名詞。

2

它可以減輕心理壓力，還可以消除疲勞。

➡ It can reduce our psychological stress **and** relieve fatigue.

解析 ▶ "and" 連接助動詞 "can" 之後的兩個原形動詞 "reduce" 和 "relieve"。

3

規律的運動可以幫助肥胖的人減肥。

➠ Regular exercise can help obese people lose weight.

解析 助動詞 "can" 之後接原形動詞 "help"，因為句子後半使用的是 "help＋sb＋Vr ..." 的句型，因此也會使用原形動詞。

4

不過，都市人常常工作忙碌且找不到適合的運動場所。

➠ However, people living in big cities are busy at work and cannot find suitable places to exercise.

解析 以對等連接詞 "and" 連接兩個動作，並且以分詞構句的形容詞子句 "living in big cities" 修飾先行詞 "people"。"beV busy at work" 是 「忙碌於工作之中」的意思，在與工作或職場相關的文章中經常 會用到，務必要記住。

5

他們只能到健身房健身，進而逐漸遠離了大自然。

➠ They can only go to gyms to do exercise, and they are becoming distant from the Mother Nature.

解析 動詞 become 是「變成」的意思，這裡使用現在進行式來表達出 「逐漸變成」的語意。

 必備字彙 與片語整理

➠ exercise	[ˈɛksɚˌsaɪz]	v./n.	運動
➠ gym	[dʒɪm]	n.	健身房
➠ Nature	[ˈnetʃɚ]	n.	大自然
➠ obese	[oˈbis]	adj.	肥胖的
➠ recreational	[ˌrɛkrɪˈeʃənəl]	adj.	休閒的
➠ regular exercise		phr.	規律運動
➠ distant from		phr.	與～疏遠
➠ lose weight		phr.	減重
➠ psychological stress		phr.	心理壓力

題目敘述

¹大多數人喜歡看新聞，而我也是。²每天的新聞中都有著大量的資訊。³不同的人喜歡不同的新聞。⁴有些人喜歡看運動新聞，有些人只看頭條新聞，有些人則喜歡娛樂新聞。⁵我最喜歡看頭條，因為頭條有最重要的國內外新聞。⁶如果你沒有太多時間可以看完所有的新聞，頭條新聞毫無疑問是你最好的選擇。

參考範文

¹Most people like to read news, and so do I. ²There is a lot of information in daily news. ³Different people like different kinds of news. ⁴Some like the sports section, some read the headlines only, and some prefer the entertainment news. ⁵My favorite kind of news is the headlines because they have the most essential national and international news. ⁶If you don't have much time to read through all kinds of news, headline news is no doubt your best choice.

範文句型解析

大多數人喜歡看新聞，而我也是。

➡ Most people **like to** read news, and **so do I**.

解析 ▶ 這裡用對等連接詞 "and" 連接兩個完整的句子。前面的句子使用了
"like ＋ to ＋ Vr" 的句型，這個句型中也可以將不定詞改為動名詞，
意思不變。後面的句子則使用了倒裝句型 "so/neither ＋助動詞＋ S"
表示「……也是」。

每天的新聞中都有著大量的資訊。

➡ There is a lot of **information** in daily news.

解析 ▶ 這裡要特別注意的是 information（資訊）是不可數名詞，因此句
型中出現的 beV 必須使用單數的 is。

不同的人喜歡不同的新聞。

➡ Different people like different kinds of news.

解析 ▶ "S＋V＋O" 的基本句型。動詞 "like" 前後都有 "different"（不同
的），描述每個人都有各自喜好的新聞種類。

有些人喜歡看運動新聞，有些人只看頭條新聞，有些人則喜歡
娛樂新聞。

➡ Some like the sports section, some read the headlines
only, and some prefer the entertainment news.

解析 ▶ 用 "A＋B＋, and＋C." 的句型來連接三個地位相同的句子。

我最喜歡看頭條，因為頭條有最重要的國內外新聞。

➡ My favorite kind of news is the headlines because they
have the most essential national and international news.

解析 ▶ 用 "主要子句＋because＋從屬子句." 的句型來表達「原因」。

205

如果你沒有太多時間可以看完所有的新聞，頭條新聞毫無疑問是你最好的選擇。

➡ If you don't have much time to **read through** all kinds of news, headline news is no doubt your best choice.

解析 ▶ "If＋從屬子句，＋主要子句." 的句型，是典型的條件句句型。"through" 有「從頭到尾；徹底」的意思，所以 "read through" 就是「從頭看到尾」的意思。

 必備字彙 與片語整理

➡ entertainment	[ɛntə`tenmənt]	n.	娛樂
➡ essential	[ɪ`sɛnʃəl]	adj.	重要的；必須的
➡ favorite	[`fevərɪt]	adj.	最喜愛的
➡ headline	[`hɛd͵laɪn]	n.	大標；頭條新聞
➡ information	[͵ɪnfə`meʃən]	n.	資訊
➡ international	[͵ɪntə`næʃənḷ]	adj.	國際的
➡ national	[`næʃənḷ]	adj.	國內的
➡ news	[njuz]	n.	新聞（不可數）
➡ prefer	[prɪ`fɝ]	v.	比較喜歡
➡ section	[`sɛkʃən]	n.	版面；部分
➡ choice	[tʃɔɪs]	n.	選擇
➡ headline news		phr.	頭條新聞
➡ no doubt		phr.	無疑地
➡ read through		phr.	從頭看到尾

題目敘述

　　1 上個月，我在回家途中看見一個大箱子。**2** 我打開箱子，發現裡面有好幾隻小貓。**3** 牠們幾乎快要餓死了；我想不透是誰會對牠們這麼狠心。**4** 我一衝動就把牠們帶回家了，可是我媽媽從來就不喜歡貓。**5** 很幸運地，有兩個鄰居喜歡貓，立刻收養了牠們。

參考範文

　　1Last month, I saw a big box on my way home. **2**I opened the box and found that there were several kittens in the box. **3**They nearly starved to death; I wondered who could be so cruel to put them through this situation. **4**I brought them home on an impulse, but my mother has never liked cats. **5**Luckily, two of my neighbors loved cats and adopted them immediately.

範文句型解析

1

上個月，我在回家途中看見一個大箱子。

➠ Last month, I saw a big box on my way home.

解析 ▶ "on one's way＋to＋地點" 的句型表達「在……途中」。例如 "on my way to school"。"home" 之前的介系詞 "to" 通常會被省略。

2

我打開箱子，發現裡面有好幾隻小貓。

➠ I opened the box and found **that there were several kittens in the box**.

解析 ▶ 對等連接詞 "and" 連接兩個過去簡單式動詞 "opened" 和 "found"。由 "that" 引導的名詞子句是動詞 "found" 的受詞。

3

牠們幾乎快要餓死了；我想不透是誰會對牠們這麼狠心。

➠ They nearly starved to death; I wondered who could be so cruel to put them through this situation.

解析 以分號隔開兩個完整的句子。後面的句子用了 "I wonder＋以疑問詞引導的名詞子句." 的句型，意為「我想不透……」。"be cruel＋to" 意為「對……狠心」。

4

我一衝動就把牠們帶回家了，可是我媽媽從來就不喜歡貓。

➠ I brought them home **on an impulse**, but my mother has never liked cats.

解析 對等連接詞 "but" 連接兩個完整的句子。前面的句子用了 "on an impulse" 的表達方式，意為「衝動之下」，類似的表達方式還有 "in a haste"（匆忙之下）。

5

很幸運地，有兩個鄰居喜歡貓，立刻收養了牠們。

➠ Luckily, two of my neighbors loved cats **and** adopted them immediately.

解析 情狀副詞有時會放在句首以加強語氣，這裡的 "Luckily" 就是這種用法。句子以對等連接詞 "and" 連接兩個過去簡單式動詞 "loved" 和 "adopted"。

 必備字彙 與片語整理

➠ adopt	[ə`dɑpt]	v.	認養、收養
➠ find	[faɪnd]	v.	發現
➠ kitten	[`kɪtn̩]	n.	小貓
➠ neighbor	[`nebɚ]	n.	鄰居
➠ open	[`opən]	v.	打開
➠ be cruel to		phr.	對……狠心
➠ on an impulse		phr.	衝動之下
➠ starve to death		phr.	餓死

TEST 20

陳年舊物篇

解析篇

題目敘述

¹很多人喜歡老舊的束西。²老音樂和老電影既感人又浪漫。³老古董是無價之寶，而且充滿回憶。⁴陳年老酒香醇可口。⁵老人仁慈而有智慧。⁶這些人事物越老就越珍貴。

參考範文

¹Many people love old things. ²Old music and old movies are touching and romantic. ³Antiques are invaluable and full of memories. ⁴Old wine is mellow and tasty. ⁵Old people are kind and wise. ⁶The older they are, the more valuable they become.

範文句型解析

1

很多人喜歡老舊的束西。

➠ Many people love old things.

解析 ▶ "S + V + O." 的基本句型。陳述現在的事實，使用現在簡單式。

2

老音樂和老電影既感人又浪漫。

➠ Old music and old movies are touching and romantic.

解析 ▶ 延續前文使用現在簡單式。這裡使用的是 "S + beV + SC." 的基本句型，其中，主詞和主詞補語的部分都使用對等連接詞 "and" 來連接。

209

3

老古董是無價之寶，而且充滿回憶。

➡ Antiques are invaluable and full of memories.

解析 ▶ 延續前文使用現在簡單式。對等連接詞 "and" 連接 be 動詞片語 "are invaluable and (are) full of memories"，這裡省略了句中重複的第二個 be 動詞。

4

陳年老酒香醇可口。

➡ Old wine is mellow and tasty.

解析 ▶ 延續前文使用現在簡單式。採用 "S + beV + SC." 的基本句型，其中，主詞補語的部分以對等連接詞 "and" 來連接兩個形容詞 "mellow" 和 "tasty"。

5

老人仁慈而有智慧。

➡ Old people are kind and wise.

解析 ▶ 延續前文使用現在簡單式。採用 "S + beV + SC." 的基本句型，其中，主詞補語的部分以對等連接詞 "and" 來連接兩個形容詞 "kind" 和 "wise"。

6

這些人事物越老就越珍貴。

➡ The older they are, the more valuable they become.

解析 ▶ 延續前文使用現在簡單式。使用 "The ＋比較級，＋ the ＋比較級" 的句型，表示「越……就越……」的意思。

 必備字彙 與片語整理

antique	[æn`tik]	n.	古董
become	[bɪ`kʌm]	v.	變得
invaluable	[ɪn`væljəbḷ]	adj.	無價的，非常貴重的
kind	[kaɪnd]	adj.	仁慈的
mellow	[`mɛlo]	adj.	香醇的；成熟的
memory	[`mɛmərɪ]	n.	回憶
old	[old]	adj.	老舊的
romantic	[rə`mæntɪk]	adj.	浪漫的
tasty	[`testɪ]	adj.	可口的
touching	[tʌtʃɪŋ]	adj.	感人的
valuable	[`væljʊəbḷ]	adj.	貴重的
wine	[waɪn]	n.	（葡萄）酒
wise	[waɪz]	adj.	有智慧的
be full of		phr.	充滿

unit 2 英文作文

英文作文的考題包含「看圖寫作」、「故事接龍」、「書信寫作」三種題型,考生必須按照各題型的要求來作答,才能拿到滿意的分數,因此務必要多做練習,才能在限定的時間之內,以足夠的句數及字數充分切題發揮。

2-1 模擬試題篇

TEST 1 兩代之間篇

請根據下面所提供的圖片以及文字提示,寫一篇英文作文,長度約 120 字(8 至 12 句)。答案請寫在答案欄內(評分重點包括內容、組織、文法、用字遣詞、標點符號與大小寫)。

台灣現代社會的老年人與年輕人間的代溝越來越加深。身為台灣的一分子,請說明老年人與年輕人該如何共同相處並互相協助。

_____

_____

_____

_____

恐怖的旅遊篇

請用 120 字（8 至 12 句）完成以下的故事。主題是 "A Terrible Trip"，故事的開頭如下。答案請寫在答案欄內，開頭的部分不需重謄（評分重點包括內容、組織、文法、用字遣詞、標點符號與大小寫）。

My girlfriend and I took a trip to Hawaii last year. My brother and his wife lived in Hawaii and they wanted us to come to visit them. We had tickets for an early flight to Hawaii, so we got up before the sun rose. This is where our problems started. On our way to the airport, we had a flat tire. This made us miss our flight ...

_____

_____

_____

商業拜訪篇

請依照下面所提供的文字提示，寫一篇長度約 120 字（8 至 12 句）的英文信件，請將答案寫在答案欄內（評分重點包括內容、組織、文法、用字遣詞、標點符號與大小寫）。

你商業上的夥伴（Mr. Brown）來信表示希望來台灣一趟，與他們公司長期合作的你，將寫一封信向 Mr. Brown 說明你打算如何歡迎他來到台灣。

_____

_____

_____

213

 樹木篇

請根據下面所提供的圖片以及文字提示，寫一篇英文作文，長度約 120 字（8 至 12 句）。答案請寫在答案欄內（評分重點包括內容、組織、文法、用字遣詞、標點符號與大小寫）。

樹木是有用且美麗的植物，請說明樹木的生長過程，並說明它每一個部位的功能為何。

_____

_____

_____

_____

 婚宴篇

請用 120 字（8 至 12 句）完成以下的故事。主題是 "A Special Experience in Wedding"。答案請寫在答案欄內，開頭的部分不需重謄（評分重點包括內容、組織、文法、用字遣詞、標點符號與大小寫）。

Last weekend, I had the most wonderful experience! I attended the wedding of two of my friends from college. I was really excited. Actually, I haven't attended wedding parties for a long time. Let me tell you what I saw at the party. First, ...

_____

_____

_____

_____

共進晚餐篇

書信寫作

請依照下面所提供的文字提示，寫一篇長度約 120 字（8 至 12 句）的英文信件，請將答案寫在答案欄內（評分重點包括內容、組織、文法、用字遣詞、標點符號與大小寫）。

　　上學期你參加了英文的密集訓練課程，而你真的很喜歡那位外籍老師 Mr. Charles Smith。於是你代表你的同學們寫一封信給他，表達你們對他課程的喜愛並邀請他與大家一起出遊或共進一餐。

阿姆斯壯篇

看圖寫作

請根據下面所提供的圖片以及文字提示，寫一篇英文作文，長度約 120 字（8 至 12 句）。答案請寫在答案欄內（評分重點包括內容、組織、文法、用字遣詞、標點符號與大小寫）。

　　尼爾・阿姆斯壯（Neil Armstrong）是家喻戶曉的傳奇人物，請描述他的著名事蹟，並論述你對他的豐功偉業有什麼看法。

美化環境篇

故事接龍

請用 120 字（8 至 12 句）完成以下的故事。主題是 "To Improve Quality of Life"。答案請寫在答案欄內，開頭的部分不需重謄（評分重點包括 內容、組織、文法、用字遣詞、標點符號與大小寫）。

Taiwan is a small island; however, there are more than 23-million people dwelling in this island. The consequence of population explosion is that too much land is used to build houses, shopping malls, supermarkets, movie theaters and highways, but not used to grow trees. It is impossible for those who live in a big city to be close to Nature. When doors are opened, they immediately face a lot of cars, polluted air, concrete buildings, and crowds ...

離鄉背井篇

書信寫作

請依照下面所提供的文字提示，寫一篇長度約 120 字（8 至 12 句）的英文信件，請將答案寫在答案欄內（評分重點包括內容、組織、文法、用字遣詞、標點符號與大小寫）。

妳考上了大學，離家到外地念書。為了不讓妳的母親擔心，妳寫了一封家書，告訴母親妳已平安到達學校，並且和母親分享學校生活的點滴。

華盛頓的童年篇

看圖寫作

請根據下面所提供的圖片以及文字提示,寫一篇英文作文,長度約 120 字
(8 至 12 句)。答案請寫在答案欄內(評分重點包括內容、組織、文法、
用字遣詞、標點符號與大小寫)。

美國的第一任總統喬治·華盛頓
(George Washington)小時候發生了一
個有趣的故事,這個故事家喻戶曉,常
被用來說明「誠實」這個人格特質。

_____

_____

_____

朋友篇

故事接龍

請用 120 字(8 至 12 句)完成以下的故事。主題是 "Friends"。答案請寫
在答案欄內,開頭的部分不需重謄(評分重點包括內容、組織、文法、用
字遣詞、標點符號與大小寫)。

Friends are very important in our lives. Whether we are children or
adults, we need friends, and they enrich our knowledge and mind. When
we get into troubles, friends always stay with us, help us, and encourage
us to look at the bright side of life. When we have a doubt, we feel free to
discuss it with them, and they try their best to give us some suggestions ...

_____

_____

_____

TEST 12　道歉信函篇

書信寫作

請依照下面所提供的文字提示，寫一篇長度約 120 字（8 至 12 句）的英文信件，請將答案寫在答案欄內（評分重點包括內容、組織、文法、用字遣詞、標點符號與大小寫）。

有一天，你的小狗出門玩耍，不知為何竟然把鄰居家的小孩子咬傷了。請寫一封道歉信向對方的家長（Mr. and Mrs. Smith）道歉。

_____

_____

_____

_____

TEST 13　道歉篇

看圖寫作

請根據下面所提供的圖片以及文字提示，寫一篇英文作文，長度約 120 字（8 至 12 句）。答案請寫在答案欄內（評分重點包括內容、組織、文法、用字遣詞、標點符號與大小寫）。

保羅把車子借給凱文，結果隔天卻收到一封由凱文寫來的道歉信。請試著描述他們之間可能發生了什麼事，以及整件事情發生的經過。

_____

_____

_____

失蹤的貓咪篇

請用 120 字（8 至 12 句）完成以下的故事。主題是 "A Lost Cat"。答案請寫在答案欄內，開頭的部分不需重謄（評分重點包括內容、組織、文法、用字遣詞、標點符號與大小寫）。

I have a cat whose name is Toro. His favorite food is canned tuna, and his favorite toys are little paper balls. Everyday when I go back to my house in the evening, he always sits in front of the door to welcome me home. However, one day when I came back home at the usual time, something out of the ordinary happened. I did not see him sitting in front of the door ...

取消約會篇

請依照下面所提供的文字提示，寫一篇長度約 120 字（8 至 12 句）的英文信件，請將答案寫在答案欄內（評分重點包括內容、組織、文法、用字遣詞、標點符號與大小寫）。

妳和男朋友約好了下個禮拜要去花蓮旅行，但是住在日本的表姊卻意外來訪，並且表示要小住一段時間，所以原定的旅行計畫必須要取消了，請寫一封信向男朋友說明事由。

禁止吸菸篇

看圖寫作

請根據下面所提供的圖片以及文字提示，寫一篇英文作文，長度約 120 字（8 至 12 句）。答案請寫在答案欄內（評分重點包括內容、組織、文法、用字遣詞、標點符號與大小寫）。

公共場所是大家的空間，在公共場所抽菸不只是危害自己的健康，還會影響別人。請說明你是否同意公共場所禁菸的規定。

綁架電話篇

故事接龍

請用 120 字（8 至 12 句）完成以下的故事。主題是 "A Ransom Call"。答案請寫在答案欄內，開頭的部分不需重謄（評分重點包括內容、組織、文法、用字遣詞、標點符號與大小寫）。

Last Monday morning, while I was sound asleep, my roommate knocked on my door heavily. She called my name loudly until I opened the door to see what on earth was going on outside my room ...

 **遲交報告篇**

請依照下面所提供的文字提示，寫一篇長度約 120 字（8 至 12 句）的英文信件，請將答案寫在答案欄內（評分重點包括內容、組織、文法、用字遣詞、標點符號與大小寫）。

　　老師規定今天下午四點以前要交出學期報告，遲交的一律以零分計算。但是上個禮拜你家因為颱風帶來的大雨而成為了一片汪洋，電腦中的檔案也全部泡湯了，因此無法如期交出報告。請寫一封信請求老師延長繳交報告的期限。

TEST 19 **優柔寡斷篇**

故事接龍

請用 120 字（8 至 12 句）完成以下的故事。主題是 "Indecision"。答案請寫在答案欄內，開頭的部分不需重謄（評分重點包括內容、組織、文法、用字遣詞、標點符號與大小寫）。

　　I always have difficulty making decisions. For instance, last weekend when I went shopping for a dress, I had no idea which dress I should buy ...

TEST 20 失戀心情篇

書信寫作

請依照下面所提供的文字提示,寫一篇長度約 120 字(8 至 12 句)的英文信件,請將答案寫在答案欄內(評分重點包括內容、組織、文法、用字遣詞、標點符號與大小寫)。

　　上個星期你(妳)和情人分手了,你(妳)的心情很低落,想要寫一封信給你(妳)最好的朋友,告訴他(她)發生了什麼事情,並和他(她)分享自己的心情。

_____

_____

_____

_____

_____

TEST 1 兩代之間篇

解析篇

題目敘述

台灣現代社會的老年人與年輕人間的代溝越來越加深。身為台灣的一分子，請說明老年人與年輕人該如何共同相處並互相協助。

Is there some one to help me out?

參考範文

1Our society is composed of various kinds of people, and we meet people from different age groups in our daily life. 2If we get along with people who are older or younger than us, we can also learn something from them. 3Older people usually have more experience in studying and working. 4Moreover, they can give advice to younger people when the latter are confused about the same problems. 5On the other hand, younger people often own the creativity and courage that older people lack. 6These qualities can help older people who always worry too much when they face some new situations. 7In conclusion, both older and younger people have advantages of their own and can offer to help to each other.

1 我們的社會是由各式各樣的人所組成的,而且我們在日常生活中會遇到不同年紀的人。2 假如我們和比我們年長或年輕的人相處,我們也可以從他們身上學到一些束西。3 年長者通常在學習與工作上有較多的經驗。4 此外,他們可以給予年輕人忠告,當後者正在為同樣的問題感到困惑時。5 另一方面,年輕人常擁有年長者缺乏的創造力與勇氣。6 這些特質可以幫助在面臨一些新的狀況時總是過度焦慮的年長者。7 總之,年長者與年輕人都有他們的優勢,可以彼此提供協助。

範文句型解析

1

Our society is composed of various kinds of people, and we meet people from different age groups in our daily life.
我們的社會是由各式各樣的人所組成的,而且我們在日常生活中會遇到不同年紀的人。

解析 ▶ "A + beV + composed + of + B" 的句型表示「A 是由 B 組成的」。"composed of" 是固定的表達方式,不可以使用其他的介系詞。

2

If we get along with people who are older or younger than us, we can also learn something from them.
假如我們和比我們年長或年輕的人相處,我們也可以從他們身上學到一些束西。

解析 ▶ 連接詞 "if" 連接表示條件的從屬子句,修飾後面的主要子句 "we can also learn something from them"。從屬子句中還用了由關係代名詞引導的形容詞子句修飾先行詞 "people"。

3

Older people usually have more experience **in studying and working**.

年長者通常在學習與工作上有較多的經驗。

解析 頻率副詞一般會放在 beV 和助動詞之後、一般動詞之前。這裡使用介系詞 "in" 來說明是在哪方面的經驗。

4

Moreover, they can **give advice to** younger people when the latter **are confused about** the same problems.

此外,他們可以給予年輕人忠告,當後者正在為同樣的問題感到困惑時。

解析 "Moreover, ..." 的表達方式也可以用 "What is more, ..." 來代替。"the latter" 指的是前面句子中的 "younger people"。"give advice to" 意為「給……忠告」,"be confused about" 意為「為……感到困惑」。

5

On the other hand, younger people often own the creativity and courage **that** older people lack.

另一方面,年輕人常擁有年長者缺乏的創造力與勇氣。

解析 在寫作時常會使用 "on one hand"(一方面)和 "on the other hand"(另一方面)來陳述事情的一體兩面。關係代名詞 "that" 引導形容詞子句,說明年輕人所擁有的創造力和勇氣是「年長者所缺乏的」。

6

These qualities can help older people who always worry too much **when** they face some new situations.

這些特質可以幫助在面臨一些新的狀況時總是過度焦慮的年長者。

解析 關係代名詞 "who" 所引導的形容詞子句修飾先行詞 "older people",這裡的連接詞 "when" 引導表示時間點的副詞子句,補充說明前面的整個句子。

> **In conclusion**, both older and younger people have advantages of their own and can offer to help to each other.
>
> 總之，年長者與年輕人都有他們的優勢，可以彼此提供協助。

 解析 寫作時可以用來帶出結論的表達方式有："In conclusion, ..."（總之）、"To sum up, ..."（總地來說）、"In one word, ..."（總而言之）、"In short, ..."（簡而言之），適時使用這些用來總結的表達方式，可以使文章架構更顯完整。

必備字彙 與片語整理

advantage	[əd`væntɪdʒ]	n.	優點
courage	[`kɝɪdʒ]	n.	勇氣
creativity	[͵krie`tɪvətɪ]	n.	創造力
experience	[ɪk`spɪrɪəns]	n.	經驗
lack	[læk]	v.	缺乏
latter	[`lætɚ]	adj.	後面的
moreover	[mor`ovɚ]	adv.	除此之外
own	[on]	v.	擁有
quality	[`kwɑlətɪ]	n.	特質
society	[sə`saɪətɪ]	n.	社會
worry	[`wɝɪ]	v.	擔憂
be composed of		phr.	由……組成
be confused about		phr.	為……感到困惑
different from		phr.	和……不同
give advice to		phr.	給……建議
in conclusion		phr.	總之
on the other hand		phr.	另一方面
various kinds of		phr.	各式各樣的

恐怖的旅遊篇

解析篇

題目敘述

　　My girlfriend and I took a trip to Hawaii last year. My brother and his wife lived in Hawaii and they wanted us to come to visit them. We had tickets for an early flight to Hawaii, so we got up before the sun rose. This is where our problems started. On our way to the airport, we had a flat tire. This made us miss our flight ...

　　我和女朋友去年一起去了夏威夷旅行。我的哥哥和嫂嫂住在夏威夷，要我們過去拜訪他們。我們買的是早班機票，所以在天亮之前我們就起床了。這就是我們麻煩的開始。在我們去機場的路上，我們的車子爆胎了。這使得我們錯過了班機……

參考範文

　　¹Because we were five hours late, there was nobody at the airport to pick us up. ²Then, we called and asked them to come back to the airport to pick us up. ³We stayed for two weeks and had a terrible time. ⁴On the second day, while we were hiking up a mountain, my girlfriend fell and sprained her ankle. ⁵I had to carry her all the way down the mountain. ⁶On the third day, while I was surfing, I fell off my surfboard and hurt my face. ⁷On the fourth day, I drove my brother's car and

had a terrible car accident. ⁸In addition to that, the weather was really awful. ⁹It rained almost every day, and the sun didn't shine at all. ¹⁰When it was time to leave, we were both sad and happy. ¹¹ In short, we agreed that it was a terrible trip.

中文翻譯

1 因為我們已經遲到了五個小時，所以沒人在機場接我們。2 之後，我們打電話要求他們來接我們。3 我們待了兩個星期，玩得很不愉快。4 在第二天，當我們正在爬山時，我的女友摔倒並扭傷了腳踝。5 我必須一路背著她走下山。6 第三天，當我在衝浪時，我從衝浪板上摔下來，弄傷了我的臉。7 第四天，我開我哥哥的車，結果發生了嚴重車禍。8 除了這些之外，天氣真的很糟。9 幾乎每天都下雨，沒有一點太陽。10 當回家的時候到了，我們既難過又高興。11 簡而言之，我們都同意這是一次可怕的旅行。

範文句型解析

Because we were five hours late, there was nobody at the airport to pick us up.

因為我們已經遲到了五個小時，所以沒人在機場接我們。

解析 ▶ 「我們遲到了五個小時。」的句型是 "We were five hours late."。以這個句子為基礎，「他們遲到了二十五分鐘。」是 "They were twenty-five mimutes late. "；「我們早到了兩個小時。」則是 "We were two hours early."，這類句子在寫作測驗時經常會用到，請特別注意。

Then, we <mark>called and asked</mark> them **to** come back **to** the airport **to** pick us up.
之後，我們打電話要求他們來接我們。

We **stayed** for two weeks <mark>and</mark> **had** a terrible time.
我們待了兩個星期，玩得很不愉快。

3

解析 對等連接詞 "and" 連接兩個過去簡單式動詞。

On the second day, <mark>while</mark> we were hiking up a mountain, my girlfriend fell and sprained her ankle.
在第二天，當我們正在爬山時，我的女友摔倒並扭傷了腳踝。

4

解析 主要句型為 "While＋進行式子句, 簡單式主要子句."，因為整篇文章都在說發生在過去的事，所以使用的是過去式，句型可以變化為 "While＋過去進行式子句, 過去簡單式主要子句."。

I had to carry her <mark>all the way</mark> down the mountain.
我必須一路背著她走下山。

5

解析 "all the way"（一路）和 "all the time"（一向）常做為副詞在句中修飾動詞。例如 "She cried all the way home."（她一路哭著回家。）、"I keep early hours all the time."（我一向早睡早起。）。

On the third day, while I was surfing, I fell off my surfboard and hurt my face.

第三天，當我在衝浪時，我從衝浪板上摔下來，弄傷了我的臉。

解析 ▶ 這個句子的句型也是 "While＋進行式子句, 簡單式主要子句."。因此改成過去式就會變成 "While＋過去進行式子句, 過去簡單式主要子句."。

On the fourth day, I drove my brother's car and had a terrible car accident.

第四天，我開我哥哥的車，結果發生了嚴重車禍。

解析 ▶ 對等連接詞 "and" 連接兩個過去式動詞。

In addition to that, the weather was really awful.

除了這些之外，天氣真的很糟。

解析 ▶ "in addition to ＋ N" 相當於 "besides ＋ N"，意為「除了……之外」。

It rained almost every day, and the sun didn't shine at all.

幾乎每天都下雨，沒有一點太陽。

解析 ▶ 對等連接詞 "and" 連接兩個過去式子句，特別注意這裡 "and" 的前面要加逗點。

When it was time to leave, we were both sad and happy.

當回家的時候到了，我們既難過又高興。

解析 ▶ 句型 "it is time to ＋ Vr" 意為「是時候做～」。例如 "It is time to study."（是時候讀書了。）、"It is time to sleep."（是時候睡覺了。）。

> In short, we agreed that it was a terrible trip.
> 簡而言之，我們都同意這是一次可怕的旅行。

11

解析  用來在文章最後做結論的慣用表達有："In conclusion, ..."（總之）、"To sum up, ..."（總地來說）、"In one word, ..."（總而言之）、"In short, ..."（簡而言之），使用恰當的結論轉折語來收尾，就寫作測驗而言相當重要，務必要特別注意。

必備字彙 與片語整理

⇒ airport	[`ɛr͵port]	n.	機場
⇒ awful	[`ɔfʊl]	adj.	可怕的
⇒ carry	[`kærɪ]	v.	背；提
⇒ ankle	[æŋkl̩]	n.	腳踝
⇒ fall	[fɔl]	v.	跌倒
⇒ hike	[haɪk]	v.	健行；爬山
⇒ late	[let]	adj.	遲到的
⇒ mountain	[`maʊntn̩]	n.	山
⇒ nobody	[`nobɑdɪ]	n.	沒有人
⇒ rain	[ren]	v.	下雨
⇒ shine	[ʃaɪn]	v.	發光；照耀
⇒ sprain	[spren]	v.	扭傷
⇒ surf	[sɝf]	v.	衝浪
⇒ surfboard	[`sɝf͵bord]	n.	衝浪板
⇒ terrible	[`tɛrəbl̩]	adj.	可怕的；糟糕的
⇒ trip	[trɪp]	n.	旅行
⇒ weather	[`wɛðɚ]	n.	天氣
⇒ all the way		phr.	一路
⇒ in addition to		phr.	除了……之外
⇒ in short		phr.	簡而言之
⇒ pick up		phr.	用車子接送某人

 商業拜訪篇

TEST

題目敘述

你商業上的夥伴（Mr. Brown）來信表示希望來台灣一趟，與他們公司長期合作的你，將寫一封信向 Mr. Brown 說明你打算如何歡迎他來到台灣。

參考範文

Dear Mr. Brown,

¹Thank you very much for your letter dated February 13, 2021. ²I am pleased to learn that you are coming to visit Taiwan and will stay here for two weeks. ³If it is convenient for you, I hope I can meet you at 10:30 AM on April 18, 2021 at my Taipei office. ⁴A luncheon in your honor will follow our meeting. ⁵If you have some special people who you want us to make arrangements for you, please feel free to let me know. ⁶We would be very happy if we can be of some help in making your trip pleasant. ⁷I am proud of the warm relations between our two companies over the past two years. ⁸I look forward to hearing from you soon.

Sincerely yours,
Betty Wu

中文翻譯

親愛的伯朗先生：

1 非常感謝您在 2021 年 2 月 13 日的來信。2 我很高興得知您將來台灣拜訪並停留兩週。3 假如您方便的話，我希望能在 2021 年 4 月 18 日的上午十點半與您在我台北的辦公室見面。4 為您準備的午餐餐會安排在會議之後。5 假如您有什麼希望我們替您安排見面的特別人選，請不要客氣讓我知道。6 如果能夠幫助您度過一次愉快的旅行，我們將會感到非常高興。7 我對我們兩家公司過去兩年的熱絡情誼感到驕傲。8 期待很快收到您的回音。

真誠地
吳蓓蒂

範文句型解析

1

Thank you very much for your letter dated February 13, 2021.
非常感謝您在 2021 年 2 月 13 日的來信。

解析 ▶ 書信類文章中常用的感謝句型 "Thank you for sth ..."，意為「我為某事感謝你」。

2

I am pleased to learn that you **are coming to** visit Taiwan and will stay here for two weeks.
我很高興得知您將來台灣拜訪並停留兩週。

解析 ▶ "I am pleased to learn that ＋子句 ."，意為「我很高興得知某消息」，這是在書信中經常用到的萬用句型，語氣客氣且有禮貌地打開話題。

233

3

If it is convenient for you, I hope I can meet you at 10:30 AM on April 18, 2021 at my Taipei office.
假如您方便的話，我希望能在 2021 年 4 月 18 日的上午十點半與您在我台北的辦公室見面。

> **解析** ▶ "If it is convenient for you,＋子句 ."，意為「如果您方便的話，⋯⋯」，在書信中經常用來委婉請求對方答應自己的要求。

4

A luncheon in your honor will follow our meeting.
為您準備的午餐餐會安排在會議之後。

> **解析** ▶ "in sb's honor"、"in honor of sb"、"in sth's honor"、"in honor of sth" 意為「出於對某人或某事的敬意」，在正式書信中是很重要的表達句型。

5

If you have some special people who you want us to make arrangements for you, please feel free to let me know.
假如您有什麼希望我們替您安排見面的特別人選，請不要客氣讓我知道。

> **解析** ▶ 在商業書信中，如果想要請對方提出意見，可以使用 "Please feel free to let me know."（請不要客氣讓我知道。）、"Kindly contact with us."（煩請與我們聯絡。）、"Please do not hesitate to let us know."（請不要猶豫讓我們知道。）、"Please contact us any time."（請隨時與我們聯絡。）。

6

We would be very happy if we can be of some help in making your trip pleasant.
如果能夠幫助您度過一次愉快的旅行，我們將會感到非常高興。

> **解析** ▶ "We would be very happy if we can be of some help in ..."，意為「如果能夠幫助您⋯⋯，我們將會感到非常高興」，這是相當客氣有禮的表達方式。

I am proud of the warm relations between our two companies over the past two years.

我對我們兩家公司過去兩年的熱絡情誼感到驕傲。

解析 ▶ "S＋be＋proud＋of＋N ..." 意為「對……感到驕傲」。

I look forward to hearing from you soon.

期待很快收到您的回音。

解析 ▶ "I look forward to hearing from you soon." 是在書信結尾委婉請求對方盡快回信的常用表達方式。

 必備字彙 與片語整理

➡ arrangement	[ə`rendʒmənt]	n.	安排
➡ convenient	[kən`vinjənt]	adj.	方便的
➡ dear	[dɪr]	adj.	親愛的
➡ luncheon	[`lʌntʃən]	n.	午餐餐會
➡ meet	[mit]	v.	會面，見面
➡ meeting	[`mitɪŋ]	n.	會議
➡ pleasant	[`plɛzənt]	adj.	令人愉快的
➡ pleased	[plizd]	adj.	感到愉快的
➡ relation	[rɪ`leʃən]	n.	關係
➡ trip	[trɪp]	n.	旅行
➡ visit	[`vɪzɪt]	v.	拜訪；參觀
➡ be proud of		phr.	對……感到驕傲
➡ in your honor		phr.	（為表示敬意）為您～
➡ look forward to		phr.	期待

樹木篇

題目敘述

　　樹木是有用且美麗的植物，請說明樹木的生長過程，並說明它每一個部位的功能為何。

參考範文

　　¹Trees are wonderful plants. We like to sit under a large tree on a hot summer day. ²Kids love to climb trees, and painters love to draw them. ³Old people enjoy chatting under trees as well. ⁴When we look at a tree, we may think only of its beautiful appearance, but, in fact, a tree has a complex physical structure. ⁵The structure of a tree consists of three parts: the leaves, the branches and trunk, and the roots. ⁶Under the ground, the roots spread out to anchor the tree. ⁷The root system absorbs water from the soil and sends it up to the trunk and branches. ⁸Above the ground, the roots form the trunk. The job of the trunk is to support the branches and hold them up to the sunlight. ⁹At the top of the tree, the leaves grow out of the branches. ¹⁰Trees are really beautiful and useful. That's what I know about trees.

中文翻譯

1 樹是很棒的植物。我們喜歡在炎熱的夏天坐在大樹底下。2 小孩們喜歡爬樹，畫家喜歡畫下它們。3 老人也喜歡在樹下聊天。4 當我們注視著樹時，我們可能只想到它美麗的外表，但事實上，它擁有複雜的身體結構。5 樹的結構由三部分組成：樹葉、樹枝與樹幹、根部。6 在地底下，根部向外延伸來穩固樹木。7 根部系統從土壤吸收水分再往上送到樹幹與樹枝。8 在地面上，根部形成樹幹。樹幹的工作是支撐樹枝，並支撐它們向上面對陽光。9 在樹的頂端，樹葉從樹枝上長出來。10 樹木真的既美麗又有用。這就是我所知的樹木。

範文句型解析

1

Trees are wonderful plants. We like to sit under a large tree on a hot summer day.
樹是很棒的植物。我們喜歡在炎熱的夏天坐在大樹底下。

解析 ▶ "S＋like＋to＋Vr ..." 等同於 "S＋like＋V-ing ..."，意為「喜歡做某事」。

2

Kids love to climb trees, and painters love to draw them.
小孩們喜歡爬樹，畫家喜歡畫下它們。

解析 ▶ "S＋love＋to＋Vr ..." 等同於 "S＋love＋V-ing ..."，意為「喜愛做某事」。

3

Old people enjoy chatting under trees as well.
老人也喜歡在樹下聊天。

解析 ▶ "S＋enjoy＋V-ing" 是常用於寫作測驗之中的慣用表達方式，在 enjoy 之後一定要加動名詞，意為「享受、喜愛做某事」。

When we look at a tree, we may think only of its beautiful appearance, but, in fact, a tree has a complex physical structure.

當我們注視著樹時，我們可能只想到它美麗的外表，但事實上，它擁有複雜的身體結構。

解析 這裡用 "but" 連接兩個語氣衝突的句子，後面的句子則加上轉折語 "in fact" 來加強語氣。前面的句子使用以從屬連接詞 "when" 引導 來表示時間的副詞子句 "when we look at a tree"，修飾主要子句 "we may think only of its beautiful appearance"，說明動作發生的 時間點為何。

The structure of a tree consists of three parts: the leaves, the branches and trunk, and the roots.

樹的結構由三部分組成：樹葉、樹枝與樹幹、根部。

解析 "consist of" 意為「由……組成」，等同於 "be composed of"，務 必特別留意這兩種表達方式在使用上的不同，"consist of" 是主動 語態，而 "be composed of" 是被動語態。

Under the ground, the roots spread out to anchor the tree.

在地底下，根部向外延伸來穩固樹木。

解析 不定詞可以表示目的，"to anchor the tree" 表示樹根向外延伸的目 的在於穩固樹木。

The root system **absorbs** water **from** the soil **and sends** it up **to** the trunk and branches.

根部系統從土壤吸收水分再往上送到樹幹與樹枝。

解析 連接詞 "and" 連接兩個現在式的動詞片語 "absorbs ... from ..." 和 "sends ... to ..."。"absorb sth from somewhere" 意為「從某處吸 收某物」，"send sth to somewhere" 意為「將某物送往某處」。

8

Above the ground, the roots form the trunk. The job of the trunk **is to support** the branches and **hold** them up to the sunlight.

在地面上，根部形成樹幹。樹幹的工作是支撐樹枝，並支撐它們向上面對陽光。

解析 ▶ "S＋beV＋to＋Vr ... " 的句型中，利用不定詞做為主詞補語，並以連接詞 "and" 連接兩個原形動詞。

9

At the top of the tree, the leaves grow out of the branches.

在樹的頂端，樹葉從樹枝上長出來。

解析 ▶ "at the top of ..." 的句型用來表示「在……的頂端」。例如 "at the top of the mountain"（在山頂）、"at the top of the building"（在建築物頂端）。

10

Trees are really beautiful and useful. That's what I know about trees.

樹木真的既美麗又有用。這就是我所知的樹木。

解析 ▶ 這裡的 "what" 等同於 "the things that"，舉例來說，"I don't believe what you told me." = "I don't believe the things that you told me."（我不相信你告訴我的事。）。

239

⟶ anchor	[ˋæŋkɚ]	v.	固定
⟶ branch	[bræntʃ]	n.	樹枝
⟶ chat	[tʃæt]	v.	聊天
⟶ climb	[klaɪm]	v.	攀爬
⟶ complex	[ˋkɑmplɛks]	adj.	複雜的
⟶ draw	[drɔ]	v.	畫
⟶ leaf	[lif]	n.	葉子（複數為 leaves）
⟶ physical	[ˋfɪzɪkl̩]	adj.	身體的
⟶ root	[rut]	n.	根
⟶ structure	[ˋstrʌktʃɚ]	n.	結構
⟶ sunlight	[ˋsʌnˌlaɪt]	n.	陽光
⟶ tree	[tri]	n.	樹
⟶ trunk	[trʌŋk]	n.	樹幹
⟶ useful	[ˋjusfəl]	adj.	有用的
⟶ wonderful	[ˋwʌndɚfəl]	adj.	美好的
⟶ absorbs ... from ...		phr.	從某處吸收某物
⟶ as well		phr.	也
⟶ consist of		phr.	組成
⟶ in fact		phr.	事實上
⟶ send ... to ...		phr.	將某物送往某處
⟶ spread out		phr.	延伸、展開
⟶ think of		phr.	想到

TEST
5

婚宴篇

解析篇

P
A
R
T
3

unit 2

英文作文

題目敘述

Last weekend, I had the most wonderful experience! I attended the wedding of two of my friends from college. I was really excited. Actually, I haven't attended wedding parties for a long time. Let me tell you what I saw at the party. First, ...

上個週末，我經歷了一段最棒的體驗！我參加了兩位大學朋友的婚禮。我真的很興奮。事實上，我已經很久不曾參加婚宴了。讓我告訴你我在宴會上看見了什麼。首先，……

參考範文

¹First, the guests arrived at the church. ²The ushers at the door helped them find seats. ³Next, the groom and his best man entered the church and stood in front. ⁴Then, a band began to play the "Wedding March," and the bridesmaids began to walk slowly down from the back toward the front. ⁵Eventually, the bride showed up and walked down the aisle by her father. ⁶Everyone at the church was very excited. ⁷At last, the priest said, "I pronounce you husband and wife," and the couple was now married. ⁸The last big event was the wedding reception. ⁹This was a big party after the wedding ceremony. ¹⁰Everybody at the party was very happy. ¹¹I believed that it was really a special experience for me to attend a wedding ceremony and party. ¹²I loved it so much that I won't forget it.

241

　　1 首先，賓客們來到了教堂。2 在門口的招待幫助他們找到位子。3 接下來，新郎與他的伴郎進入教堂並站在前方。4 之後，樂團開始演奏「結婚進行曲」，然後伴娘開始慢慢地從後頭走到前面來。5 終於，新娘出現了，她的父親伴隨她一起走過走道。6 在教堂裡的每個人都十分興奮。7 最後，牧師說：「我宣布你們是丈夫與妻子了」，然後這一對就結婚了。8 最後的大活動是喜宴。9 這是一個在結婚儀式後的大派對。10 每個參加這場派對的人都非常開心。11 我認為參加婚禮和婚宴對我來說真是一次特別的經驗。12 我非常喜愛這次的經驗，因而讓我難以忘懷。

範文句型解析 ◦○

1

First, the guests **arrived at** the church.
首先，賓客們來到了教堂。

解析 ▶ "First" 或 "First of all" 等表達方式常常會用來帶出故事開端所發生的事。特別要注意的是 "arrive in ＋大地點" 及 "arrive at ＋小地點" 的差異，小心不要搞混了。

2

The ushers at the door helped them find seats.
在門口的招待幫助他們找到位子。

解析 ▶ "help sb Vr ..." 的句型，意為「幫忙某人做某事」，help 之後要接原形動詞。

3

Next, the groom and his best man entered the church and stood in front.
接下來，新郎與他的伴郎進入教堂並站在前方。

解析 ▶ "Next, ..." 開頭的句子是前文 "First, ..." 的延續。

4

Then, a band began to play the "Wedding March," and the bridesmaids began to walk slowly down from the back toward the front.

之後，樂團開始演奏「結婚進行曲」，然後伴娘開始慢慢地從後頭走到前面來。

解析 ▶ 同樣延續前文的句型，形成 "First, ..."、"Next, ..."、"Then, ..." 的文章結構。

5

Eventually, the bride showed up and walked down the aisle by her father.

終於，新娘出現了，她的父親伴隨她一起走過走道。

解析 ▶ 繼續延續前文的句型，形成 "First, ..."、"Next, ..."、"Then, ..."、"Eventually, ..." 的文章結構。

6

Everyone at the church was very **excited**.

在教堂裡的每個人都十分興奮。

解析 ▶ "S ＋連綴動詞＋動詞過去分詞" 的句型用來表示感覺或情緒，例如 "I feel depressed. "（我覺得沮喪。）或 "He was surprised. "（他覺得驚訝。）。可以用在這種句型裡的動詞有：surprise, excite, depress, confuse, interest, annoy, satisfy, worry, tire 等。

7

At last, the priest said, "**I pronounce you husband and wife**," and the couple was now married.

最後，牧師說：「我宣布你們是丈夫與妻子了」，然後這一對就結婚了。

解析 ▶ 再繼續延續前文的句型，形成 "First, ..."、"Next, ..."、"Then, ..."、"Eventually, ..."、"At last, ..." 的文章結構。"S＋pronounce＋sb＋sth"，是典型命名類動詞的用法，例如 "She named her cat Mimi."（她把她的貓咪取名叫作咪咪。）。

243

The <u>last</u> big event was the wedding reception.
最後的大活動是喜宴。

8

解析 ▶ 前面文章中提及了許多重要活動，這裡提的是整場婚禮中的最後一個活動，所以加上 "last"，表示「最後的」。

This was a big party <u>after</u> the wedding ceremony.
這是一個在結婚儀式後的大派對。

9

解析 ▶ 介系詞 after 的意思是「在……以後」，介系詞之後必須要接名詞或動名詞，這裡接的是 "the wedding ceremony"，點出派對舉行的時間點。

Everybody <u>at the party</u> was very happy.
每個參加這場派對的人都非常開心。

10

解析 ▶ 介系詞片語 "at the party" 修飾前面的名詞 Everybody，說明名詞的範圍。例如 "all the birds in the trees"（所有在樹上的鳥）、"the girl in the forest"（在森林中的女孩）、"the stars in the sky"（在天空中的星辰）。

<u>I believed that</u> it was really a special experience for me to attend a wedding ceremony and party.
我認為參加婚禮和婚宴對我來說真是一次特別的經驗。

11

解析 ▶ 這裡使用 "I believe that ＋子句 ." 的句型來陳述個人的想法，例如 "I believe that one day I will succeed."（我相信我有一天會成功。）。

I loved it <u>so</u> much <u>that</u> I won't forget it.
我非常喜愛這次的經驗，因而讓我難以忘懷。

12

解析 ▶ "so ... that ..." 的句型意為「如此……以致於……」，這是寫作時經常會用到的重要句型，務必要記下來。

必備字彙 與片語整理

⇒ aisle	[aɪl]	n.	走道
⇒ band	[bænd]	n.	樂隊
⇒ bride	[braɪd]	n.	新娘
⇒ bridesmaid	[`braɪdz͵med]	n.	伴娘
⇒ ceremony	[`sɛrə͵monɪ]	n.	典禮；儀式
⇒ forget	[fɚ`gɛt]	v.	忘記
⇒ groom	[grum]	n.	新郎
⇒ pronounce	[prə`naʊns]	v.	宣布
⇒ seat	[sit]	n.	座位
⇒ usher	[`ʌʃɚ]	n.	接待員
⇒ arrive at		phr.	抵達
⇒ be married		phr.	結婚
⇒ in front		phr.	在前面
⇒ show up		phr.	出現
⇒ Wedding March		phr.	結婚進行曲
⇒ wedding reception		phr.	婚宴

PART3

unit 2

英文作文

245

題目敘述

上學期你參加了英文的密集訓練課程，而你真的很喜歡那位外籍老師 Mr. Charles Smith。於是你代表你的同學們寫一封信給他，表達你們對他課程的喜愛並邀請他一起出遊或共進一餐。

參考範文

Dear Mr. Smith,

1It was really a pleasure to be your student. 2I took your class last semester, and now I still remember everything we did during the class. 3It was an amazing and wonderful memory. 4I'd say you are the best teacher that I have ever known. 5It's been a long time since I left school and your class. 6My classmates and I miss you very much. 7If it is convenient for you, we would like to meet you again and invite you to have a dinner with us. 8What do you think about this? 9If it is OK with you, I will e-mail you or give you a call soon to tell you the exact time and place. 10I look forward to seeing you soon.

Sincerely yours,

Danny

親愛的史密斯先生：

1 能成為您的學生真是件快樂的事。**2** 我在上學期修了您的課，而現在我仍然記得我們在課堂上所做的一切。**3** 這真的是一段很棒很美好的回憶。**4** 我會說您是我認識的老師之中最棒的。**5** 我已經離開學校與您的課很長一段時間了。**6** 我的同學們和我十分想念您。**7** 如果您方便的話，我們想要再與您見面，邀您共進晚餐。**8** 您覺得怎麼樣呢？**9** 假如您可以的話，我會盡快寄電子郵件或打電話給您，告知正確的時間與地點。**10** 期待很快與您見面。

真誠地
丹尼

範文句型解析

1

It was really a pleasure to be your student.
能成為您的學生真是件快樂的事。

解析 ▶ 在 "It was really a pleasure to Vr ..." 的句型中，"it" 是虛主詞，後面的不定詞片語才是真正的主詞，也可以寫成 "To be your student was really a pleasure."。

2

I took your class last semester, and now I still remember everything we did during the class.
我在上學期修了您的課，而現在我仍然記得我們在課堂上所做的一切。

解析 ▶ 這裡利用對等連接詞 "and" 連接兩個句子，一個是過去式，一個是現在式。後面現在式的句子原本寫成 "now I still remember everything that we did during that class"，由 "that" 引導的形容詞子句修飾了前面的 "everything"。因為此處的 "that" 為受格，所以可以直接省略。

247

3

It was an **amazing** and **wonderful** memory.
這真的是一段很棒很美好的回憶。

解析 ▶ 對等連接詞 "and" 連接兩個形容詞 amazing 和 wonderful。

4

I'd say you are the best teacher that I have ever known.
我會說您是我認識的老師之中最棒的。

解析 ▶ 這裡用的是 "S＋beV＋the＋最高級形容詞＋N＋that＋S＋have＋ever＋Vpp ... " 的句型，例如 "It is the most beautiful song that I have ever heard."（這是我聽過的歌中最美的。）。

5

It's been a long time since I left school and your class.
我已經離開學校與您的課很長一段時間了。

解析 ▶ "It has been a long time since ＋過去式子句 ." 的句型表示「從發生某件事到現在已經過了很長一段時間了」。例如 "It has been a long time since I saw you in the campus."（從我上次在校園裡見到你到現在已經過了很長一段時間了。）。

6

My classmates and I miss you very much.
我的同學們和我十分想念您。

解析 ▶ "S＋V＋O＋very much." 的句型可以套用在各種情境之下。例如 "I hate traffic jam very much."（我非常討厭塞車。）、"She loves him very much."（她非常愛他。）。

7

If it is convenient for you, we would like to meet you again and invite you to have a dinner with us.
如果您方便的話，我們想要再與您見面，邀您共進晚餐。

解析 ▶ "If it is convenient for you, ＋子句 ."，意為「如果你方便的話，……」，在書信中經常用來委婉請求對方答應自己的要求。

8

What do you think about this?

您覺得怎麼樣呢？

解析 ▶ "What do you think about it?" 是用來詢問對方意願的慣用表達，在許多情境之下都可以使用。例如 "What do you think about going shopping with me?"（你覺得和我一起去購物怎麼樣？）

9

If it is OK with you, I will e-mail you or give you a call soon to tell you the exact time and place.

假如您可以的話，我會盡快寄電子郵件或打電話給您，告知正確的時間與地點。

解析 ▶ "If it is OK with you, ..." 是使用原形動詞的假設語氣，意思是「如果對你來說可以（接受）的話，……」。

10

I look forward to **seeing** you soon.

期待很快與您見面。

解析 ▶ 這裡用到的是 "look forward to＋V-ing" 的句型，本篇書信的目的是向對方提議見面吃晚餐，所以在信件的最後再次重申希望與對方見面。

 必備字彙 與片語整理

⇒ amazing	[ə`mezɪŋ]	adj.	令人吃驚的
⇒ exact	[ɪg`zækt]	adj.	確切的
⇒ invite	[ɪn`vaɪt]	v.	邀請
⇒ miss	[mɪs]	v.	想念
⇒ recently	[`risn̩tlɪ]	adv.	最近
⇒ semester	[sə`mɛstɚ]	n.	學期
⇒ wonderful	[`wʌndɚfəl]	adj.	美妙的
⇒ look forward to		phr.	期待
⇒ take class		phr.	修課

題目敘述

尼爾 ‧ 阿姆斯壯（Neil Armstrong）是家喻戶曉的傳奇人物，請描述他的著名事蹟，並論述你對他的豐功偉業有什麼看法。

參考範文

¹Many people believe Neil Armstrong is a great and hard-working person in the 20th century, and so do I. ²The first time I heard about him was in my elementary school days. ³In a class, our teacher told us he was the first man to walk on the moon. ⁴From that time on, I have had a deep impression of this legend. ⁵I think he is a very good role model for me. ⁶I always remember the speech in which he said, "That's one small step for man; one giant leap for mankind," to encourage myself to be as great as he is. ⁷I hope I will become an astronaut someday in the future. ⁸Therefore, I study very hard everyday to achieve my goal.

中文翻譯

　　1 許多人認為尼爾・阿姆斯壯是二十世紀中一位偉大而勤勉的人，我也這樣認為。2 我第一次聽到關於他的事情，是在我讀小學的時候。3 在某一堂課，我們老師告訴我們他是第一個在月球上行走的人。4 從那時開始，我就對這位傳奇人物有很深的印象。5 我認為他對我來說是一個非常好的模範。6 我始終記得他所說的那段話：「這是我的一小步，卻是人類的一大步」以激勵自己成為跟他一樣偉大的人。7 我希望未來有一天我會成為一個太空人。8 所以，為了達成我的目標，我每天都非常認真讀書。

範文句型解析

1

Many people believe Neil Armstrong is a great and hard-working person in the 20th century, **and so do I**.
許多人認為尼爾・阿姆斯壯是二十世紀中一位偉大而勤勉的人，我也這樣認為。

解析 ▶ "S + believe + (that) +子句 ." 是本句的主要句型，在句尾以 "so ＋助動詞＋主詞 " 的倒裝句型表明作者對前述觀點的贊同。如果前面是否定句意的句子，則可以使用 "neither ＋助動詞＋主詞 "，表示「某人也不是」。

2

The first time I heard about him was **in my elementary school days**.
我第一次聽到關於他的事情，是在我讀小學的時候。

解析 ▶ 本句的主要句型是 "The first time when +子句 "，以表示時間點的關係副詞 "when" 引導形容詞子句，修飾先行詞 "the first time"，而這裡的 when 可以省略。"in ... days" 表示「在……的時候」。

3

In a class, our teacher told us he was the first man to walk on the moon.

在某一堂課，我們老師告訴我們他是第一個在月球上行走的人。

解析 本句的主要句型是 "S＋tell＋O＋that＋子句."，表示「告訴某人某事」，引導子句的 that 可省略。

4

From that time on, I have had a deep impression of this legend.

從那時開始，我就對這位傳奇人物有很深的印象。

解析 "from that time on" 表示「從那時開始」，等同於 "from then on" 和 "since then"。表示某個動作或某個狀態從過去開始一直持續到現在，因此這裡會使用現在完成式。

5

I think he is a very good role model for me.

我認為他對我來說是一個非常好的模範。

解析 主要句型為 "S＋think＋子句."，表示「某人認為……」。

6

I always remember the speech **in which** he said, "That's one small step for man; one giant leap for mankind," **to encourage** myself to **be as great as he is**.

我始終記得他所說的那段話：「這是我的一小步，卻是人類的一大步」以激勵自己成為跟他一樣偉大的人。

解析 這個句子看起來有點長，但其實去掉其他的枝枝節節，最核心的句子就只有 "I always remember the speech."。"in which ..." 的部分是形容詞子句，修飾先行詞 "the speech"，子句當中還引用了阿姆斯壯的名言。不過，句子到這裡還沒有結束，接著還運用不定詞來補充說明前面核心句所想達成的目的，其中，動詞 "encourage" 之後接動詞必須是不定詞形態。最後還出現了 "beV＋as＋adj＋as＋S＋beV" 的同等比較句型。

I hope I **will** become an astronaut **someday in the future**.
我希望未來有一天我會成為一個太空人。

解析 ▶ 主要句型為 "S + hope (+ that) + 子句 ."，表示「某人希望……」。"someday in the future" 表示「未來有一天」，必須和未來式一起使用。

Therefore, I **study** very hard **everyday** to achieve my goal.
所以，為了達成我的目標，我每天都非常認真讀書。

解析 ▶ 頻率副詞 "everyday" 配合現在簡單式的句型，再用不定詞 "to achieve my goal" 表示讀書的目的。

 必備字彙 與片語整理

⇒ achieve	[əˋtʃiv]	v.	達成
⇒ believe	[bɪˋliv]	v.	相信
⇒ century	[ˋsɛntʃʊrɪ]	n.	世紀
⇒ encourage	[ɪnˋkɝɪdʒ]	v.	鼓勵
⇒ giant	[ˋdʒaɪənt]	adj.	巨大的
⇒ goal	[gol]	n.	目標
⇒ great	[gret]	adj.	偉大的
⇒ mankind	[mænˋkaɪnd]	n.	人類
⇒ moon	[mun]	n.	月亮
⇒ astronaut	[ˋæstrəˌnɔt]	n.	太空人
⇒ step	[stɛp]	n.	腳步
⇒ elementary school		phr.	國小
⇒ from that time on		phr.	從那時起
⇒ have a deep impression		phr.	有深刻的印象
⇒ someday in the future		phr.	未來有一天

P
A
R
T
3
unit 2
英文作文

253

題目敘述

Taiwan is a small island; however, there are more than 23-million people dwelling in this island. The consequence of population explosion is that too much land is used to build houses, shopping malls, supermarkets, movie theaters and highways, but not used to grow trees. It is impossible for those who live in a big city to be close to Nature. When doors are opened, they immediately face a lof of cars, polluted air, concrete buildings, and crowds ...

台灣是一座小島，然而，卻有超過兩千三百萬人居住在此。人口爆炸的後果就是太多的土地被拿來蓋房子、購物中心、超級市場、電影院和公路，而非用來種樹。住在大都市裡的人根本沒機會接近大自然。當門一打開，他們便直接面對很多汽車、污染的空氣、水泥建築物和人群……

參考範文

[1]In my opinion, the best way to raise our living standards is to improve both our living environment and spiritual environment. [2]In improving the living environment, we have to grow as many trees as we can. [3]As we know, trees are essential in purifying air. [4]Basically, they beautify our residential areas and provide fresh air. [5]Fresh and natural environments

make people healthy.

6Another way to improve our quality of lives is to change the way we think. 7Material is not the key to a good life. 8Good quality of life can also be achieved by looking on the bright side of things, and maintaining a good mood. 9To sum up, to maintain a good quality of life, we should plant trees and be optimistic.

中文翻譯

1依我之見，提升我們生活品質最好的方法，就是改善我們的居住環境和心靈環境。2在改善居住環境方面，我們必須盡可能多種樹。3如同我們所知道的，樹木在淨化空氣方面是不可或缺的。4基本上，樹可以美化我們的居住區域並提供清新空氣。5清新而自然的環境讓人健康。6另一個提升生活品質的方法是改變我們的思考方式。7物質不是美好生活的關鍵。8好的生活品質也能夠靠多看事物的光明面和保持好心情來達成。9總而言之，為了維持好的生活品質，我們應該種樹和保持樂觀。

範文句型解析

In my opinion, the best way **to** raise our living standards **is to** improve both our living environment and spiritual environment.

依我之見，提升我們生活品質最好的方法，就是改善我們的居住環境和心靈環境。

解析 ▶ 這裡用片語 "in my opinion" 開頭，表明自己的論點。後面句子的主要架構為 "to＋Vr＋beV＋to＋Vr"，前面的不定詞片語是主詞，後面的不定詞片語則是主詞補語。

2

In improving the living environment, we have to grow **as many trees as we can**.

在改善居住環境方面，我們必須盡可能多種樹。

解析 ▶ "in ..." 表示「在……方面」。 "as ... as one can " 和 "as ... as possible" 意義相近，都表示「盡量；盡可能」的意思。

3

As we know, trees are essential in purifying air.

如同我們所知道的，樹木在淨化空氣方面是不可或缺的。

解析 ▶ 用片語 "as we know" 開頭，表示後面要提出的觀點屬於大眾的共識。

4

Basically, they beautify our residential areas **and** provide fresh air.

基本上，樹可以美化我們的居住區域並提供清新空氣。

解析 ▶ 用 "basically" 開頭，帶出樹木最廣為人知的功能。這裡的對等連接詞 "and" 連接兩個現在式動詞。

5

Fresh and natural environments make people healthy.

清新而自然的環境讓人健康。

解析 ▶ "make＋O＋adj." 的句型，表示「讓某人成為某種狀態」。

6

Another way **to improve our quality** of live is to change the way we think.

另一個提升生活品質的方法是改變我們的思考方式。

解析 ▶ 以 "another way" 開頭，指出除了改善外在環境之外，還可以改變內在環境。不定詞 "to" 引導出表示目的的不定詞片語，修飾後面的句子。

Material is not **the key to** a good life.
物質不是美好生活的關鍵。

解析 ▶ "the key to ..." 這種慣用表達方式，意為「……的關鍵」，固定會使用介系詞 "to"。類似的用法還有："the answer to the question"（這個問題的答案）。

Good quality of life can also be achieved by **looking** on the bright side of things, and maintaining a good mood.
好的生活品質也能夠靠多看事物的光明面和保持好心情來達成。

解析 ▶ "by ..." 表示「以……方式」，這邊用這個句型來說明能夠達成良好生活品質的另一種方法。介系詞 "by" 的後面要加動名詞。

To sum up, to maintain a good quality of life, we should plant trees and be optimistic.
總而言之，為了維持好的生活品質，我們應該種樹和保持樂觀。

解析 ▶ 表目的的不定詞片語 "to ..." 表示「為了……」。文章結尾常會用 "To sum up" 來總結前面提出的論點，這裡帶出結論 "we should plant trees and be optimistic"。

必備字彙 與片語整理

⟹ achieve	[ə`tʃiv]	v.	達成
⟹ basically	[`besɪkḷɪ]	adv.	基本上
⟹ beautify	[`bjutə,faɪ]	v.	美化

essential	[ɪˋsɛnʃəl]	adj.	不可或缺的
fresh	[frɛʃ]	adj.	新鮮的；清新的
healthy	[ˋhɛlθɪ]	adj.	健康的
improve	[ɪmˋpruv]	v.	改進
maintain	[menˋten]	v.	維持
material	[məˋtɪrɪəl]	n.	物質
natural	[ˋnætʃərəl]	adj.	自然的
optimistic	[ˌɑptəˋmɪstɪk]	adj.	樂觀的
provide	[prəˋvaɪd]	v.	提供
purify	[ˋpjʊrəˌfaɪ]	v.	淨化
residential	[ˌrɛzəˋdɛnʃəl]	adj.	居住的
spiritual	[ˋspɪrɪtʃʊəl]	adj.	精神上的
as we know		phr.	如同我們所知道的
in a good mood		phr.	心情好
in my opinion		phr.	依我之見
living standard		phr.	生活品質，生活水準
quality of life		phr.	生活品質

題目敘述

　　妳考上了大學，離家到外地念書。為了不讓妳的母親擔心，妳寫了一封家書，告訴母親妳已平安到達學校，並且和母親分享學校生活的點滴。

參考範文

Dear Mother,

　[1]I am writing this letter to let you know that I have already arrived in the university safely. [2]I am fine here, so please do not worry about me. [3]I made a lot of friends in the dorm, and my classmates are all very friendly and courteous. [4]I think I can get along well with everybody here. [5]The food in the student restaurant is not too bad. [6]There are fried chicken, hamburgers, and wonderful Japanese food. [7]They are cheap and delicious. [8]I miss you and Father very much, and I look forward to hearing from you soon. [9]Please write to me as often as you can, and I won't suffer from homesickness so much.

Sincerely yours,
Helen

親愛的母親：

　　1 我寫這封信是為了讓您知道我已經安全抵達學校了。2 我在這裡很好，所以請不要擔心我。3 我在宿舍交了很多朋友，而且我的同班同學都很友善有禮。4 我想我可以和這裡的每個人相處愉快。5 學生餐廳的食物還不錯。6 有炸雞、漢堡和棒極了的日本料理。7 食物便宜又好吃。8 我很想念您與父親，期待盡快收到你們的消息。9 請盡量多寫信給我，這樣我就不會那麼想家了。

您真摯的
海倫

範文句型解析

1

I am writing this letter to let you know **that** I have already arrived in the university safely.

我寫這封信是為了讓您知道我已經安全抵達學校了。

解析 ▶ 表目的的不定詞片語 "to ..." 表示「為了……」。 其中，"that" 做為從屬連接詞，引導名詞子句 "I have already arrived in the university safely" 做為動詞 "know" 的受詞，這裡的 "that" 可以省略。

2

I am fine here, **so** please do not worry about me.

我在這裡很好，所以請不要擔心我。

解析 ▶ 表結果的從屬連接詞 "so" 表示「所以……」，連接有因果關係的兩個句子。

3

I made a lot of friends in the dorm, **and** my classmates are all very friendly and courteous.

我在宿舍交了很多朋友，而且我的同班同學都很友善有禮。

解析 ▶ 這裡用對等連接詞 "and" 連接兩個完整的簡單式句子，"and" 前面要加逗點。

I think I can get along well with everybody here.
我想我可以和這裡的每個人相處愉快。

解析 ▶ 主要句型為 "I think (＋that)＋子句." 其中的 "that" 是從屬連接詞，引導名詞子句做為動詞 "think" 的受詞，"that" 可以省略。

The food in the student restaurant is not too bad.
學生餐廳的食物還不錯。

解析 ▶ 主要句子為 "The food is not too bad."，是 "S＋V＋SC" 的基本句型。在主詞 "the food" 之後以介系詞片語 "in the student restaurant" 補充說明 the food 的所在地點。

There are fried chicken, hamburgers, **and** wonderful Japanese food.
有炸雞、漢堡和棒極了的日本料理。

解析 ▶ 這是以 "There ＋ beV ＋ ..." 句型為主的句子，並以 "A, B, and C" 的表達方式來列舉。

They are cheap and delicious.
食物便宜又好吃。

解析 ▶ 本句是 "S＋V＋SC" 的基本句型，主詞補語的部分使用了兩個形容詞，以對等連接詞 "and" 連接。

I miss **you and Father** very much, and I **look forward to** hearing from you soon.
我很想念您與父親，期待盡快收到你們的消息。

解析 ▶ 主要句型結構為 " 子句＋ , and ＋子句 ."。前面的子句以對等連接詞 "and" 連接兩個名詞做為動詞 "miss" 的受詞。後面的子句是 "S ＋ look forward to ＋ N/V-ing" 句型的句子。

Please write to me **as** often **as you can**, and I won't **suffer from homesickness** so much.

請盡量多寫信給我，這樣我就不會那麼想家了。

解析 ▶ 主要的句型結構為 " 子句＋ , and ＋子句 ." 。前面的子句使用了 "as ... as you can" 的句型，意為「盡量……，盡可能……」。後面子句中的 "suffer from homesickness" 意為「受思鄉之苦」，是常見的表達方式。

 必備字彙 與片語整理

⇒ cheap	[tʃip]	adj.	便宜的
⇒ courteous	[`kɝtjəs]	adj.	有禮貌的
⇒ delicious	[dɪ`lɪʃəs]	adj.	美味的
⇒ dorm	[dɔrm]	n.	宿舍
⇒ friendly	[`frɛndlɪ]	adj.	友善的
⇒ hamburger	[`hæmbɝgɚ]	n.	漢堡
⇒ homesickness	[`hom͵sɪknɪs]	n.	思鄉之情
⇒ restaurant	[`rɛstərənt]	n.	餐廳
⇒ worry	[`wɝɪ]	v.	擔憂
⇒ arrive in		phr.	抵達
⇒ fried chicken		phr.	炸雞
⇒ get along with		phr.	與……相處
⇒ look forward to		phr.	期待……
⇒ make friends		phr.	交朋友
⇒ suffer from		phr.	受……之苦

題目敘述

　　美國的第一任總統喬治‧華盛頓（George Washington）小時候發生了一個有趣的故事，這個故事家喻戶曉，常被用來說明「誠實」這個人格特質。

參考範文

　　¹When George Washington was a little boy, he was very smart and naughty. ²One day he was playing in the yard, and he came up with a very bad idea. ³He wanted to try his new hatchet, and he cut down his father's favorite cherry tree. ⁴Later on, his father found the chopped cherry tree and was very furious. ⁵He asked little George if he cut down the cherry tree. ⁶Little George told his father the truth, and his father forgave him because of his honesty. ⁷After George grew up, he became the first president of the United States. ⁸Now parents around the world love to tell the story to teach their children to be honest. ⁹Moreover, children all over the world love to tell the same story to ask their parents to be forgiving.

1 當喬治・華盛頓還是個小男孩時，他非常聰明而且調皮。2 有一天他在院子裡玩耍，想到了一個很糟糕的點子。3 他想要試試他的新斧頭，就砍倒了父親最心愛的櫻桃樹。4 後來，他的父親發現了被砍倒的櫻桃樹便勃然大怒。5 他問小喬治是不是他砍倒了櫻桃樹。6 小喬治告訴了父親事實，而父親因為他的誠實而原諒了他。7 在喬治長大之後，成為了美國的第一任總統。8 現在全世界的父母親都喜歡跟孩子說這個故事，教導他們的小孩要誠實。9 除此之外，全世界的孩子也同樣喜歡跟父母說這個故事，要求他們的父母要寬容。

範文句型解析 ●

1

When George Washington **was** a little boy, he **was** very smart and naughty.
當喬治・華盛頓還是個小男孩時，他非常聰明而且調皮。

解析 ▶ 主要句型結構為 "When＋從屬子句,＋主要子句."。描述過去發生的事實，使用過去簡單式。

2

One day he was playing in the yard, and he came up with a very bad idea.
有一天他在院子裡玩耍，想到了一個很糟糕的點子。

解析 ▶ 延續前文的時態，使用過去簡單式。時間副詞 "one day" 可以用於過去式和未來式，"some day" 通常只會用於未來式。

He wanted to try his new hatchet, **and** he cut down his father's favorite cherry tree.

他想要試試他的新斧頭,就砍倒了父親最心愛的櫻桃樹。

解析 ► 延續前文的時態,用對等連接詞 "and" 連接兩個過去簡單式的句子。

Later on, his father **found** the chopped cherry tree **and was** very furious.

後來,他的父親發現了被砍倒的櫻桃樹便勃然大怒。

解析 ► "later on" 是固定的慣用表達,意為「後來,之後」。繼續延續前文的時態,這裡用對等連接詞 "and" 連接兩個過去簡單式的句子。

He asked little George **if he cut down the cherry tree.**

他問小喬治是不是他砍倒了櫻桃樹。

解析 ► 這裡用到 "ask+sb+sth" 的句型,意為「問某人某事」。本句中 "sth" 的部分是由 "if" 所引導的名詞子句。

Little George **told his father the truth,** and his father forgave him **because of** his honesty.

小喬治告訴了父親事實,而父親因為他的誠實而原諒了他。

解析 ► 主要句型結構為 "子句+, and+子句."。前面的子句使用了 "tell+sb+sth" 的句型,"tell the truth" 意為「說實話」,因為真相只有一個,所以在 truth 的前面必須要加上定冠詞 the。後面的子句用了 "because of+N" 的句型,意為「因為……」。

7

After George grew up, he became the first president of the United States.

在喬治長大之後，成為了美國的第一任總統。

解析 ▶ 這裡使用從屬連接詞 "after" 引導表時間的副詞子句，修飾後面的主要子句。

8

Now parents around the world love **to** tell the story **to** teach their children **to** be honest.

現在全世界的父母親都喜歡跟孩子說這個故事，教導他們的小孩要誠實。

解析 ▶ 介系詞片語 "around the world" 修飾主詞 "parents"，句子的後半部用了三個不定詞 "to＋Vr"。第一個不定詞句型是 "love＋to＋Vr"，也可以使用 "love＋V-ing" 的方式來表達，意義相同。第二個不定詞的句型是用來表示目的。第三個不定詞是 "teach＋sb＋to＋Vr ..." 的句型，意為「教某人做某事」，例如 "teach me to write"（教我寫字）。

9

Moreover, children all over the world love **to** tell the same story **to** ask their parents **to** be forgiving.

除此之外，全世界的孩子也同樣喜歡跟父母說這個故事，要求他們的父母要寬容。

解析 ▶ 介系詞片語 "all over the world" 修飾主詞 "children"，句子後半部用了三個不定詞 "to＋Vr"。第一個不定詞句型是 "love＋to＋Vr"，可以替換成 "love＋V-ing"，意義相同。第二個不定詞的句型是用來表示目的。第三個不定詞是 "ask＋sb＋to＋Vr ..." 的句型，意為「要求某人做某事」，例如 "ask me to leave"（要求我離開）。

必備字彙 與片語整理

⇒ forgiving	[fə`gɪvɪŋ]	adj.	寬容的
⇒ furious	[`fjʊərɪəs]	adj.	狂怒的
⇒ hatchet	[`hætʃɪt]	n.	短柄小斧
⇒ honest	[`ɑnɪst]	adj.	誠實的
⇒ naughty	[`nɔtɪ]	adj.	調皮的
⇒ try	[traɪ]	v.	試圖；嘗試
⇒ yard	[jard]	n.	院子
⇒ all over the world		phr.	全世界的
⇒ around the world		phr.	全世界的
⇒ came up with		phr.	想出
⇒ cherry tree		phr.	櫻桃樹
⇒ cut down		phr.	砍倒
⇒ grow up		phr.	長大
⇒ later on		phr.	後來，之後
⇒ one day		phr.	有一天
⇒ tell the truth		phr.	說實話
⇒ the United States		phr.	美國

題目敘述

Friends are very important in our lives. Whether we are children or adults, we need friends, and they enrich our knowledge and mind. When we get into troubles, friends always stay with us, help us, and encourage us to look at the bright side of life. When we have a doubt, we feel free to discuss it with them, and they try their best to give us some suggestions...

朋友在我們生活中是非常重要的。不論我們是孩子還是大人，都需要朋友，而他們會豐富我們的知識和心靈。當我們遇到麻煩的時候，朋友總是待在我們身邊，幫助我們、鼓勵我們往好的方面想。當我們困惑時，我們可以盡情地與他們討論，他們也會盡可能提供我們一些建議……

參考範文

¹Moreover, friends share our happiness and joy. ²They are happy for us when we achieve our goals. ³Friendship does not consist in forcing two people to stay together twenty-four hours a day. ⁴Friendship means that two people protect, help, and love each other.

⁵However, as we all know, he who keeps company with the wolf will learn to howl. ⁶When we make

friends, we should realize their influence upon us. ⁷If we don't choose friends carefully, we may start to smoke, be addicted to drugs, or become violent. ⁸Bad habits are easy to fall into but not so easy to fall out of. ⁹Therefore, before we enjoy friendship, we have to know what kinds of friends are good for us.

中文翻譯

1 此外，朋友和我們分享快樂和喜悅。2 當我們達成目標時，他們為我們感到欣喜。3 友誼不在於強迫兩個人一天二十四小時待在一塊。4 友誼指的是兩個人彼此保護、扶持、相愛。

5 然而，大家都知道，近朱者赤，近墨者黑。6 交朋友時，我們應該要體認到朋友對我們的影響。7 如果我們不慎選朋友，我們可能會開始抽菸、吸毒，或是變得暴力。8 養成壞習慣很容易，要戒掉卻很難。9 因此，在我們享受友誼之前，我們必須曉得什麼樣的朋友對我們有益。

範文句型解析

1

Moreover, friends share our happiness and joy.
此外，朋友和我們分享快樂和喜悅。

解析 ▶ share 常見的另一表達句型是 "share＋sth＋with＋sb"，意為「和某人分享某事物」，在寫作測驗中經常會用到這個句型，請一併記下來。

2

They are happy for us when we achieve our goals.
當我們達成目標時，他們為我們感到欣喜。

解析 ▶ "beV＋happy＋for＋sb" 意為「為某人感到高興」。

3

Friendship does not consist in forcing two people to stay together twenty-four hours a day.

友誼不在於強迫兩個人一天二十四小時待在一塊。

解析 ▶ "A＋consists in＋B" 意為「A（的意義或基本概念）在於 B」。在這個句子裡的 B 是由動名詞片語 "forcing two people to stay together twenty-four hours a day" 所構成。

4

Friendship means that two people **protect, help, and love** each other.

友誼指的是兩個人彼此保護、扶持、相愛。

解析 ▶ 主要句型是 "Friendship means＋that＋子句."，以 "that＋子句" 來說明友誼的定義。子句中一連用了三個動詞，採用的是 "A, B, and C" 的句型。

5

However, **as we all know**, he who keeps company with the wolf will learn to howl.

然而，大家都知道，近朱者赤，近墨者黑。

解析 ▶ 在這之前寫的都是交朋友的正面影響，從這裡開始轉換語氣，提出交朋友可能會有的負面影響，所以使用轉折語 "however" 開頭。接著用 "as we all know" 來提出一個眾所皆知的事實或真理，後面則使用切題的俗語「近朱者赤，近墨者黑」表明接下來的論點，這樣的處理方式，可以讓文章雖有語氣上的轉折，卻不會顯得太過突兀。

6

When we make friends, we should realize their **influence upon** us.

交朋友時，我們應該要體認到朋友對我們的影響。

解析 ▶ "When ＋從屬子句，＋主要子句." 是以副詞子句表示時間的表達方法，這裡在主要子句中使用了 "influence ＋ upon ＋ sb" 的句型，意思是「對某人造成影響」，這裡的 upon 也可以改用 on。

7

If we don't choose friends carefully, we may **start** to smoke, **be** addicted to drugs, **or become** violent.

如果我們不慎選朋友，我們可能會開始抽菸、吸毒，或是變得暴力。

解析 ▶ 主要的句型是 "If ＋條件子句 , ＋主要子句 ."，這裡的條件子句也可以寫成 "we don't choose the friends (who) we make"，其中 "(who) we make" 是形容詞子句，修飾名詞 "friends"。主要子句在助動詞 "may" 之後一連放了三個原形動詞，使用的是 "A, B, and C" 的句型。

8

Bad habits are **easy to fall into** but **not so easy to fall out of**.

養成壞習慣很容易，要戒掉卻很難。

解析 ▶ 這裡以對等連接詞 "but" 連接前後兩個對比的情況 "easy to fall into" 和 "not so easy to fall out of"。

9

Therefore, **before** we enjoy friendship, **we have to know what kinds of friends are good for us**.

因此，在我們享受友誼之前，我們必須曉得什麼樣的朋友對我們有益。

解析 ▶ 這裡利用 "Therefore" 來總結全文論點，清楚點出具體結論。主要使用的句型是 "before ＋從屬子句 , ＋主要子句 "。主要子句是 "we have to know what kinds of friends are good for us"，在這個子句之中，是以由 what 所引導的名詞子句，來當作動詞 know 的受詞。

271

⇒ addict	[əˋdɪkt]	v.	使成癮
⇒ adult	[əˋdʌlt]	n.	成人
⇒ carefully	[ˋkɛrfəlɪ]	adv.	小心地
⇒ encourage	[ɪnˋkɝɪdʒ]	v.	鼓勵
⇒ enrich	[ɪnˋrɪtʃ]	v.	豐富
⇒ friend	[frɛnd]	n.	朋友
⇒ friendship	[ˋfrɛndʃɪp]	n.	友誼
⇒ habit	[ˋhæbɪt]	n.	習慣
⇒ howl	[haʊl]	v.	吼叫
⇒ influence	[ˋɪnflʊəns]	n.	影響
⇒ realize	[ˋrɪəˏlaɪz]	v.	體認
⇒ share	[ʃɛr]	v.	分享
⇒ smoke	[smok]	v.	抽菸
⇒ trouble	[ˋtrʌbḷ]	n.	麻煩
⇒ violent	[ˋvaɪələnt]	adj.	暴力的
⇒ wolf	[wʊlf]	n.	狼
⇒ consist in		phr.	在於
⇒ fall into		phr.	養成
⇒ fall out of		phr.	戒除
⇒ make friends		phr.	交朋友

題目敘述 ▸●

　　有一天，你的小狗出門玩耍，不知為何竟然把鄰居家的小孩子咬傷了。請寫一封道歉信向對方的家長（Mr. and Mrs. Smith）道歉。

參考範文 ▸●

Dear Mr. and Mrs. Smith,

　¹I am terribly sorry that my dog bit your daughter. ²Usually he is a mild pet. ³I have no idea why he became so wild and attacked an innocent little girl. ⁴Please forgive my carelessness, and I owe you an apology for my dog's horrible behavior. ⁵I will pay all the medical expenses, and I will keep my dog on a leash. ⁶This is what I have to do, though it seems to be a little too late. ⁷Do you mind if I visit your daughter? ⁸If you don't mind, please tell me which hospital she is in. ⁹I would like to say sorry to her in person. ¹⁰If there is anything I can do for her, please tell me. ¹¹I am willing to do anything for her.

Truly yours,
Clark

中文翻譯

親愛的史密斯先生與太太：

　　1 我非常抱歉我的狗咬傷了你們的女兒。2 他平時是一隻很溫和的寵物。3 我不知道他為什麼會變得這麼不受控制，還攻擊了一個無辜的小女孩。4 請原諒我的疏失，我為我的狗的可怕行為向你們道歉。5 我會付所有的醫藥費，也會把狗拴好。6 這是我必須要做的，雖然似乎有點太遲了。7 你們介意我去探望你們的女兒嗎？8 如果不介意，請告訴我她在哪一家醫院。9 我想親自跟她道歉。10 如果有任何我能為她做的事，請告訴我。11 我很樂意為她做任何事。

真誠地
克拉克

範文句型解析

1

I am terribly sorry that my dog bit your daughter.
我非常抱歉我的狗咬傷了你們的女兒。

解析 ▶ 這裡使用 "I am sorry that ＋子句 ." 的句型，意為「我為某件事感到抱歉」，特別以副詞 "terribly" 來強調感到抱歉的程度。

2

Usually he is a mild pet.
他平時是一隻很溫和的寵物。

解析 ▶ 主要的句型結構為 "S＋beV＋SC."，並以副詞 Usually（通常地；慣常地）來修飾整個句子，指出小狗「平時」是很溫和的寵物，帶出下文的「我不知道他為什麼會變得這麼不受控制……」。

3

I have no idea **why** he became so wild and attacked an innocent little girl.

我不知道他為什麼會變得這麼不受控制，還攻擊了一個無辜的小女孩。

解析 ▶ 主要句型為 "I have no idea ＋以疑問詞引導的間接問句 ."，意為「我不知道……」。在這個句型中，以疑問詞引導的間接問句其實就是名詞子句，代替一般名詞做為動詞的受詞。

4

Please forgive my carelessness, **and** I owe you an apology for my dog's horrible behavior.

請原諒我的疏失，我為我的狗的可怕行為向你們道歉。

解析 ▶ 以對等連接詞 "and" 連接兩個完整的句子。"I owe you an apology for ..." 意為「我為……向你道歉」。

5

I will pay all the medical expenses, and I will keep my dog on a leash.

我會付所有的醫藥費，也會把狗拴好。

解析 ▶ 以對等連接詞 "and" 連接兩個未來式的句子，也可以將重複的主詞和助動詞省略，把句子簡化為 "I will pay all the medical expenses and keep my dog on a leash."。

6

This is what I have to do, **though** it seems to be a little too late.

這是我必須要做的，雖然似乎有點太遲了。

解析 ▶ "what I have to do" = "the things that I have to do"。這裡用 "though" 引導表示讓步的副詞子句，修飾前面的主要子句。"though" 的句型也可以用 "but" 來改寫，本句即可寫成 "It seems to be a little too late, but this is what I have to do."。

7

Do you mind if I visit your daughter?
你們介意我去探望你們的女兒嗎？

解析 "Do you mind if ＋子句 ?" 和 "Do you mind ＋ N/Ving?" 句型，意為「你介不介意……」，是委婉詢問對方意願的表達方式。例如 "Do you mind if I open the window?" 和 "Do you mind me opening the window?"（你介意我把窗戶打開嗎？）。

8

If you don't mind, please tell me **which hospital she is in**.
如果不介意，請告訴我她在哪一家醫院。

解析 "If you dont mind, ＋主要子句." 是「如果你不介意，……」的意思，延續前文的詢問內容，主要子句的部分以委婉口吻提出請求。"which hospital she is in" 是間接問句，原句是 "Which hospital is she in?"，在這裡做為 "tell" 的受詞。

9

I would like to say sorry to her in person.
我想親自跟她道歉。

解析 "I would like to ＋ Vr ..." 也是語氣較為委婉的表達方式，比起 "I want to ＋ Vr ..." 的句型，這種委婉的口吻更適合用在道歉信裡。

10

If there is anything I can do for her, please tell me.
如果有任何我能為她做的事，請告訴我。

解析 ▶ "If there is anything I can do, ..." 是委婉表示願意為對方做事的表達方式，商業書信中經常使用類似的句型 "If there is anything I can be a help, ..."（如果有我幫得上忙的地方，……）來詢問客戶需求。

11

I am willing to do anything for her.
我很樂意為她做任何事。

解析 ▶ "I am willing to ＋ Vr ..." 是積極表示自己意願的句型。例如 "She is willing to come with us."（她願意和我們一起去。）。

 必備字彙 與片語整理

P
A
R
T
3

unit 2

英
文
作
文

⟶ attack	[əˋtæk]	v.	攻擊
⟶ behavior	[bɪˋhevjɚ]	n.	行為
⟶ bite	[baɪt]	v.	咬
⟶ carelessness	[ˋkɛrlɪsnɪs]	n.	疏失
⟶ daughter	[ˋdɔtɚ]	n.	女兒
⟶ forgive	[fəˋgɪv]	v.	原諒
⟶ horrible	[ˋhɔrəbḷ]	adj.	可怕的；令人毛骨悚然的
⟶ hospital	[ˋhɑspɪtḷ]	n.	醫院
⟶ innocent	[ˋɪnəsn̩t]	adj.	無辜的
⟶ leash	[liʃ]	n.	（拴狗等的）鏈繩
⟶ mild	[maɪld]	adj.	溫和的
⟶ sorry	[ˋsɑrɪ]	adj.	抱歉的
⟶ terribly	[ˋtɛrəbḷɪ]	adv.	非常地
⟶ usually	[ˋjuʒʊəlɪ]	adv.	通常地；慣常地
⟶ visit	[ˋvɪzɪt]	v.	探望
⟶ wild	[waɪld]	adj.	粗野的；不受控制的
⟶ willing	[ˋwɪlɪŋ]	adj.	願意的，樂意的
⟶ have no idea		phr.	不曉得
⟶ in person		phr.	親自
⟶ medical expenses		phr.	醫藥費
⟶ owe sb an apology for sth		phr.	為某事向某人道歉

題目敘述

保羅把車子借給凱文，結果隔天卻收到一封由凱文寫來的道歉信。請試著描述他們之間可能發生了什麼事，以及整件事情發生的經過。

參考範文

¹Kevin had a date with his girlfriend last Friday. ²He drove the car he borrowed from Paul to pick up his girlfriend at seven o'clock in the evening. ³After dinner, Kevin and his girlfriend decided to go for a drive along the eastern coast. ⁴The scenery along the coast was so beautiful that Kevin paid little attention to his driving. ⁵When he tried taking a sudden turn to the right, they hit a rock. ⁶Although Kevin and his girlfriend were both unhurt, Paul's car was seriously damaged. ⁷When Kevin drove the damaged car back to Taipei, it was almost dawn. ⁸Kevin parked it in front of Paul's house and left a message on it. ⁹In the early morning, Paul found his car badly damaged and he felt really heartbroken.

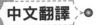

中文翻譯

　　1 上星期五凱文和女朋友去約會。**2** 他開著向保羅借來的車子在晚上七點去接女友。**3** 晚飯過後，凱文和女友決定要沿著東海岸兜風。**4** 沿岸的風景美得讓凱文開車不太專心。**5** 當他試著向右急轉彎時，撞上了一塊岩石。**6** 雖然凱文和女友兩人都沒受傷，保羅的車卻壞得很嚴重。**7** 當凱文把那一輛壞掉的車開回台北的時候，天都快要亮了。**8** 凱文把車停在保羅家前面，然後在車上留了言。**9** 一大清早，保羅就發現他的車子壞得很嚴重，他真的覺得很心碎。

範文句型解析

1

Kevin **had a date with** his girlfriend last Friday.
上星期五凱文和女朋友去約會。

解析 ▶ 因為敘述的內容是過去所發生的事實，所以整篇文章都使用過去簡單式。"have a date with sb" 意為「與某人約會；和某人有約」。

2

He drove the car **he borrowed from Paul** to pick up his girl-friend **at seven o'clock in the evening**.
他開著向保羅借來的車子在晚上七點去接女友。

解析 ▶ 這裡的 "(which) he borrowed from Paul" 是形容詞子句，修飾先行詞 "the car"。時間副詞 "at seven o'clock in the evening" 中的時間單位是從小 (o'clock) 到大 (evening) 排列。

PART 3 / unit 2 英文作文

3

After dinner, Kevin and his girlfriend decided to **go for a drive** along the eastern coast.

晚飯過後，凱文和女友決定要沿著東海岸兜風。

解析 "decide＋to＋Vr ..." 意為「決定要做某事」。"go for a drive" 則是「兜風」的意思。

4

The scenery along the coast was so beautiful that Kevin **paid little attention to** his driving.

沿岸的風景美得讓凱文開車不太專心。

解析 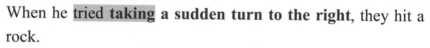 "so ... that ..." 的句型表示「太……以致於……」的意思。"pay attention to＋N" 的句型表示「專心在……」，"pay little attention to＋N" 的句型則是「不太專心在……」，這些句型都是寫作時經常會用到的表達方式，請務必特別留意。

5

When he tried **taking a sudden turn to the right**, they hit a rock.

當他試著向右急轉彎時，撞上了一塊岩石。

解析 "try＋V-ing" 和 "try to＋Vr" 在語意上有一點差別，前者是「試著，嘗試」，後者則是「努力要；試圖要」，兩者相較之下，前者較不認真，帶點漫不經心、隨意的感覺，所以在這裡使用 "try＋V-ing" 較為合適。"take a turn" 是「轉彎」，"take a sudden turn" 則是「急轉彎」，"turn to the right" 是「向右轉」，"turn to the left" 則是「向左轉」。

6

Although Kevin and his girlfriend were both unhurt, Paul's car **was seriously damaged**.

雖然凱文和女友兩人都沒受傷，保羅的車卻壞得很嚴重。

解析 ▶ "although" 引導表示讓步的副詞子句，修飾後面的主要子句。主要子句是被動語態，特別要注意的是，因為整篇文章都是過去式，所以這裡的被動語態也是用過去簡單式的 "was/were + Vpp"，並且用了副詞 "seriously" 強調被破壞的程度。

7

When Kevin drove the damaged car **back** to Taipei, it was almost dawn.

當凱文把那一輛壞掉的車開回台北的時候，天都快要亮了。

解析 ▶ 由 "when" 引導的時間副詞子句修飾後面的主要子句。副詞 "back" 常用來表示「回到」的意思，例如 "I went to the park." 的意思是「我去了那個公園。」而 "I went back to the park." 則是「我回去了那個公園。」

8

Kevin **parked** it in front of Paul's house and **left** a message on it.

凱文把車停在保羅家前面，然後在車上留了言。

解析 ▶ 這裡用 "and" 連接兩個過去簡單式動詞 "parked" 和 "left"。

9

In the early morning, Paul found his car badly **damaged** and he **felt really heartbroken**.

一大清早，保羅就發現他的車子壞得很嚴重，他真的覺得很心碎。

解析 ▶ 這裡用了兩個重要的句型，第一個是 "find＋sth＋adj"，表示「發現某人事物在某狀態」，在這裡將過去分詞 damaged 當成形容詞。第二個句型是 "S＋feel＋adj" 意為「某人覺得……」，這裡也是利用過去分詞來做為形容詞。

⇒ almost	[`ɔl‚most]	adv.	幾乎，快要
⇒ back	[bæk]	adv.	回到（原處）
⇒ damage	[`dæmɪdʒ]	v.	損壞
⇒ date	[det]	n.	約會
⇒ girlfriend	[`gɝl‚frɛnd]	n.	女朋友
⇒ heartbroken	[`hɑrt‚brokən]	adj.	心碎的
⇒ park	[pɑrk]	v.	停泊
⇒ scenery	[`sinərɪ]	n.	景色
⇒ decide to		phr.	決定……
⇒ go for a drive		phr.	兜風
⇒ hit on		phr.	撞上……
⇒ in front of		phr.	在……的前面
⇒ leave a massage		phr.	留言
⇒ pay attention to		phr.	專心在……
⇒ pick up		phr.	用汽車接送某人
⇒ so ... that ...		phr.	太……以致於……
⇒ take a sudden turn		phr.	急轉彎
⇒ to the right		phr.	向右
⇒ try＋V-ing		phr.	試著，嘗試

題目敘述

I have a cat whose name is Toro. His favorite food is canned tuna, and his favorite toys are little paper balls. Everyday when I go back to my house in the evening, he always sits in front of the door to welcome me home. However, one day when I came back home at the usual time, something out of the ordinary happened. I did not see him sitting in front of the door ...

我有一隻貓，他的名字叫做 Toro。他最愛的食物是鮪魚罐頭，最愛的玩具是小紙球。每天傍晚我回家時，他總是會坐在門前歡迎我回家。但是，有一天當我在平常時間回到家時，發生了一件不尋常的事。我沒看見他坐在門前……

參考範文

¹I wondered why he was not where he used to be. ²I felt uneasy and searched for my pet everywhere in the house. ³I searched all the places where he usually loved to stay, but in vain. ⁴I was terrified and was about to cry. ⁵I stood helplessly and called his name as loudly as I could. ⁶Then, I heard Toro meowing in the distance. ⁷I paid full attention to the sound to find out where it came from and found that he was stuck in the

ceiling. [8]I wondered how he could slip into the space. [9]What I could do at that very moment was to take apart the boards of the ceiling to rescue my pet. [10]He looked extremely hungry and tired, so I fed him his favorite canned tuna. [11]Afterward, I sealed all the cracks in the ceiling to make sure that he would never be trapped again.

中文翻譯

[1]我很納悶他為什麼不在他常待的地方。[2]我感到不安,在屋子裡到處找我的寵物。[3]我找遍所有他平時喜歡待的地方,卻徒勞無功。[4]我嚇壞了,幾乎快哭了出來。[5]我無助地站著,盡全力大聲呼喚他的名字。[6]然後,我聽到了 Toro 在遠處喵喵叫。[7]我聚精會神地聽著叫聲以找出聲音的來源,結果發現他卡在了天花板裡面。[8]我想不透他是怎麼溜進那個地方的。[9]在那一刻我所能做的就是拆開天花板把我的寵物救出來。[10]他看起來很餓很累,所以我餵他吃他最愛的鮪魚罐頭。[11]之後,我把天花板所有的縫隙都封死了,確保他不會再被困住。

範文句型解析

I wondered why he was not where he used to be.
我很納悶他為什麼不在他常待的地方。

解析 主要句型為 "I wonder +以疑問詞引導的間接問句 .",意為「我想不通……」、「我很納悶……」。在這個句型中,以疑問詞引導的間接問句是名詞子句,代替一般名詞做為接受動作的受詞。

2

I felt uneasy and searched for my pet everywhere in the house.

我感到不安，在屋子裡到處找我的寵物。

解析 ▶ "everywhere ＋地點"，表示「某個地點裡的每一處」。例如 "everywhere in the forest"（在森林裡的每一處）。

3

I searched all the places where he usually loved to stay, **but in vain**.

我找遍所有他平時喜歡待的地方，卻徒勞無功。

解析 ▶ "where" 引導形容詞子句修飾先行詞 "the places"。"..., but in vain." 是寫作時常用的表達方式，表示「……，但徒勞無功。」

4

I was terrified and **was about to** cry.

我嚇壞了，幾乎快哭了出來。

解析 ▶ 這裡用對等連接詞 "and" 連接兩個過去式動詞。"be about to ＋Vr" 的句型，表示「幾乎要……」。

5

I stood helplessly and called his name **as loudly as I could**.

我無助地站著，盡全力大聲呼喚他的名字。

解析 ▶ 這裡用對等連接詞 "and" 連接兩個過去式動詞。"as ... as I can" 的表達方式，也可以改用 "as ... as possible" 表示「盡量」、「盡己所能」。因為這整篇文章都是在描述過去發生的事情，所以會把助動詞改成過去式的 "could"。

6

Then, I **heard** Toro **meowing** in the distance.

然後，我聽到了 Toro 在遠處喵喵叫。

解析 ▶ 以時間副詞 "Then, ..." 開頭，表示「然後，……」。感官動詞 "hear" 後面要接原形動詞或動名詞。

285

I paid full attention to the sound to find out where it came from and found **that he was stuck in the ceiling**.

我聚精會神地聽著叫聲以找出聲音的來源，結果發現他卡在了天花板裡面。

解析 ▶ 這裡用對等連接詞 "and" 連接前後兩個過去式動詞 "paid" 和 "found"。其中，"(the place) where it came from" 是省略了先行詞 the place 的名詞子句，做為 "find out" 的受詞；另外，從屬連接詞 "that" 引導的名詞子句 "that he was standing on the ceiling"，是動詞 "found" 的受詞。

I wondered how he could slip into the space.

我想不透他是怎麼溜進那個地方的。

解析 ▶ 主要句型為 "I wonder＋以疑問詞引導的間接問句 ."，意為「我想不透……」。在這個句型中，以疑問詞引導的間接問句是名詞子句，代替一般名詞做為接受動作的受詞。

What I could do at that very moment was to take apart the boards of the ceiling to rescue my pet.

在那一刻我所能做的就是拆開天花板把我的寵物救出來。

解析 ▶ 主要的句型結構為 "What＋子句＋beV＋to＋Vr ..."，意為「……就是……」，例如 "What I want to do is to travel around the world." （我想做的事就是環遊世界。）。不過要注意，因為這篇文章描述的是在過去發生的事，所以 beV 也要改成過去式的 "was"。

He looked extremely hungry and tired, **so** I fed him his favorite canned tuna.

他看起來很餓很累，所以我餵他吃他最愛的鮪魚罐頭。

解析 ▶ 從屬連接詞 "so" 連接後面表示結果的子句，修飾前面的主要子句。其中，主要子句使用了 "S＋look＋adj" 的句型，並以對等連接詞 "and" 連接兩個形容詞 hungry 和 tired，做為主詞補語。從屬子句中使用了 "feed＋sb＋sth" 的句型，意為「餵某人吃某物」。

Afterward, I sealed all the cracks in the ceiling to make sure **that he would never be trapped again**.

之後，我把天花板所有的縫隙都封死了，確保他不會再被困住。

解析 副詞 "afterward" 是美式用法，"afterwards" 則是英式用法。從屬連接詞 "that" 引導的名詞子句 "that he would never be trapped again"，在這裡是動作 "make sure" 的受詞。

 必備字彙 與片語整理

afterward	[ˋæftɚwɚd]	adv.	之後，後來
ceiling	[ˋsilɪŋ]	n.	天花板
crack	[kræk]	n.	裂縫
everywhere	[ˋɛvrɪ͵hwɛr]	adv.	到處
favorite	[ˋfevərɪt]	adj.	最愛的
feed	[fid]	v.	餵食
helplessly	[ˋhɛlplɪslɪ]	adv.	無助地
meow	[mɪˋaʊ]	v.	喵喵叫
rescue	[ˋrɛskju]	v.	拯救
trap	[træp]	v.	使陷入困境
uneasy	[ʌnˋizɪ]	adj.	不安的
usual	[ˋjuʒʊəl]	adj.	慣常的；平常的
welcome	[ˋwɛlkəm]	v.	歡迎
be about to		phr.	幾乎要……
canned tuna		phr.	鮪魚罐頭

⇒ in front of	phr.	在……的前面
⇒ in vain	phr.	徒勞無功
⇒ pay attention to	phr.	專注在……
⇒ slip into	phr.	溜進……
⇒ stuck in	phr.	卡在……裡面
⇒ take apart	phr.	拆開
⇒ used to	phr.	過去經常……

題目敘述

　　妳和男朋友約好了下個禮拜要去花蓮旅行，但是住在日本的表姊卻意外來訪，並且表示要小住一段時間，所以原定的旅行計畫必須要取消了，請寫一封信向男朋友說明事由。

參考範文

Dear William,

　　1I am sorry but I have to tell you bad news. **2**I am afraid that our plan to travel to Hualien next week has to be cancelled. **3**My cousin, who lives in Japan, came to visit me unexpectedly yesterday, and she said that she will stay in Taiwan for two weeks. **4**I haven't seen her since her family moved to Japan ten years ago. **5**She missed the scenery in Taiwan very much and asked me to accompany her to do some sightseeing in the following two weeks. **6**I don't know when she will visit Taiwan next time. **7**Maybe it will be another ten years for me to wait. **8**Do you mind if I suggest that our plan be cancelled? **9**We can still plan another trip to Hualien or anywhere you want to go. **10**Thank you for understanding.

Lovingly yours,
Ariel

中文翻譯

親愛的威廉：

1 我很抱歉有壞消息要告訴你。**2** 我們下個禮拜到花蓮旅行的計畫恐怕要取消了。**3** 我住在日本的表姊昨天意外地來找我，她說她會在台灣待兩個禮拜。**4** 自從十年前她們一家搬到日本後，我就沒有再見過她了。**5** 她很想念台灣的景色，所以請我在接下來的兩個禮拜之間陪她去觀光。**6** 我不知道她下一次來台灣會是什麼時候。**7** 也許又要再等十年。**8** 你介意我提議將計畫取消嗎？**9** 我們還是可以計畫另一次旅行，去花蓮或任何你想去的地方。**10** 謝謝你的諒解。

愛你的
愛莉兒

範文句型解析

1
I am sorry but I have to tell you bad news.
我很抱歉有壞消息要告訴你。

解析 ► "I am sorry but＋子句 ." 的句型，意為「我很抱歉（可是）……」。

2
I am afraid that our plan to travel to Hualien next week has to be cancelled.
我們下個禮拜到花蓮旅行的計畫恐怕要取消了。

解析 ► "I am afraid＋that＋子句 ." 的句型表達的是「恐怕……」。這樣的句型常常被用來委婉告知不好的消息。

3

My cousin, who lives in Japan, came to visit me unexpectedly yesterday, and she said that she will stay in Taiwan for two weeks.

我住在日本的表姊昨天意外地來找我，她說她會在台灣待兩個禮拜。

解析 ▶ 整個句子的主幹是 "My cousin came to visit me."，本句句尾加上了情狀副詞 "unexpectedly" 和時間副詞 "yesterday" 來補充說明相關的更多資訊，並以同位語的形容詞子句 "who lives in Japan" 修飾主詞 "My cousin"。

4

I haven't seen her since her family moved to Japan ten years ago.

自從十年前她們一家搬到日本後，我就沒有再見過她了。

解析 ▶ 主要句型是 " 完成式句子＋ since ＋過去式句子 ."。

5

She missed the scenery in Taiwan very much and asked me to accompany her to do some sightseeing **in the following two weeks**.

她很想念台灣的景色，所以請我在接下來的兩個禮拜之間陪她去觀光。

解析 ▶ 對等連接詞 "and" 連接兩個過去簡單式動詞 "missed" 和 "asked"。"in ＋一段時間 " 表示「在某段時間之內」的意思，不過也有可能會是「在某段時間之後」的意思，但這時會和未來式一起使用，例如 "She will come back in a few days."（幾天後她會回來。）。

6

I don't know when she will visit Taiwan next time.

我不知道她下一次來台灣會是什麼時候 。

解析 ▶ 這裡將疑問句 "When will she visit Taiwan next time?" 改為名詞子句 "when she will visit Taiwan next time" 做為動詞 "know" 的受詞。

7

Maybe it will be another ten years for me to wait.
也許又要再等十年。

解析 ▶ 因為要表達的是未來的事，因此這裡要用未來式表達。

8

Do you mind if I **suggest that** our plan **be** cancelled?
你介意我提議將計畫取消嗎？

解析 ▶ "Do you mind if ＋子句 ?" 和 "Do you mind ＋ N/V-ing?" 意為「你介不介意……」，是委婉詢問對方意願的表達方式。其中還用了 "S1 ＋ suggest ＋ that ＋ S2 (+should) ＋ Vr ... " 句型，即使這裡省略了助動詞 "should"，被動語態的 beV 仍然要使用原形的形態。在這裡特別以被動語態來提出令人難以啟齒的提議，語氣在表達上較為委婉，因此會比使用主動語態來得恰當。

9

We can still plan another trip to Hualien **or** anywhere **you want to go**.
我們還是可以計畫另一次旅行，去花蓮或任何你想去的地方。

解析 ▶ "plan a trip to ＋地點" 意為「計畫到某處旅行」，本句以對等連接詞 "or" 連接兩個地點 "Hualien" 和 "anywhere"，並且用了形容詞子句 "(which) you want to go" 來修飾名詞 "anywhere"。

10

Thank you for understanding.
謝謝你的諒解。

解析 ▶ "Thank you for ＋ N" 是英文書信中經常出現的句型。在書信開頭的話，經常是用來感謝對方已經做過的事，例如 "Thank you for your prompt reply."（感謝您的迅速回應。），出現在書信結尾的話，則多半是針對信中提出的內容事先感謝對方。

 **必備字彙** 與片語整理

⇒ accompany	[ə`kʌmpənɪ]	v.	陪伴
⇒ cancel	[`kænsḷ]	v.	取消
⇒ cousin	[`kʌzṇ]	n.	表親；堂親
⇒ following	[`faləwɪŋ]	adj.	接下來的
⇒ Hualien	[`hua`lɪɛn]	n.	花蓮
⇒ Japan	[dʒə`pæn]	n.	日本
⇒ news	[njuz]	n.	消息（不可數）
⇒ scenery	[`sinərɪ]	n.	景色（不可數）
⇒ sightseeing	[`saɪt‚siɪŋ]	n.	觀光（不可數）
⇒ suggest	[sə`dʒɛst]	v.	建議
⇒ understand	[‚ʌndɚ`stænd]	v.	理解
⇒ unexpectedly	[‚ʌnɪk`spɛktɪd]	adv.	出乎意料地
⇒ wait	[wet]	v.	等待
⇒ be afraid that		phr.	恐怕……
⇒ I am sorry that		phr.	我很抱歉……

題目敘述

公共場所是大家的空間，在公共場所抽菸不只是危害自己的健康，還會影響別人。請說明你是否同意公共場所禁菸的規定。

參考範文

1When it comes to banning smoking in public, I believe that it is a very good idea. 2As we all know, smoking is bad for health. 3According to a research, people who smoke will be more likely to get lung cancer than those who don't smoke. 4What is more, even though a person does not smoke, he may get lung cancer owing to the effects of secondhand smoke. 5If you smoke in a public place, there will be so many innocent people who are forced to be secondhand smokers. 6Lately, there are more and more places where smoking is not allowed. 7 When someone smokes in a public place, we have to say to him, "No smoking in public." bravely. 8It's for everybody's health.

中文翻譯

1 談到在公共場所禁止吸菸的這件事，我認為這是一個非常好的想法。**2** 吸菸有害健康是眾所皆知的。**3** 根據研究，抽菸的人比沒有抽菸的人更有可能罹患肺癌。**4** 除此之外，一個人就算不吸菸，也有可能會因為二手菸的影響而罹患肺癌。**5** 如果你在公共場所抽菸，會有很多無辜的人都被強迫吸進了二手菸。**6** 最近有越來越多地方都禁止吸菸。**7** 當有人在公共場所抽菸的時候，我們必須勇敢說出「不要在公共場所抽菸」。**8** 這是為了大家的健康著想。

範文句型解析

When it comes to banning smoking in public, **I believe that** it is a very good idea.
談到在公共場所禁止吸菸的這件事，我認為這是一個非常好的想法。

1

解析 ▶ "When it comes to + N/V-ing, ＋主要子句." 意為「談到……，……」，先以從屬子句點出討論主題，並在主要子句的部分直接提出自己針對主題所有的觀點，是撰寫議論文時經常使用的句型。這裡用 "I believe that ＋子句" 的句型開門見山地提出自己的見解或信念。

2

As we all know, smoking is bad for health.
吸菸有害健康是眾所皆知的。

解析 ▶ 這裡利用 "As we all know, ＋子句." 的句型，陳述一般大眾普遍採信的觀點，帶出吸菸有害健康的事實。

3

According to a research, people **who smoke** will be more likely to get lung cancer than those **who don't smoke**.
根據研究，抽菸的人比沒有抽菸的人更有可能罹患肺癌。

解析  介系詞片語的句型 "According to ＋ N, ..." 意為「根據……，……」。後面的句子看起來有點長，這是因為在句子裡用了兩個形容詞子句 "who smoke" 和 "who don't smoke" 分別修飾了先行詞 "people" 和 "those"，並利用比較級句型將兩者相比較。

4

What is more, **even though** a person does not smoke, he may get lung cancer owing to the effects of secondhand smoke.
除此之外，一個人就算不吸菸，也有可能會因為二手菸的影響而罹患肺癌。

解析 這裡利用 "What is more, ..." 的句型，指出抽菸除了會影響自己的健康，所產生的二手菸也會對別人造成影響，正式帶出在公共場所禁止吸菸的主題。"even though ＋從屬子句，＋主要子句." 是表示讓步的表達方式。

5

If you smoke in a public place, there will be so many innocent people **who are forced to be secondhand smokers**.
如果你在公共場所抽菸，會有很多無辜的人都被強迫吸進了二手菸。

解析 "If ＋從屬子句，＋主要子句." 是以 if 引導從屬子句來表示條件的副詞子句的表達方式。"who are forced to be secondhand smokers" 是形容詞子句，修飾先行詞 "people"。

6

Lately, there are more and more places **where smoking is not allowed**.
最近有越來越多地方都禁止吸菸。

解析 比較級的 "more and more" 意為「越來越多」。"where smoking is not allowed" 是形容詞子句，修飾先行詞 "places"。

7

When someone smokes **in a public place**, we have to say to him, "No smoking in public." bravely.

當有人在公共場所抽菸的時候，我們必須勇敢說出「不要在公共場所抽菸」。

解析 "When ＋從屬子句 ," 是表示時間的副詞子句，修飾了後面的主要子句，點明主要子句中所提到的事件發生時間點為何。"in public"、"in a public place"、"in public places" 都可以用來表示「在公共場所」。

8

It's for everybody's health.

這是為了大家的健康著想。

解析 "for" 可以用來表示「為了」。例如 "The colonizers in the North America fought for liberty."（北美的殖民開拓者為自由而戰。）。

 必備字彙 與片語整理

➠ allow	[əˋlaʊ]	v.	允許
➠ ban	[bæn]	v.	禁止
➠ bravely	[ˋbrevlɪ]	adv.	勇敢地
➠ for	[fɔr]	prep.	為了
➠ force	[fors]	v.	強迫
➠ health	[hɛlθ]	n.	健康
➠ innocent	[ˋɪnəsn̩t]	adj.	無辜的
➠ lately	[ˋletlɪ]	adv.	最近
➠ research	[rɪˋsɝtʃ]	n.	研究
➠ secondhand	[ˋsɛkəndˌhænd]	adj.	二手的
➠ smoke	[smok]	v.	抽菸

⇒ according to	phr.	根據……
⇒ be likely to	phr.	很可能……
⇒ even though	phr.	即使
⇒ lung cancer	phr.	肺癌
⇒ more and more	phr.	越來越多
⇒ public place	phr.	公共場所
⇒ owing to	phr.	由於
⇒ secondhand smoking	phr.	二手菸
⇒ what is more	phr.	除此之外
⇒ when it comes to	phr.	談到……

題目敘述

Last Monday morning, while I was sound asleep, my roommate knocked on my door heavily. She called my name loudly until I opened the door to see what on earth was going on outside my room ...

上星期一早上，正當我熟睡的時候，我的室友重重地敲我的門。她大聲叫著我的名字，直到我把門打開，看看房門外到底發生了什麼事……

參考範文

1She looked astonished, so I asked her what had happened.　2She did not reply but used her cellular phone to tell someone that I was safe and sound in my room.　3I wondered who she was speaking with and whether I was dreaming or not.　4She passed the phone to me, and I was surprised to hear my mother's voice. 5My mother said that she just received a phone call in which a man said I was kidnapped and asked my mother to pay the ransom by ATM.　6She called my school for help, and therefore, my school contacted all my classmates to make sure whether I was really kidnapped or not.　7My mother said that she had nearly called the police, but now she was relieved at last.

8However, for me, it was where the nightmare started because all my classmates and teachers were all searching for me, and I had to tell each of them the same story again and again.

中文翻譯

1 她看起來很驚訝,所以我問她發生了什麼事。2 她沒有回答,而是用行動電話告訴某人我安然無恙地在我的房間裡。3 我很納悶她是在跟誰講話,還有我是不是還在作夢。4 她把電話遞給我,我很驚訝地聽到媽媽的聲音。5 媽媽說她剛剛接到了一通電話,電話裡頭有一個男人說我被綁架了,要求我媽媽用自動提款機付贖金。6 她打電話到我的學校求援,於是學校聯絡了我所有的同學,想確定我是不是真的被綁架了。7 媽媽說她差一點就要報警了,不過現在總算放心了。8 可是,對我來說,這正是惡夢的開始,因為所有同學和老師都在找我,而我必須一次又一次地告訴他們每個人同樣的故事。

範文句型解析

She **looked** astonished, so I **asked** her what had happened.
她看起來很驚訝,所以我問她發生了什麼事。

2

解析 ▶ 由連接詞 "so" 引導表示結果的副詞子句,修飾前面的主要子句。連綴動詞的句型 "S + look + adj." 意為「看起來……」。"ask + sb + sth" 的句型意為「問某人某事」,這句中的 "sth" 是名詞子句 "what had happened"。

2

She did not reply but used her cellular phone to **tell someone that I was safe and sound in my room**.

她沒有回答，而是用行動電話告訴某人我安然無恙地在我的房間裡。

解析 ▶ "not ... but ..." 是「沒有……而是……」的意思。"tell + sb + sth" 的句型意為「告訴某人某事」，這一句之中的 "sth" 是名詞子句 "that I was safe and sound in my room"。

3

I wondered **who she was speaking with** and **whether I was dreaming or not**.

我很納悶她是在跟誰講話，還有我是不是還在作夢。

解析 ▶ 主要句型為 "I wonder ＋以疑問詞引導的名詞子句 ."，意為「我很納悶……」。這裡使用對等連接詞 "and" 連接兩個名詞子句。

4

She passed the phone to me, and I **was surprised to** hear my mother's voice.

她把電話遞給我，我很驚訝地聽到媽媽的聲音。

解析 ▶ "pass + sth + to + sb"，也可以改用 "pass + sb + sth" 的句型來表達，意為「將某物遞給某人」，"be surprised to + Vr" 表示「很驚訝……」，類似的句型還有 "be glad + to + Vr"（很高興……）和 "be sorry to + Vr"（很遺憾……），都是寫作時經常會用到的表達方式，請特別留意。

5

My mother said that she just received a phone call **in which a man** said **I was kidnapped and** asked **my mother to pay the ransom by ATM**.

媽媽說她剛剛接到了一通電話，電話裡頭有一個男人說我被綁架了，要求我媽媽用自動提款機付贖金。

解析 ▶ 本句結構比較複雜，首先出現的是 "My mother said (+that)＋子句." 句型，且利用 "in which a man said (that)＋子句." 這麼長的形容詞子句來修飾前面子句中的先行詞 "a phone call"。而對等連接詞 "and" 連接形容詞子句中的兩個過去式動詞 "said" 和 "asked"。

301

6

She called my school for help, and therefore, my school contacted all my classmates to make sure **whether I was really kidnapped or not**.

她打電話到我的學校求援，於是學校聯絡了我所有的同學，想確定我是不是真的被綁架了。

解析 以對等連接詞 "and" 連接前後兩個句子。其中，後面的句子使用了名詞子句 "whether I was really kidnapped or not" 來當作 "make sure" 的受詞。

7

My mother said that she **had nearly called** the police, but now she **was** relieved at last.

媽媽說她差一點就要報警了，不過現在總算放心了。

解析 對等連接詞 "but" 連接前後兩個句子，前後的語氣和時態都不相同。

8

However, for me, it was **where the nightmare started** because all my classmates and teachers were all searching for me, and I had to tell each of them the same story again and again.

可是，對我來說，這正是惡夢的開始，因為所有同學和老師都在找我，而我必須一次又一次地告訴他們每個人同樣的故事。

解析 這個句子和前文，在語氣上有著對比的效果，所以使用轉折語 "however" 開頭。"where the nightmare started" 是名詞子句，做為主詞 "it" 的補語。接著則用表示原因的副詞子句 "because ..." 來說明之所以是惡夢開端的原因。

 必備字彙 與片語整理

⇒ astonished	[ə`stɑnɪʃt]	adj.	驚訝的
⇒ contact	[kən`tækt]	v.	聯絡
⇒ kidnap	[`kɪdnæp]	v.	綁架
⇒ nightmare	[`naɪt͵mɛr]	n.	惡夢，夢魘
⇒ pay	[pe]	v.	支付
⇒ ransom	[`rænsəm]	n.	贖金
⇒ receive	[rɪ`siv]	v.	接到
⇒ relieved	[rɪ`livd]	adj.	放心的
⇒ reply	[rɪ`plaɪ]	v.	回應
⇒ again and again		phr.	一次又一次
⇒ at last		phr.	終於
⇒ call the police		phr.	報警
⇒ cellular phone		phr.	行動電話
⇒ make sure		phr.	確定
⇒ pass sth to sb		phr.	將某物遞給某人
⇒ safe and sound		phr.	安然無恙
⇒ search for		phr.	尋找……
⇒ the same		phr.	同樣的
⇒ whether ... or not		phr.	是否……

303

題目敘述

老師規定今天下午四點以前要交出學期報告，遲交的一律以零分計算。但是上個禮拜你家因為颱風帶來的大雨而成為了一片汪洋，電腦中的檔案也全部泡湯了，因此無法如期交出報告。請寫一封信請求老師延長繳交報告的期限。

參考範文

Dear Professor Wang,

¹I know that all the students in our class should hand in their term paper before four o'clock this afternoon. ²I have worked very hard to prepare for the term paper for at least one month. ³Nevertheless, last week there was a typhoon which brought such heavy rain that our neighborhood was swallowed by the floods. ⁴My computer was damaged, and the data I prepared for my term paper was ruined too. ⁵I have already borrowed my classmate's computer to rewrite my paper. ⁶However, although I have tried my best, I still could not finish and hand in my term paper in time. ⁷Would you please give me one more week to finish it? ⁸Thank you very much for your kindness.

Sincerely yours,

Jack

親愛的王教授：

　　1 我知道我們班所有學生都應該要在今天下午四點以前交出學期報告。**2** 我已經非常努力準備這份學期報告至少一個月了。**3** 但是，上個禮拜的颱風帶來了大雨，以致於我們家附近都被洪水吞沒了。**4** 我的電腦毀了，而且我為學期報告所準備的資料也完了。**5** 我已經跟同學借了電腦來重寫報告。**6** 可是，僅管我已經盡了力，還是無法及時完成並繳交我的學期報告。**7** 可否請您再給我一個禮拜的時間來完成報告？**8** 非常感謝您的仁慈。

真誠地
傑克

1

I know that all the students in our class should hand in their term paper before four o'clock this afternoon.

我知道我們班所有學生都應該要在今天下午四點以前交出學期報告。

解析 ▶ "I know that ＋子句 ." 的意思是「我知道……」，這裡的子句部分是 "all the students in our class ... this afternoon"。

2

I have worked very hard to prepare for the term paper for at least one month.

我已經非常努力準備這份學期報告至少一個月了。

解析 ▶ "S ＋ have ＋ Vpp ＋ for ＋一段時間 ." 是完成式的典型句型。

3

Nevertheless, last week there was a typhoon which brought such heavy rain that our neighborhood was swallowed by the floods.

但是，上個禮拜的颱風帶來了大雨，以致於我們家附近都被洪水吞沒了。

解析 由 "which" 引導的形容詞子句修飾先行詞 "typhoon"，在這個形容詞子句中還使用了 "such ... that ..."（如此……以致於……）的句型。

4

My computer was damaged, and the data I prepared for my term paper was ruined too.

我的電腦毀了，而且我為學期報告所準備的資料也完了。

解析 對等連接詞 "and" 連接前後兩個過去式的句子，其中，"(which) I prepared for my term paper" 是形容詞子句，修飾先行詞 "data"。

5

I have already borrowed my classmate's computer to rewrite my paper.

我已經跟同學借了電腦來重寫報告。

解析 "borrow" 是「向別人借進來」，"lend" 則是「借出去給別人」。

6

However, although I have tried my best, I still could not finish and hand in my term paper in time.

可是，僅管我已經盡了力，還是無法及時完成並繳交我的學期報告。

解析 "Although ＋從屬子句，＋主要子句 ."，是寫作時經常用到的表示讓步的副詞子句經典句型。

7

Would you please give me one more week to finish it?

可否請您再給我一個禮拜的時間來完成報告？

解析 "Would you please ＋ Vr ...?" 是委婉對他人提出請求的常用句型。

Thank you very much for your kindness.
非常感謝您的仁慈。

8

解析 "Thank you for ＋ N." 是英文書信中經常出現的句型。在書信開頭經常被用來感謝對方已經做過的事，例如 "Thank you for your prompt reply."（感謝您的迅速回應。），在書信結尾則是針對信中提出的內容事先感謝對方。

 必備字彙 與片語整理

borrow	[`bɑro]	v.	借入
damage	[`dæmɪdʒ]	v.	毀壞
finish	[`fɪnɪʃ]	v.	結束；完成
flood	[flɑd]	n.	洪水
neighborhood	[`nebɚ͵hʊd]	n.	鄰近地區
professor	[prə`fɛsɚ]	n.	教授
rewrite	[ri`raɪt]	v.	重寫
ruin	[`rʊɪn]	v.	毀壞
swallow	[`swɑlo]	v.	吞沒
typhoon	[`taɪ`fʊn]	n.	颱風
at least		phr.	至少
hand in		phr.	繳交
heavy rain		phr.	大雨
in time		phr.	及時
prepare for		phr.	為……做準備
term paper		phr.	學期報告
this afternoon		phr.	今天下午
try one's best		phr.	盡某人的全力

307

題目敘述

I always have difficulty making decisions. For instance, last weekend when I went shopping for a dress, I had no idea which dress I should buy ...

我總是很難做出決定。舉例來說，上個週末我去逛街買洋裝的時候，我不知道該買哪一件……

參考範文

¹At first, I was fond of a pink dress which was not too expensive. ²However, I am a perfectionist, and I would like to purchase the best dress. ³The clerk showed me another dress which was the prettiest one in the store. ⁴However, it was too expensive for me. ⁵Then, the clerk showed me dozens of dresses, but the more dresses the clerk showed me, the more indecisive I became. ⁶I could not decide which one was the best dress for me to buy, so I just chose not to make any decision at all. ⁷I went to another store where I hoped I could find the perfect dress to purchase. ⁸In the end, I went to one store after another, but I did not buy anything, which made me really angry with myself.

中文翻譯

　　1 起初，我喜歡一件粉紅色的洋裝，它的價格並不貴。**2** 可是，我是個完美主義者，所以我想要買最完美的洋裝。**3** 店員給我看了另一件洋裝，那件洋裝是整間店裡面最漂亮的。**4** 然而，它對我來說太貴了。**5** 接著，店員拿了很多洋裝給我看，可是店員給我看越多洋裝，我就變得越優柔寡斷。**6** 我無法決定買哪一件洋裝對我而言才是最棒的，所以我選擇乾脆不要買。**7** 我去了另一家店，希望我能在那裡找到完美的洋裝來買。**8** 最後，我去了一家又一家店，可是我什麼都沒買，這讓我真的很氣我自己。

範文句型解析

1

At first, I was fond of a pink dress which was not too expensive.

起初，我喜歡一件粉紅色的洋裝，它的價格並不貴。

解析 這裡以形容詞子句 "which was not too expensive" 修飾先行詞 "dress"。

2

However, I am a perfectionist, and I would like to purchase the best dress.

可是，我是個完美主義者，所以我想要買最完美的洋裝。

解析 使用對等連接詞 "and" 連接兩個完整的句子。

309

3

The clerk showed me another dress **which was the prettiest one in the store**.

店員給我看了另一件洋裝，那件洋裝是整間店裡面最漂亮的。

解析 ▶ "show + sb + sth" 的句型表示「向某人展示某物」。形容詞子句 "which was the prettiest one in the store" 修飾先行詞 "dress"。

4

However, it was too expensive for me.

然而，它對我來說太貴了。

解析 ▶ "too ... to ..." 的句型表示「太……以致於無法……」，原本句尾會出現的 "to buy" 被省略不寫。本句亦可改寫成 "The dress is so expensive that I cannot afford it."。

5

Then, the clerk showed me dozens of dresses, but **the more** dresses the clerk showed me, **the more** indecisive I became.

接著，店員拿了很多洋裝給我看，可是店員給我看越多洋裝，我就變得越優柔寡斷。

解析 ▶ 這裡用對等連接詞 "but" 連接兩個完整的句子。在後面的句子裡還用上了 "the more ..., the more ..." 的句型，讓表達更生動。

6

I could not decide which one was the best dress for me to buy, **so** I just chose not to make any decision at all.

我無法決定買哪一件洋裝對我而言才是最棒的，所以我選擇乾脆不要買。

解析 ▶ 主要的句型結構為 " 主要子句 + ,so + 從屬子句 ."。其中，主要子句還使用了名詞子句 "which one was the best dress for me to buy" 做為動詞 "decide" 的受詞。

7

I went to another store where I hoped I could find the perfect dress to purchase.

我去了另一家店，希望我能在那裡找到完美的洋裝來買。

解析 ▶ 形容詞子句 "where I hoped I could find the perfect dress to purchase" 修飾前面的先行詞 "store"。

8

In the end, I went to **one store after another**, but I did not buy anything, which made me really angry with myself.

最後，我去了一家又一家店，可是我什麼都沒買，這讓我真的很氣我自己。

解析 ▶ 對等連接詞 "but" 連接兩個完整的句子。在前面的句子中還使用了 "one ... after another"（一個又一個……）的句型。

必備字彙 與片語整理

⇒ clerk	[klɝk]	n.	店員
⇒ dress	[drɛs]	n.	洋裝
⇒ perfectionist	[pɚˋfɛkʃənɪst]	n.	完美主義者
⇒ purchase	[ˋpɝtʃəs]	v.	購買
⇒ show	[ʃo]	v.	展示
⇒ at first		phr.	起初
⇒ be fond of		phr.	喜愛……
⇒ dozens of		phr.	許多……
⇒ go shopping		phr.	去購物
⇒ have difficulty in V-ing		phr.	在……有困難
⇒ have no idea		phr.	不知道
⇒ make a decision		phr.	做出決定

題目敘述

　　上個星期你（妳）和情人分手了，你（妳）的心情很低落，想要寫一封信給你（妳）最好的朋友，告訴他（她）發生了什麼事情，並和他（她）分享自己的心情。

參考範文

Dear Jean,

　　1Last week, my boyfriend told me that he had fallen in love with another girl. **2**He wanted to break up with me no matter how deep I loved him. **3**What was worse is that the girl was my best friend. **4**I cry every day, and I cannot eat or sleep. **5**Every time I think of the fact that he does not love me anymore, I feel miserable. **6**I tried to call him, but he did not even want to answer my call. **7**I feel abandoned, and I feel like dying. **8**Yet I know I cannot kill myself and break my parents' hearts. **9**Then, what should I do to ease the pain? **10**Would you please help me get over it?

Cindy

中文翻譯

親愛的吉恩：

　　1 上個禮拜，我的男朋友告訴我他愛上了另一個女孩。**2** 無論我有多愛他，他都要和我分手。**3** 更糟糕的是，那個女孩曾是我最好的朋友。**4** 我每天哭，不能吃也不能睡。**5** 每當我想到他不再愛我了的事實，我就覺得很悲慘。**6** 我試著打電話給他，但是他甚至不想接我的電話。**7** 我覺得自己被遺棄了，我覺得想死。**8** 可是我知道我不能夠輕生而傷了父母的心。**9** 那麼，我該做什麼來減輕痛苦呢？**10** 妳可以幫我克服嗎？

辛蒂

範文句型解析

Last week, my boyfriend told me that he had **fallen in love with** another girl.

上個禮拜，我的男朋友告訴我他愛上了另一個女孩。

解析 ▶ "tell ＋ sb ＋ sth" 的句型意為「告訴某人某事」，這一句裡的 "sth" 使用了由 "that" 引導的名詞子句。"fall in love" 的意思是「墜入愛河」，也可以加上 "with ＋ sb" 說明墜入愛河的對象。

He wanted to break up with me no matter how deep I loved him.

無論我有多愛他，他都要和我分手。

2

解析 ▶ "no matter how ..." 的句型意為「無論有多……」，例如 "no matter how hard I tried"（無論我多努力嘗試）。類似的句型還有 "no matter who you are"（無論你是誰）、"no matter where you go"（無論你去哪裡）、"no matter what they say"（無論他們說什麼）等。

What was worse is that the girl was my best friend.

更糟糕的是，那個女孩曾是我最好的朋友。

3

解析 ▶ 表達現在的心情因此會使用現在簡單式的 be 動詞 is。"What was worse is that + 子句." 的句型意為「（之前發生的事對現在來說）更糟糕的是……」，類似的句型還有 "What is the most important is that ..."（最重要的是……）、"What is the most interesting is that ..."（最有趣的是……）、"What is the weirdest is that ..."（最奇怪的是……）等。

I cry every day, and I cannot eat or sleep.

我每天哭，不能吃也不能睡。

4

解析 ▶ 以對等連接詞 "and" 連接兩個完整的句子，"or" 連接助動詞 "cannot" 之後的兩個原形動詞 "eat" 和 "sleep"。

Every time I think of **the fact that he does not love me anymore**, I feel miserable.

每當我想到他不再愛我了的事實，我就覺得很悲慘。

5

解析 ▶ 主要句型為 "Every time when ＋從屬子句 , ＋主要子句 "，其中，從屬子句的部分還用了 "that" 所引導的名詞子句做為 "the fact" 的同位語，補充說明 the fact 的內容為何，用來引導從屬子句的 when 在這裡可以省略。主要子句的部分則用了連綴動詞 "feel ＋ adj" 的句型，表示「感到……」。

6

I tried to call him, but he **did not even want to** answer my call.
我試著打電話給他，但是他甚至不想接我的電話。

解析 以對等連接詞 "but" 連接兩個完整的句子，"do not even want to + Vr ..." 的句型表示「甚至不想……」。

7

I feel abandoned, and I **feel like** dying.
我覺得自己被遺棄了，我覺得想死。

解析 以對等連接詞 "and" 連接兩個完整的句子，連綴動詞 "feel + adj" 的句型，意思是「感到……」，特別要注意的是與 "feel + adj." 很相似的 "feel + like + Ving/N" 的句型，意思是「想要……」，使用時請小心不要搞混了。

8

Yet I know I cannot kill myself **and** break my parents' hearts.
可是我知道我不能夠輕生而傷了父母的心。

解析 主要句型是 "I know (+ that) + 子句."，這邊的子句是名詞子句，做為動詞 "know" 的受詞。其中，以對等連接詞 "and" 連接助動詞 "cannot" 之後的兩個原形動詞 "kill" 和 "break"。

9

Then, what should I do to ease the pain?
那麼，我該做什麼來減輕痛苦呢？

解析 "What should I do to + Vr ..." 的句型意為「我該做什麼來……」，例如 "What should I do to stop the machine?"（我該做什麼來使機器停下來？）。

10

Would you please **help me get** over it?
妳可以幫我克服嗎？

解析 "Would you please + Vr ...?" 是委婉請求他人幫忙的句型。"help + sb + Vr ..." 句型的意思是「幫助某人做某事」。

315

 必備字彙 與片語整理

abandon	[ə`bændən]	v.	拋棄，遺棄
anymore	[`ɛnɪmɔr]	adv.	再也不……
boyfriend	[`bɔɪˌfrɛnd]	n.	男朋友
call	[kɔl]	v.	打電話
cry	[kraɪ]	v.	哭
eat	[it]	v.	吃
even	[`ivən]	adv.	甚至
miserable	[`mɪzərəbḷ]	adj.	悲慘的
sleep	[slip]	v.	睡
worse	[wɝs]	adj.	更糟糕的
answer a call		phr.	接電話
break one's heart		phr.	傷某人的心
break with		phr.	跟……分手
ease the pain		phr.	減輕痛苦
fall in love with sb		phr.	愛上某人
feel like＋V-ing		phr.	覺得想要……
get over		phr.	克服；恢復
no matter		phr.	無論
think of		phr.	想到……

Part 4

寫作測驗模擬試題

除了兩大題型的練習題外，若能利用完整且擬真的模擬試題，模擬考場情境並實際作答，便能讓考生實際運用前面學到的各種重要文法及句型、作答技巧、字彙、慣用表達等應考知識，且能及時檢驗自己的學習成果。請務必抱持實際上考場的心態作答，才能發揮最大的學習效果。

Look Inside

UNIT1 模擬試題
UNIT2 試題解析

全民英檢複試應考當天的注意事項

☆當天所須攜帶的物件

□有效身分證件：中華民國身分證（或有效期限內的護照、駕照）正本。國中生可用：中華民國身分證、有效期限內的護照正本、印有相片之健保IC卡正本。外籍人士可用：有效期內的台灣居留證正本。

□考試通知

□普通黑色鉛筆或藍／黑色原子筆、橡皮擦、修正液

☆當天應試前的準備與注意事項

1. 以鉛筆作答者，請準備兩枝以上削尖的鉛筆或自動筆，因為考試開始後不可能有時間削鉛筆。以原子筆作答者，請準備兩枝以上的黑／藍色原子筆，並事先確認不會中途斷水，以防止因沒水而無法完成考試。

2. 務必提早到考場，給自己充裕時間確認貼在入口處／走廊上的考試教室與座位，並做考前複習。以免在快到測驗時間時，才與其他考生擠著確認自己的教室／座位，若遇到特殊情況（例如當天臨時換教室）也會沒有足夠的時間應對。

3. 在測驗教室前排隊等候時，請利用時間保持英文思考的環境。一般到了考試現場，許多考生習慣以中文聊天，這其實會扼殺自己的考試能力，因為在寫作／口說測驗中，若能直接以英文的思考邏輯來答題，表達出來的內容就會更為流暢。因此，建議在入場前閱讀（或朗讀）英文的文章或句子，也可以聽英文廣播，來掌握英文的思考結構並提升流暢度。

4. 在進入考場之前，請先把有效證件、考試通知，以及相關文具都準備好，取消所有電子儀器的鬧鈴設定，以便於入場後能迅速將不需帶入座位的物品擺至測驗教室的前方地板上，並馬上找到自己的座位入座。

5. 為了順利進行口說測驗，在正式考試前考務人員會要求考生檢查錄音設備，此時務必詳細檢查座位上的耳機、錄音設備是否都正常，而且不會干擾作答，否則若因錄音設備而影響到考試成績，那就太可惜了。

寫作能力測驗答題注意事項

1. 本測驗共有兩部分。第一部分為中譯英，第二部分為英文作文。測驗時間為 40 分鐘。

2. 請利用試題紙空白處及背面擬稿，但正答務必書寫在「寫作能力測驗答案紙」上。在答案紙以外的地方作答，不予計分。

3. 第一部分中譯英請在答案紙第一頁作答，第二部分英文作文請在答案紙第二頁作答。

4. 作答時請勿隔行書寫，請注意字跡應清晰可讀，並保持答案紙之清潔，以免影響評分。

5. 測驗時，不得在考試通知或其他物品上抄題，亦不得有傳遞、夾帶小抄、左顧右盼或交談等違規行為。

6. 意圖或已經將試題紙攜出試場者，五年內不得報名參加本測驗。請人代考者，連同代考者，三年內不得報名參加本測驗。

7. 測驗結束時，須立即停止作答，在原位靜候監試人員收回全部試題紙及答案紙，清點無誤後，宣布結束始可離場。

8. 應試者入場、出場及測驗中如有違反上列規則或不服監試人員之指示者，監試人員得取消其應試資格並請其離場，且作答不予計分。

全民英語能力分級檢定測驗

中級寫作能力測驗

本測驗共有兩部分。第一部分為中譯英,第二部分為英文寫作。測驗時間為 40 分鐘。

一、中譯英 (40%)

說明:請將下列的一段中文翻譯成通順、達意且前後連貫的英文。

通過中級英檢是我這幾年來的一個理想目標。俗話說:「一分耕耘,一分收穫」。因此,為了通過測驗,我一直很努力,而且我的英文成績也一直都很好。然而,我仍然不敢大意,因為測驗內容並不簡單。總而言之,學好一種外語絕不容易,必須勤加練習才能熟能生巧。我相信只要我願意付出時間,要成功通過測驗絕非難事。

二、英文作文 (60%)

說明:請依下面所提供的文字提示寫一篇英文作文,長度約 120 字(8 至 12 個句子)。作文可以是一個完整的段落,也可以分段。(評分重點包括內容、組織、文法、用字遣詞、標點符號、大小寫。)

提示:在現今競爭的社會之中,每個人都必須不斷學習。有人在學習的過程中會遭遇挫折且無法有效學習,然而有些人卻能夠有效學習。請寫一篇文章說明:

1. 你認為有效學習的重點是什麼?
2. 你在學習過程中是否友遵循這些重點?你覺得自己的學習是否有效?

全民英語能力分級檢定測驗中級寫作能力測驗答案紙

第一部分：中譯英（40%），請由第 1 行開始並於<u>框線</u>內作答，勿隔行書寫。

第 1 頁

5

10

15

20

（第二部分：英文作文，請翻至背面作答。）

25

30

35

40

寫作能力測驗 解析

▶▶▶ 第一部分 **中譯英** (40%)

請將下列的一段中文翻譯成通順、達意且前後連貫的英文。

　　通過中級英檢是我這幾年來的一個理想目標。俗話說：「一分耕耘，一分收穫」。因此，為了通過測驗，我一直很努力，而且我的英文成績也一直都很好。然而，我仍然不敢大意，因為測驗內容並不簡單。總而言之，學好一種外語絕不容易，必須勤加練習才能熟能生巧。我相信只要我願意付出時間，要成功通過測驗絕非難事。

翻譯範例

Passing GEPT has been an <u>ideal</u> goal of mine for the past several years. "You <u>reap</u> what you <u>sow</u>," goes a <u>saying</u>. <u>Therefore</u>, for passing the exam, I have been <u>working hard</u> on my studies, and my English grades have been very good. <u>Nevertheless</u>, the <u>difficulty</u> of the test <u>prevents</u> me <u>from slacking off</u>. <u>In short</u>, mastering a foreign language is never easy, and <u>perfection</u> only comes with <u>diligent practice</u>. I believe that as long as I <u>am willing to</u> <u>devote</u> my time to the test, passing the test <u>successfully</u> won't be a hard thing.

字彙解析

1. ideal [aɪˋdiəl] adj. 理想的
2. reap [rip] v. 收穫
3. sow [so] v. 播種
4. saying [ˋseɪŋ] v. 格言，警語（= proverb）
5. therefore [ˋðɛr͵for] adv. 因此（= thus = hence = consequently = as a result 等等）

6. work hard phr. 努力

7. nevertheless [ˌnɛvəðəˋlɛs] adv. 然而（= however = nonetheless 等等）

8. difficulty [ˋdɪfəˌkʌltɪ] n. 困難；難處

9. prevent from phr. 防止；避免

10. slack off phr. 鬆懈；偷懶

11. in short phr. 總而言之（= to sum up = in conclusion = in sum = all in all 等等）

12. perfection [pəˋfɛkʃən] n. 完美

13. diligent practice phr. 勤加練習

14. be willing to phr. 願意做……（後加原形動詞）

15. devote [dɪˋvot] v. 把……投入

16. successfully [səkˋsɛsfəlɪ] adv. 成功地

    （動詞為 succeed、形容詞為 successful、名詞為 success）

句型解析

1. 通過中級英檢是我這幾年來的一個理想目標。

   Passing GEPT has been an ideal goal of mine for the past several years.

   解析 ▶ 這是一個以動名詞（V-ing）做為主詞的句子。因為時間副詞 for the past several years（在過去的幾年）強調的是「這個狀態已經持續了一段時間」，因此這裡會使用現在完成式（has been）來表達。

2. 俗話說：「一分耕耘，一分收穫」。

   "You reap what you sow," goes a saying.

   解析 ▶ 在引用「一分耕耘，一分收穫」這種格言或諺語時，句子的前後需加上引號。goes a saying 則是「俗話說……」或「有句老話說……」的意思。必須特別注意的是，前一句的逗點須放置在引號內，而非引號之外。

3. 因此，為了通過測驗，我一直很努力，而且我的英文成績也一直都很好。

   Therefore, for passing the exam, I have been working hard on my studies, and my English grades have been very good.

   解析 ▶ therefore（因此）是表轉折的副詞，通常會在句與句間語氣轉換時使用。表達因果關係的常用轉折語還有：therefore = thus = hence = consequently = as a result 等。因為要表現出「動作一直持續」，所以這裡也會使用現在完成式（has/have been）來表達。

4. 然而，我仍然不敢大意，因為測驗內容並不簡單。

   Nevertheless, the difficulty of the test prevents me from slacking off.

   解析 ▶ nevertheless（然而）也是表轉折的副詞，同樣會在句與句間語氣轉換時使用。表達對比或讓步等句意時，常用的轉折語還有：nevertheless = however = nonetheless 等等。本句的時態是現在簡單式，因為這句話的內容是一種「常態」。prevent A from B 是「讓 A 免於 B」的意思，如果這裡的 B 是動作，則必須將動詞改成動名詞（V-ing）的形態，就如本句中出現的 slacking off。

5. 總而言之，學好一種外語絕不容易，必須勤加練習才能熟能生巧。

   In short, mastering a foreign language is never easy, and perfection only comes with diligent practice.

   解析 ▶ 表達「總而言之」的 in short 也是表轉折的副詞，同樣用於文章中句與句間語氣轉換的時候。其他用來下結論的轉折語還有：in short = to sum up = in conclusion = in sum = all in all 等等。句子裡的 come with 是「伴隨……」的意思，diligent practice 則是「勤加練習」的意思。

325

6. 我相信只要我願意付出時間，要成功通過測驗絕非難事。

I believe that as long as I am willing to devote my time to the test, passing the test successfully won't be a hard thing.

解析 ▶ 這個句子是 I believe that 的句型，在 that 之後要接上完整子句。as long as 是表「只要……」的連接詞片語。be willing to 是「願意做……」的意思，在 to 之後會接原形動詞。

▶▶▶ 第二部分 英文作文 (60%)

請依下面所提供的文字提示寫一篇英文作文,長度約 120 字（8 至 12個句子）。作文可以是一個完整的段落,也可以分段。（評分重點包括內容、組織、文法、用字遣詞、標點符號、大小寫。）

作文題目

提示 在現今競爭的社會之中,每個人都必須不斷學習。有人在學習的過程中會遭遇挫折且無法有效學習,然而有些人卻能夠有效學習。請寫一篇文章說明:

1. 你認為有效學習的重點是什麼?
2. 你在學習過程中是否友遵循這些重點?你覺得自己的學習是否有效?

作文解答範例

Learning successfully is a difficult <u>task</u>. I think there are some <u>fundamental</u> <u>principles</u> we need to <u>follow</u> first, and then successful learning can be <u>achieved</u>. Among these principles, <u>in my opinion</u>, <u>diligence</u> and <u>devotion</u> are the most important. <u>First of all</u>, all things can be done through diligent <u>efforts</u>. People say that a diligent fool will <u>accomplish</u> more than a lazy wit. For example, when we are learning a language, we always need to work hard on all the materials and practice a lot, so that we can <u>master</u> the language. Second, devotion means focusing. People who cannot be focused on what they learn often fail to learn successfully. That is to say, their lack of devotion makes them learn things <u>inefficiently</u> and <u>ineffectively</u>.

<u>To be honest</u>, I am the kind of person who always keeps these principles in my mind when learning. I am not only <u>diligent</u> but also

devoted. Therefore, I can learn new things very quickly. <u>For instance,</u> I have been learning cooking these days <u>in order to</u> get me a culinary <u>certificate</u>. To learn it successfully, I practice cooking every day, and I always pay full attention to what my <u>instructor</u> teaches me in class. I believe I can cook many <u>tasty</u> dishes <u>in the near future</u>.

作文解答翻譯

成功學習是一件困難的任務。我認為有一些基本原則是我們必須先遵守的，然後才能達到成功的學習。在這些原則之中，依我來看，勤奮和投入是最重要的。首先，所有事情都可以透過勤奮的努力來達成。人們說一個勤奮的傻子會比一個懶惰的聰明人完成更多。舉個例子，當我們在學習語言的時候，我們一定必須努力看所有的資料並大量練習，這樣我們才能精通這個語言。第二，投入就是專注的意思。無法專注所學的人經常無法成功學習。這也就是說，他們的缺乏專注會使他們的學習變得沒有效率也沒有效果。

老實說，我是那種在學習時總將這些原則謹記在心的人。我不只勤奮，也很投入。因此，我可以很快速地學會新事物。舉例來說，我最近為了要拿一張烹飪的證照而一直在學烹飪。為了成功學習，我每天都練習烹飪，而且總是全神貫注在老師上課時教給我的東西上。我相信我在不久的將來就能做出很多美味的料理。

字彙解析

1. task [tæsk] n. 任務
2. fundamental [ˌfʌndə`mɛntl] adj. 基本的；十分重要的
3. principle [`prɪnsəpl] n. 原則
4. follow [`fɑlo] v. 遵守
5. achieve [ə`tʃiv] v. 達成
6. in my opinion phr. 依我來看（= from my point of view = if you ask me）
7. diligence [`dɪlədʒəns] n. 勤勉

8.　devotion [dɪˋvoʃən] n. 投入，專注

9.　first of all phr. 首先（＝ in the first place ＝ first ＝ firstly）

10. effort [ˋɛfət] n. 努力

11. accomplish [əˋkɑmplɪʃ] n. 達成

12. master [ˋmæstə] v. 精通，掌握

13. inefficiently [ɪnəˋfɪʃəntlɪ] adv. 無效率地

　　（形容詞為 inefficient、名詞為 efficiency、反義詞為 efficient）

14. ineffectively [ɪnəˋfɛktɪvlɪ] adv. 無效果地

　　（形容詞為 ineffective、名詞為 effect、反義詞為 effective）

15. to be honest phr. 老實說

　　（＝ honestly ＝ honestly speaking ＝ frankly ＝ frankly speaking）

16. diligent [ˋdɪlədʒənt] adj. 勤奮的（名詞為 diligence）

17. for instance phr. 舉例來說（＝ for example）

18. in order to phr. 為了（＝ so as to）

19. certificate [səˋtɪfəkɪt] n. 證照；結業證書

20. instructor [ɪnˋstrʌktə] n. 講師；教練

21. tasty [ˋtestɪ] adj. 美味的

22. in the near future phr. 在不久的將來

句型解析

1. **Learning successfully is a difficult task.**

   成功學習是一件困難的任務。

   解析 ▶ 這是一句以動名詞（V-ing）當作主詞的句子。這個句子是文章結構中的主題句（Topic Sentence），直接表明作者對於成功學習的看法，清楚說明作者認為成功學習這件事很困難。

2. **I think there are some fundamental principles we need to follow first, and then successful learning can be achieved.**

   我認為有一些基本原則是我們必須先遵守的，然後才能達到成功的學習。

這個句子以「我認為（I think）」開頭，後面接的名詞子句即是作者針對主題的個人觀點，亦可視為是支撐主題句的支持句（Supporting Sentence）。其中的 we need to follow first（我們必須先遵守）用來修飾前面的 principles，後面的 can be achieved（可以達到）是被動語態的表達方式，被動語態（Passive Voice）是一種相當重要的寫作必備句型。

3. Among these principles, in my opinion, diligence and devotion are the most important.

在這些原則之中，依我來看，勤奮和投入是最重要的。

解析 ▶ 本句以 in my opinion（依我來看）帶出作者的個人意見與想法。本句亦可寫成 In my opinion, diligence and devotion are the most important among these principles，或是 Among these principles, diligence and devotion are the most important, in my opinion，也就是說，in my opinion 可以置於句首、句中或是句尾。而 in my opinion（依我來看）也可以用 from my point of view 或 if you ask me 來替換表達。

4. First of all, all things can be done through diligent efforts.

首先，所有事情都可以透過勤奮的努力來達成。

解析 ▶ 本句以 first of all（首先）開頭，並包含了一句以被動語態 can be done（Can＋be＋Vpp）寫成的句子，through 在這裡是「藉由，透過」的意思。

5. People say that a diligent fool will accomplish more than a lazy wit.

人們說一個勤奮的傻子會比一個懶惰的聰明人完成更多。

解析 ▶ 本句以 People say 開頭，並以 that 引導後面的名詞子句。其中 a diligent fool will accomplish more than a lazy wit 一句中，包含了比較級 more than 的表達方式，這種表現方式亦可增加句子的深度與可看度。

6. **For example**, when we are learning a language, we always need to **work hard on** all the materials and practice a lot, **so that** we can master the language.

舉個例子，當我們在學習語言的時候，我們一定必須努力看所有的資料並大量練習，這樣我們才能精通這個語言。

> **解析** ▶ 當要以實際例子來支持前面論點時，可以用 For example（舉個例子）帶出後面的例子，請注意 For example 的後面要先加上逗點，才可以接句子。work hard on 是「努力做……」的意思，這裡的 material 是「資料」的意思，也就是指與學語言相關的各種資料，material 做為「資料」之意時，和 information（資訊；資料）一樣都是不可數名詞，因此字尾不可以加上 s，這點請特別注意。so that 是表示因果關係「以致於；以便」的連接詞，so that 的後面常會出現表達能力、意願、請求或猜測等語氣或態度的情態助動詞，如：can、may、should、will 等等。

7. **Second**, devotion means focusing.

第二，投入就是專注的意思。

> **解析** ▶ 本句以 second（第二）開頭，表示這是作者的第二項觀點論述。在寫作時以順序式列點來呈現自己的論點，會讓文章顯得更有層次。

8. People **who cannot be focused on what they learn** often **fail to** learn successfully.

無法專注所學的人經常無法成功學習。

> **解析** ▶ 本句的主詞為 People who cannot be focused on what they learn，其中以關係代名詞 who 引導形容詞子句，修飾先行詞 people，在寫作時須善用形容詞子句的句型，來替文章加分。fail 是動詞「失敗」的意思，經常以「fail to＋原形動詞」的方式使用，表達「無法做……」的意思。

9. That is to say, their lack of devotion makes them learn things inefficiently and ineffectively.

這也就是說，他們的缺乏專注會使他們的學習變得沒有效率也沒有效果。

解析 ▶ That is to say 是「這也就是說；就是」的意思，可以用來總結前面的論點及例子。lack 是「缺乏」的意思，在這裡是做為名詞使用，所以後面要加上介系詞 of，當 lack 做為動詞使用時，後面則可直接加上名詞。

10. To be honest, I am the kind of person who always keeps these principles in my mind when learning.

老實說，我是那種在學習時總將這些原則謹記在心的人。

解析 ▶ 本句以轉折語 to be honest（老實說）開頭，其他意義相似的表達方式還有 honestly = honestly speaking = frankly = frankly speaking 等等。另外，以關係代名詞 who 開頭的形容詞子句 who always keeps these principles in my mind when learning，修飾的是先行詞 person。作答時務必要善用形容詞子句的句型，替文章加分。

11. I am not only diligent but also devoted.

我不只勤奮，也很投入。

解析 ▶ 本句用了對等連接詞 not only A but also B（不只 A，也 B）來表達，其中的 A 與 B 必須對等，像這個句子，即是形容詞對形容詞，即 diligent（勤奮）對應 devoted（專注的）。此外，not only A but also B 裡的 also 可以省略。

12. Therefore, I can learn new things very quickly.

因此，我可以很快速地學會新事物。

解析 ▶ 本句以轉折語 therefore（因此）開頭，意義相似的表達方式還有 thus = hence = consequently = as a result = as a consequence 等。

13. **For instance, I have been learning cooking these days <u>in order to</u> get me a culinary certificate.**

舉例來說，我最近為了要拿一張烹飪的證照而一直在學烹飪。

解析 ▶ For instance 和前面出現過的 for example（舉個例子）意思相同，兩者可替換使用。另外，「in order to ＋原形動詞」的意思是「為了……」，是以不定詞表示「目的」的表達方式。

14. **To learn it successfully, I practice cooking every day, and I always pay full attention to <u>what my instructor teaches me in class</u>.**

為了成功學習，我每天都練習烹飪，而且總是全神貫注在老師上課時教給我的東西上。

解析 ▶ 這裡以不定詞來表達「目的」。另外，pay full attention to ... 的意思是「全神貫注在……上」，介系詞 to 的後面要接名詞，這裡則是接了名詞子句 what my instructor teaches me in class。

15. **I believe I can cook many tasty dishes <u>in the near future</u>.**

我相信我在不久的將來就能做出很多美味的料理。

解析 ▶ 本句以 I believe（我相信……）開頭，原本接在後方的從屬連接詞 that 被省略，直接接上名詞子句表達作者相信的事物為何。另外，in the near future 直翻的話是「在很近的未來」，也就是「不久的將來」，這個表達方式經常會應用在英文寫作上，請務必要記下來。

台灣廣廈 國際出版集團
Taiwan Mansion International Group

國家圖書館出版品預行編目（CIP）資料

NEW GEPT 新制全民英檢中級寫作測驗必考題型 /
陳頎著；國際語言中心委員會監修. -- 初版. -- 新北市：
國際學村, 2021.09
　　面；　公分
　ISBN 978-986-454-176-8（平裝）
　1. 英語　2. 寫作法

805.1892　　　　　　　　　　　　　　110012458

國際學村

NEW GEPT 新制全民英檢中級寫作測驗必考題型
一本掌握命題趨勢、文法句型、常考情境、字彙、慣用表達，只給你最完整、最有用的必考重點！

作　　　者／陳頎　　　　　　　編輯中心編輯長／伍峻宏・編輯／徐淳輔
監　　　修／國際語言中心委員會　封面設計／何偉凱・內頁排版／東豪印刷事業有限公司
　　　　　　　　　　　　　　　　製版・印刷・裝訂／東豪・紘億・明和

行企研發中心總監／陳冠蒨　　　線上學習中心總監／陳冠蒨
媒體公關組／陳柔彣　　　　　　數位營運組／顏佑婷
綜合業務組／何欣穎　　　　　　企製開發組／江季珊、張哲剛

發　行　人／江媛珍
法 律 顧 問／第一國際法律事務所 余淑杏律師・北辰著作權事務所 蕭雄淋律師
出　　　版／國際學村
發　　　行／台灣廣廈有聲圖書有限公司
　　　　　　地址：新北市235中和區中山路二段359巷7號2樓
　　　　　　電話：（886）2-2225-5777・傳真：（886）2-2225-8052
讀者服務信箱／cs@booknews.com.tw

代理印務・全球總經銷／知遠文化事業有限公司
　　　　　　地址：新北市222深坑區北深路三段155巷25號5樓
　　　　　　電話：（886）2-2664-8800・傳真：（886）2-2664-8801
郵 政 劃 撥／劃撥帳號：18836722
　　　　　　劃撥戶名：知遠文化事業有限公司（※單次購書金額未滿1000元需另付郵資70元。）

■出版日期：2021年09月　　　ISBN：978-986-454-176-8
　　　　　　2024年07月3刷　　版權所有，未經同意不得重製、轉載、翻印。